Tony Brookes

A first time author with a flair for characterisation and description, Tony Brookes has lived in Manchester for fifteen years after moving from Chesterfield in Derbyshire.

In Our Life Time

Tony Brookes

In Our Life Time

ARTEMIS PUBLISHERS

© Copyright 2014 Tony Brookes

The right of Tony Brookes to be identified as author of
This work has been asserted by him in accordance with the
Copyright, Designs and Patents Act 1988

All Rights Reserved No part of this publication may be
reproduced, stored or transmitted in any form without
written permission of the publisher. Any person who does
any unauthorised act in relation to
This publication may be liable to criminal prosecution and
civil claims for damage.

ISBN-978-1-907785-14 6

First Published in 2014
ARTEMIS PUBLISHERS LTD.

Hamilton House
Mabledon Place
Bloomsbury
London
WC1H 9BB

www.artemispublishers.com

Printed & Bound in Great Britain

Dedication

To my lovely wife for her love, support and happiness and to Rob Bathie for his inspiration.

Chapter 1

"Graham? Oh sweetie, come here you charming devil; meet my dear friend Florence."

Florence was dressed entirely in a flowing, fawn outfit that clung to her body sensuously into and attractively out of every curve. Effortlessly she turned briskly on her heels taking her attention away from the scenes of vigorous dancing and frivolous excess and faced her new company. You couldn't fail to notice her standing on high heels and being over five and a half feet tall with a presence befitting a Hollywood actress. Despite this stature and expressive pout, her frowning face looked bored to tears. Even standing seemed too much bother for her but she attempted a smile anyway.

Ottoline spoke to her friend in an excited and compelling manner, standing up straight and launching into vocal action as she slipped her shoes back and forth across the shiny and perfectly polished floor beneath her feet.

"Florence, this is my *love*...Graham Wright."

Florence looked up and down Ottoline's tall and slim body, acknowledging the introduction by a slight sideways nod of her head and by raising her painted black eyebrows to show at least *some* kind of interest, despite not moving her body in the slightest. Graham Wright transferred his stale Martini from the right hand to his left, bent at his waist and then delicately kissed her hand, his attentions focused on the glum face of the woman before him.

He'd seen Florence at dances and social occasions before but at that point had not yet been introduced to or spoken to her. He'd often realised her attractiveness, not that he'd ever let his date know that of course. Faceless people acted gaily whilst sloshing alcoholic drinks about the room, choking on old tobacco smoke and acting like a group of rather unsophisticated animals.

Graham looked great amongst these Neanderthals and threw his drinks, loudness and crisp white bank notes about the place as well, if not even more grandly than the rest of them. He didn't think he was one of them at all and always believed that somehow he was different but, whether he liked it or not, he was just one more animal in the high society rule-less zoo.

Graham was driven by society and was a heavyweight within this bubbling new post Great War Britain and looked disdainfully at the old ways; fully launching himself at just about anything new or exciting just for the sake of doing it. If it cost money, was taxed, could be dangerous or had alcohol and ladies as accompaniments, then he would almost definitely be involved.

He had always seen himself as a ladies' man, and indeed he was, especially in the eyes of affluent, fickle or just dreaming women. He was a young, wealthy charming man with cheeky mannerisms, a slim waist and a persistent confidence that was both controlled and yet wildly unrestrained at the same time. He always wore a suit well and he could always manage to know just what to say, when to say it and to whom. His glance was one of those that exploded warmth and reassurance around any situation and to anyone that noticed it. You could never fail to notice it either, he and the smile that he proudly wore seemed to be everywhere. It was a smile that always attracted attention and especially from the female of the species.

Graham, feeling that the moment was right, reached into his breast pocket and removed a slim and finely engraved gold cigarette case, before offering the now open vessel to his date. Ottoline looked into the gold container that that sparkled under the bright lights above. She took a moment or so longer deciding which of the ten identical cigarettes to choose and slip into a black cigarette holder she held between her bony fingers. Her eyes flicked around the room for a light, Graham acknowledged with the engraved match vesta that came as an expensive partner to the cigarette case.

Graham took the match and struck it on the side of the vesta, instantly sparking it into life. The burning orange flame lapped around the white paper that surrounded the Egyptian tobacco as Ottoline greedily inhaled the dark gritty smoke into her lungs through the excessively long black holder. Eagerly, Florence took a step forward, implying her desire to do just as her friend was doing. Florence didn't smoke unless she were in the company of others and in twenties society, smoking was definitely the thing. As Ottoline was smoking Florence childishly wasn't going to sit out the moment without doing likewise and that was a certainty. She looked across to Graham and met his slightly glazed eyes with her stare. He knew what he was required to do.

Again he held out the container and watched once more as the woman before him peered wide eyed into the case and somehow seemed to be able to see each cigarette as unique and dissimilar from the others. She was of course going to choose for just a second or two longer than Ottoline had done ensuring that she could be viewed as the more particular; should, anyone be watching and should that matter at all either. After the pause of thought she eventually picked out the one that was the best in her opinion and inserted it into the ivory and mother of pearl holder that was produced from her black crocodile skin clutch bag that was instantly snapped shut immediately afterwards.

He selected a cigarette for himself, in contrast not seeing the obvious differences between them before loosely holding it in his lips. Florence's eyes seemed to sparkle as the black smoke rose from her exhalation, she shifted her attention away quickly from Graham and back to her friend. Graham eventually lit his own and replaced both the match vesta and cigarette case in his top pocket. He too now blew a stream of smoke out between them, through his nose, as it slowly drifted towards the perfectly white plaster ceiling rose above them.

Florence and Ottoline greedily took further gulps of smoke from their loosely held cigarette holders as they stood a few feet apart trying to mentally out-do the other whilst pretending not to care that the other were doing it back to them in return. Ottoline had apparently finished her cigarette and carelessly dropped the still burning white stick onto the shiny surface below. Florence looked at her friend and quickly realised that she did not want to be smoking alone and therefore flicked her cigarette away as her friend had done.

The couple began to talk now in earnest and transferred mental one-up-man-ship to that of drunkenly audible chatter. The transfer of gossip, although totally based on subjects relating only to them, was purposely audible for most of the people in the club to hear. Ottoline looked around to see if she were being watched and proclaimed with as much false expression as she could manage,

"Oh and I tell you Florence, if he were a drug, I guess I'd be a hopeless addict."

She followed it with a wide smile and another over exuberantly and entirely fake laugh. Florence smiled to mimic the look on her friend's face and then partook in much artificial and raucous laughter to accompany it. There was a break in the sparring and Graham edged forward. Wanting anything than to be ignored at a party, he inserted himself into the conversation, speaking rather vaguely with the only thing he could find in his thoughts, directly towards Florence.

"Smashing swing again wouldn't you say?"

Florence did not look amused, as was usually the case.

"Lovely dress, I must say you look quite charming."

Florence looked up catching Graham's eye as she did so. The eye contact continued for all but the briefest of moments before it was broken by the advancing Ottoline who didn't like what she had seen. She was clearly jealous of Florence, or at least the attention she was getting from Graham and saw her chance to arrest it, moving in front of her to block her friend's view or opportunity to receive further positive comment.

She looked at her date and grimaced before she grasped her man's arm spilling his drink again as she did so. Looking up disdainfully at her he began to brush the liquid off the arm of his jacket as his hand was now snatched and pulled in the direction of the dance floor.

"Come on, we're to dance," she forcefully projected.

As usual when confronted with a hot-tempered woman he was unable to utter a suitable reply and therefore thought it better not to try. With uneasy gaze he balanced his glass on a table; entering the arena for the one-step. Another gentleman appeared amongst the thirty or so others on the scene at this time dragging Florence onto the floor with him. A tray of glasses smashed at the back of the hall, accompanied by an inebriated cheer; but few on the dance floor turned to look as the riotous 'shimmy shake' had been struck up by the energetic band, whilst one man standing on a table reaped in the laughs with his Noel Coward impersonations and witticisms.

Ottoline stopped dancing almost suddenly and turned to face him, grabbing his throat, turning his head to face hers and then apathetically kissed his cheek leaving a smudge of thick red lipstick on his otherwise clean-shaven and expensively fragranced white face. Twisting almost elegantly she moved on to another gentleman swaying her slight hips as she did so. She looked at him as if he were the only man she had ever laid her eyes and proceeded to produce that well practiced and yet rather intriguing smile towards the man. It was clearly not the first time that they had met; the whole room knew that much at least but apparently not Graham.

Graham continued to dance but his eyes remained fixed on his date's unpredictable actions. She seemed to be talking quite feverishly to the man before her and she moved so that her back was positioned so that it prevented Graham from observing her actions. Swiftly she kissed him passionately on the lips in a wholly exuberant and extraordinary manor. Graham had however, managed to spot the latest indiscretion and he knew all too well that he had seen it so many times before.

Graham's jealously of the unknown man grew wildly out of his control as it had a habit of doing so. He felt his temperature rise and his blood pulse through his veins and he decided he had to intervene in some way. He strode over to the table and took up his drink, sloshing a big swig into the back of his mouth before grandly striding over to the couple, his wide eyes glaring at them as he did so.

On the one hand, it was only Ottoline and she had never been even close to playing fair in the games of assumed love that they played, this time was no exception. Her stature as a socialite came with a label of being 'loving' towards Graham and it was viewed widely that one day the two would be married.

Ottoline did offer intimacy of a sort when it suited her and warmth was something she got from the times that Graham or others praised her in order to stave off a moody outburst or period of sulking for a while or so. She needed it to live. On the other side of her, she was his girl and for honour, even if it was just his, he had to defend that fact.

Graham thought that there was much more to him than Ottoline had about her but in reality he too was as fickle as the seasons were and would help himself in immense portions to anything that he could derive pleasure from, however shallow or short lived it may have been. As confident and heroic as he always believed himself to be, he strode over to the couple now even closer, amorously gazing into each other's eyes it seemed. He placed his expensively tailored black leather shoes toe to toe with his latest opposition and forced his hand into Ottoline's, gripping it tight and squeezing as he did so.

"I don't think we've met *Ottoline,*" he said with venom.

Both parties looked surprised or pretended to at least. Graham continued with a steely eyed glare and accusing tongue and pushed her harder to explain herself whilst she stood next to a man that Graham didn't know.

"Ottoline you really have gone too far this time, did you think I didn't see you two?"

She started to reply but stuttered and stammered in an attempt to make out that she were a little unsure as to exactly who the man was and why she had been talking to him. The men looked at one another; Graham spoke whilst making and holding eye contact with the man before him, the man met his stare and equalled it with well practiced menace. Graham felt he had to speak again.

"This is Miss Barker; if you were wondering, Mr..?"

"It's Charles, Charles Henry. I was..."

Graham interjected before a proper reply could be given. "...kissing her was it? You know this woman do you?" he asked before starting to rant and rave about just who his girl was and indeed who Graham Wright was and what he was angry about. He implied that he *did not* know her and therefore should not be in a posture that he termed as close. The fact was; Wright hardly knew her either.

The man before him was around thirty years in age and was quite a bit shorter than Graham was but was also clearly a player in the social game that they all played. His wildly long hair was different to the style of the time and Graham picked on that as another reason why he should dislike the man. It was as if he saw him as more than just a threat to his girl but also as a stag may view an opponent just for standing in the same forest. Graham was ready to rut.

Ottoline summoned up yet another practiced smile from her back catalogue and smugly looked up at Graham Wright with a half drunken and semi-pretty gaze. With that one look his ranting and impolite tone of voice seemed to drift off into the massive void of space above their heads. Even his anger towards the other stag now ebbed away and he realised that nothing had changed and therefore, as usual, Ottoline had won the battle and the war.

She bent almost delicately at the waist and kissed this same cheek as she had done whilst they had been dancing before forcing a cosmetic smile towards them both. The party was over for them and it seemed that she wanted to be taken home. Graham glanced up and casually winked his right eye, teasing Charles Henry with his immature mocking; the man raised his eyebrows to imply 'why should he care anyway?' Both men had lost it seemed.

The evening air was crisp and quite bracing; this was a sudden change to the stuffy heat of the club and the warmth of the last few days. The stars were sadly just dim specks of light and covered with thick grey night-time cloud; the moon to the left was still only an early crescent. The couple walked out of the building and towards the car outside on the street side by side but not hand in hand or even close to each other. Graham's beautifully, expensively, exuberant white car roared with passion and excitement once it was started and leapt into action as he depressed the silver pedal beneath his right foot.

He drove through the blackened smoggy streets of London with only the headlights of the car lighting the dark rough streets before them. On street corners, small gas lamps lit the cobbles below them casting shadows upwards across the red brick buildings that surrounded the sparsely populated roads.

Victoria Terrace stood at the end of the short journey garishly illuminated by numerous lamps on its facade at the end of Clarence Road on otherwise blackened streets. An uneasy silence had excited since they had started off and Graham thinking out the subject over and over in his mind felt he could bear it no longer. His anger had grown in his head as it always did and he had to speak up there and then.

"Ottoline, I'm sick and tired of this furtiveness all the time, this selfish abandon, this frivolous excess; you said you would be mine; for some foolish reason I believed that."

He looked away as he said it but even if he had faced her the result would be no different. His heart rose and fell like the wooden roller-coasters on the popular destinations at sea fronts at Blackpool and his stomach seemed to be within his mouth rather than where it should have been. He was angry and yet he knew that his argument would do nothing but heap pressure upon himself.

Ottoline looked up at him like a small wide eyed puppy as if shocked that he should have even noticed or that he'd have the audacity to comment on *anything* she said or did. Her pale, lifeless face told him she was merely humouring him and she refused to listen, her usual cunning science said more than any words she could ever manage. Her eyes were a pale washed out green and wildly insincere, her face, an open and well read book, a book however that he had always failed to read.

She had been like this since she had first set eyes on him a year ago and yet he had failed to ever tame the beast behind the furrowed brow. Her erratic yet predictable eruption and forced glaring eyes was meaningless and impolite but no less than what he had deserved he felt. He carried on his futile battle to push her to admit or resign herself to something and questioned her again.

"At least you're not bloody drunk again, acting like some kind of hopeless fool..." He stopped, thinking for a moment, frowning at his thought and then glancing across to her said.

"...but you're no fool are you? The fool's right here, sitting next to you."

His energetic speech floated off into the void that hung between them as the spoilt little girl before him manifested another one of her faces before him whilst puffing out more dense smoke from yet another cigarette. *His girl,* socially beautiful, with small, well proportioned features and such high society charm; seemed more interested in the latest off the shelf loose clothing and raging parties than in sharing anything with him.

They only things they ever shared were upset and grief. She'd again managed to dispel any grievances that Graham had by doing a cruelly precise and well practiced nothing. She could see little wrong in spreading herself around when and wherever she liked and knew full well that Graham would do anything she demanded in the end. She had him, as always, under her thumb and whatever squealing he did, she knew she could cry and then be forgiven, welcomed back with open arms and sincere apologies.

She sat there in total silence, smugly examining the intricate details of her spindly white fingers in the darkness of the car; yet her face tactfully revealed the sorry, sweet and delicate figure she was everything but. "Oh Graham you..."

She started to speak but Graham Wright sensed a slight whimper in Ottoline's throat as she did so and jumped to prevent the inevitable with his own words. "I just can't stand it," He paused before raising his voice further and continuing.

"Don't cry, I know that you're going to, you do it all the time. Every argument, each time you can't find an answer you blubber and cry in a hope that I'm just going to shut up, just going to let you win...not this time, oh no."

Ottoline interjected in another attempt to throw her frustrated date to her knifing mental shadows, "You're just jealous of that Charles aren't you?"

He immediately shrugged off the accusation, despite the fact that it was the truth. She always had the ability, in one way or another, of finding and then speaking the truth, in turn getting deep into him. "No!" He said bluntly. "If I was, which obviously I'm not, I'd have every bloody reason to be wouldn't I? I'm flirtatious am I? I do it to you, do I?"

He knew this was also a lie, and so of course did she, saying it only made his argument seem all the more futile, if not pathetic. The argument was slipping and his words as always were on the verge of hypocrisy. His drunken gaze and hazy mind were not helping his argument as he reverted to the insecure person he was on the inside. He stopped speaking and instead looked down towards the wooden steering wheel and then back to the road.

Again his girl sat still hidden amongst the shadows and remained quite content to let Graham's fires burn themselves out before making any kind of move to extinguish them further. She played him like a game of cards, she always held the aces somehow; usually sneaking them in half way through a game from underneath the table or from her sleeve. She thought her words out carefully in her head before uttering them in her all too over polite and shrill feminine tones. Graham sat tight in his seat and tried to ignore the implications that he knew were on their way.

"I know you love me." She smiled whilst looking away from Graham and out of the passenger window before continuing. "I know you couldn't leave me and it's just not my fault Graham that you are an upright, rotten traditionalist. What's wrong with a little fun here and there anyway, what kind of world do you still think this is anyway?"

With this she angrily slapped her hand onto her knee, her words, he knew, probably marked the end to the conversation. Graham urgently wished Ottoline's terrace would appear, in the vain hope that she would get out, somehow fall out or just totally disappear. He attempted to answer the questions posed again against the barrage of argument with his own words.

He stared across at her as if she had now revealed some sacred secret that only he had been permitted to say. She mentioned the word love and that put him on the spot, it was a word he feared and a word that always would provoke a reaction. He floundered for a second or two not knowing how to deal with the love issue, whatever that was.

"What's love got to do with it?" he suddenly blurted out.

"I don't love you, I never have oh, and yes, there is everything wrong with a little fun 'here and there' as you put it actually." He had already gone too far he felt but his anger was such that he could not stop the advance on his so called girlfriend. "Do you just have fun? Or do you also sleep with them?" He looked her straight in her shadow covered face and then continued.

"Is that the fun you mean? Is it?"

He looked back to the road in front of him but he knew he'd crossed the line. He didn't need to look back across to her to know that. There was always a line and he always crossed it somehow even if she moved it so that he could step or fall flat on his face over it. He had been driven to it once again but had failed to notice its cunningly disguised appearance when it appeared, he always did.

Without care or thought, Ottoline swung a slap at his face forcing the car to swerve and career towards a white painted gate-post. Graham's beautiful white coloured and highly polished expensive car hit the gate. Smashing glass and twisting chrome metal broke the stillness of the quiet evening as the light and wing took the punishment from Ottoline's rage in a shower of splintering wood and metal. Graham's face hit the polished walnut wooden dashboard hard.

Dazed and confused, Graham sat back upright and touched his forehead with his left hand, and felt fresh warm blood running down his cheek and neck then onto his pristine white starched collar. Ottoline was shaken but un-harmed. They sat quietly for a moment just looking at still shadows in the darkness of night. Graham reversed back onto the road and sheepishly gave her a look that suggested acceptance of blame for the whole incident. Despite this still he battled on as she twisted the already imbedded knife.

"Look, just stop this, you know I'll leave you, don't you realise that?"

Graham's armour was now low and all his heavy guns seemed to have been abandoned further down the road. Ottoline laughed at his precariousness, that he could lose the trend-setter of the entire West-End party scene. He knew he was out of his own league and said no more. He knew he could do little without her for now and sympathetically kissed her cheek before parking at the front of the terrace, turning off the engine and getting out.

Getting out he walked over to the passenger door and opened it, helping Ottoline out, with a firm and ridged hand and shut the door with a frustrated slam. She still looked as if she were painfully suffering his attentions and probably was. The moon gleamed over them, peering over the vivid green ivy that coated and clung to the terrace wall and with half cocked face at the numerous lights that lit the facade. She looked her pale faced self again under those lights and appeared to glow with some kind of radiance.

Making sure that she were again dramatically portraying an over-zealous show of forced emotion, she took a large gulp of stale air and sighed, shaking her head slightly as she did so before turning to face Graham.

"You're not staying then?" She proceeded to bluntly ask, removing her new French silk cloth hat as she did so. She waited no more than a moment before angrily turning her head with her usual exuberance and marching off in the direction of the apartment's entrance.

Graham stood amongst the silent shadows and silver moonlight and remained in two minds as to whether he should get into the battered car and drive home as a mark of his feelings against her insensibility or to stay just as Ottoline again required. He wanted to just get in the car and slam the door as hard as he could, not saying a word as he did so. He wanted to then drive back home as fast as he could make it and then have nothing more to do with that woman ever again and yet somehow, despite the feelings deep inside, he seemed compelled to follow her.

He did just that and they walked; Ottoline two steps ahead of him towards the door of that cold stone building and the hard steps that lead up to the front door. All that had been said appeared to melt into the night's sky, just as it always did. Tricked, beaten and betrayed he knew, but even that said he dutifully followed. One day he wished he could be free of her, but it suited him at the moment to share his life with her, whatever her scorn and scavenging mind ripped from him. It suited her to be with him and that was how it was going to be.

The trim figure led him to the iron lift and then pressed the control for the fourth level. The lift was a wonderful mixture of solid iron and hand carved Italian marble panelling. It looked quite beautiful under the dim amber lights. The doors impolitely slammed shut and then with a jolt the lift creaked and shook its way to Ottoline's floor.

Graham's face remained positioned towards the wall and his disinterested gaze was just a timid protest to his girlfriend's sour attitude for all that had gone before him that night that had just transpired around them. Ottoline again had that look of ultimate control on her face and again she was just that, in charge. They alighted from the lift and walked to the door of the flat that she shared with her two female friends. Inside they said and did little, the interaction was minimal and all the emotion that Graham felt was to imagine how life could have been with someone else.

There was little to do other than the inevitable as there always was in Graham's opinion it stopped him having to speak with her for a while at least. For half an hour into the morning the couple kissed and held each other, searching for something they both needed that evidently was not there. Each realised that one day, one time when perhaps it was maybe more acceptable for both parties that they should end the falsity that they clung to with every living breath. But now was all that mattered and they both pretended that they were enjoying it.

It was what Graham perceived as a blind well of excitement, the deeper and deeper that he reached into its richness, the more and more he realised that he should be as far apart as from it as he could possibly manage. It was a relationship built on the music that animated a generation, not on love or value or emotion. It was something deep and thrilling, bubbling in their blood, something neither of them nor any other could control, a world that had for now spun wildly out of control.

They knew that the relationship was built on wild and unfounded gossip, fluid hot Martini evenings, youth gaiety and frivolity; and that made no hell of difference to them. He believed in love, he'd never received it neither had he given it, Ottoline was a mere substitute and an excuse.

She knew she could play him just like she had played the others and whilst they were the talk of high society they would remain together on the pretext of love and the satisfaction of physical sex for fulfilment purposes. She believed in love as he did, she believed she gave it, she believed she received it; nothing was further from the truth. But with the free love culture and time gleefully breaking away from the shackles of the past, but who could spare a care?

What was love anyway? What did it mean when they could have the fox-trot and a fever in the blood? What did it matter when a new superficial energy could illuminate an entire life time. Why suffer risky pain and suffering when social matchmaking would suffice: when the flappers could have comfort and convenience and gentlemen could have all the bathing beauty contests and days out in the country that they liked.

There they were in bed together, yet it seemed that they should be far apart they were not a couple that should have been together that was for sure but they were a couple that had been thrown together for the purpose of society. They shared parts of their life with each other but not each other's heart, not each other's feelings or their emotions. They shared each other's bodies but not for love.

Graham took off his clothes and rose to the occasion but didn't feel that he should have done nor was he satisfied that he had done. He still felt angry with the whole concept of it and was clearly and massively disjointed from love, yet there he was with trousers around his ankles having sexual intercourse with the woman before him thinking of someone else whilst he did it, he did not make love that evening.

She lay there showing yet another face as Graham sweated in a vain attempt to satisfy her. This time was predictably just like all the others had been, impassive, cold and loveless and the peaceful two o'clock drive seemed more enjoyable.

He wished he could leave her: the longer he was with her, the more he thought of Maria Taumont, Sally Wentingham, Bonny Pickford and now Florence Morrell. He was beginning to see through Ottoline's thin, skin deep ,disguise and false sincerity. He was the last to do so but finally it had come.

He'd made all the newspapers and been to more riotous themed parties than even he could remember; his associations with Miss Ottoline Barker had made him even more of a desirable person, someone that excited all for many reasons be it money, spectacle or sexual interest. It was always easier to play along than to return to the honest and truthful man he was before and was inside.

Her talk of women's rights and zeal for revolutionary change had begun to bore him and only when drunk did he even dare to put his point forward. One moment he was the party animal, or her sweet love, the next, he was a bastion of the evil and the wasteful old world. In her mind however she just wanted it all, all of the time.

Graham spent the next day at home with his father; feeling strangely at ease with him and conversed for almost an hour on any topical subject that came to mind and there seemed to be a few on this occasion. Graham was especially pleased that his father had asked him about last night's dance at the Embassy club on Bond Street.

"You had a smashing time at the dance last night Graham I presume?"he said in his pompously official way. He paused a moment slowly moving his attention from his newspaper to Graham. "How was the dancing?"

He continued in his gruff, gentleman's voice. Graham was a little surprised to listen to his father expressing interest but it pleased him that he did so. There was a lot that had happened that night but very little that his father would have been impressed with so he decided to just scout around the edges. Instead, in reply to his father's question he gave, as he always did, the impression of a civilised and enjoyable evening. Graham's father was from the old world, more interested in the financial times, warfare and dead soldiers and the way that society had become de-valued over the decade since the Great War.

The large figure of Robert William Wright had been a well respected engineer and latterly, over the last few years, had held the seat of driver for the Bentley racing team bringing success and fortune over the first four formative years of the motor sport pastime. Graham's father had previously held charge of a battalion of infantry during the battle of the Somme and served in the Irish territories, amassing much wealth, honour and experience for his service to the King and country. The newspapers loved him and wrote even more in there columns about him than they did about his son and his riotous parties.

The family's house was a grand one within a large number of acres of wooded and agricultural land and pasture near London. The wealth that they and the family had lived in had always surrounded them and Graham, despite his job as junior partner in a solicitors practice didn't need to work as his father's income and family inheritance was enough to see him through his expensive lifestyle of women and cars.

The front of the house was in the classic English style with large hand cut stone on the front of the large building and finely hand crafted blocks of limestone to the exterior of the rest of the age old structure. Powerful columns rose from the ground supporting a triangular roof with a shield, in carved stone. of the family coat of arms at the centre of it. The building and the grand grounds that it stood in, were the product of years of ancestry, wealth and achievement and Graham Wright took his part within that.

Graham's father's opinion of wealth and honour and in serving king and country with the old lie had often clashed with Graham's and he blamed 'his type' for the old wasteful society and looked disdainfully at people that didn't relish the younger generation and its constantly changing moods and morals.

Graham sat with his father as the maid brought in breakfast consisting of amongst other things; eggs of three types and toast of both English and French varieties. Jam from a local farm and freshly imported fruit from all over the empire. They ate and conversed on matters that seemed relevant at the time. Graham tried to avoid any questions relating to his social life and managed to keep it to topics that his father would like to discuss.

After a full breakfast, conversation seemed to be drying up and Graham excused himself from his father's company to call on Sally Wentingham. He perceived a drive to Brighton sea front along the promenade in the brisk sea air and to show Sally the new flat he had recently had built for him, possibly getting the car repaired on the return journey.

At Sally's house he positively pulled the bell chain and waited for the large figure of Mrs Herring to appear from the depths of the house to open the door. She arrived in a puff having run up the stairs but she smiled in her usual jovial manor anyway. She showed Mr Wright into the lounge where she produced a freshly brewed cup of tea from a silver pot before climbing the stairs to Sally's bedroom.

The slight figure of the auburn haired girl who arrived at the bottom of the stairs was again a pleasure for him to behold. Her well mannered character and pretty face were the things he enjoyed most about her, that and the relief from Ottoline that she gave him from time to time. He always found her to be different from the other girls he had known, she seemed a little more honest and thoughtful, it was just a shame that Graham had always been cheating on her with Ottoline.

"Oh Graham!" she pronounced in her velvety, soft, smooth voice as a tiny smile of delight appeared on her slightly parted and moist pink lips. Her eye contact dropped towards the floor and her expression changed as she evidently recalled something she had momentarily tried to push out of her mind when Graham arrived.

She walked over to a set of oak drawers and after some foraging retrieved a letter, holding it out for Graham's attention. He watched her lightly freckled face change again to a figure of concern and thought; her little, trembling white fingers loosely feeling the paper as the document changed between her hands. She sat down, taking in a deep breath of air before she spoke. "There's something you should know Graham, I think maybe I should have told you earlier but I...."

She stopped half way through her sentence it seemed with a shortness of breath. He looked at her eyes. They were eyes that desperately feared that something from within her would strike her down. She closed them in mid sentence. Instead of reading the letter, she passed it over to Graham to read for himself. He began to read, after glancing up once more as she moved her colourful ardent flamed hair from her eyes to behind her ears.

Graham started to read the letter:

'My dearest divine Sally I'm unable to hold inside me a feeling as powerful as this any longer and with glee I write to explain my heart once more. My love for you is undying, unsurpassed by any other and is as pure as any in their wildest dreams could imagine.

My heart does sing all the joys and warmth of summer evenings, all the blissful comfort of silver moonlight on still, starlit waters and does burn with an invigorating, ardent flame of my burning desire.

I have never loved you nor any other so much as I proudly proclaim today and wish for you to share all the love I know we need to hold. Never has there been someone I needed more, never someone I could do without less.

Dance with your ever living fascination through flowers mixed, vivid and scented, through vales and streams of crystal radiance. So long as the wind breathes life to the earth and that the sun and moon reflect their glory upon me, I shall love you with all my heart and soul.

I have prayed in vain for months, with pain swelling inside my aching body, that I could once more be with you. It is with pounding heart and utter excitability that I can reveal that tomorrow I will be with you, in the arms of the woman I do so love.

All of my love as always; William.

Graham nearly choked as he read the words, the thought of another man ever meaning anything to his girl was an extraordinary thing for him even to contemplate. He started to smile as he thought about how crazy the man who wrote the letter must have been. Sally spoke before Graham had time to comment on what he had just read.

"Graham, it's over, our..." she paused, trying to phrase the remark in the best way she could think of and the one that would cause her the least pain. She continued "...little thing, it's over, I'll have to ask you to leave." Sally turned her head away from Graham. She clearly felt as sick as she had ever done before but could not add anything else. Graham looked up, sighed then frowned angrily at her suggestion; he was shocked that she should say such a thing. He was more surprised and indeed angry that she had kept such a secret from him. His tone was strongly abrasive and assertive as it had a tendency to be when confronted with home truths. He spoke with the first words that came into his head.

"Look the man is obviously crazy, he writes some flowery letter with some poetic words on it and you think it's love or something! He's hardly a mint to his name anyway and just where has he been lately, loving you? From America? I don't think so."

Graham loved these little outbursts of his and relished the power he could wield with his words, especially over a woman, even his own. "Why does he think he can just `have` you like some object. He writes a letter, all is forgotten and you come running? Don't you have anything about you?"

The words were harsh, even from his lips especially as they were directed to a young girl who was far more fragile than the women he had ever had outbursts towards. In response to his tirade she didn't offer any words but instead she began to cry into a small lace embroidered white handkerchief that she took out from a pocket in the side of her dress. Graham wasn't ready to go easy on her just yet, even the remotest thought that he was being cheated on was too powerful for him to leave it just yet.

He scoffed at her whimpering attempt to intervene and turned to face the window and the sunlight in the garden huffing to himself as he did so. She turned also and appeared even more hurt, replying with her back towards him; looking out of the opposite window with an intense stare, gazing at the finely manicured lawn as if some historic event were occurring on the other side of the glass. Graham turned back to face her, remaining relaxed. His right arm rested heavily on the marble fire-place, tea in the other hand rapidly going cold as the drama continued to unfold. Sally eventually found the composure to reply

"He's not crazy, he's a loving man, a decent man and don't speak to me like that Graham, you don't even know him. No he's not got your money or style, but he's sensible and honest and what's more he *loves* me, you don't."

Sally's tears and dramatically emotive arm and hand gesturing had left Graham feeling uneasy and a little shameful of his outburst. Graham was again taken aback and fought hard to maintain his cool exterior before offering more comment.

"Oh look I didn't mean it, I really like you and the times we have shared together, that's why I got upset."

He had a way, a reassuring smile and crafty glint in his eye. He was a good looking young man, well dressed and had charm in abundance but his attitude was often abrupt and self-opinionated. He didn't suffer fools gladly that was for sure but he could always seem to get out of a difficult circumstance by a smooth move or sentence that could melt a heart or heal a wound.

A smile reappeared for a fleeting moment as she understood that he really liked her, despite falling short of loving her; even though she already knew it. That was all that she was going to get and in that way she was happy. Graham decided to continue his quest to make amends.

"Why can't we go out today, and when he comes back we'll see if you're ready to decide between us?"

Sally's face changed with Graham's suggestion and her whole attitude seemed lighter in an instant. She clearly didn't enjoy having to decide between two men she liked for differing reasons, but it was a whole day away and this was *the* Graham Wright. She agreed to Brighton and would decide when the two men were together the following day; until then she would put the whole thing out of her mind until then. Graham continued.

"You'll have to visit the new place...Ottoline thinks it's divine."

Sally swung a hand on the keys of the piano and began playing furiously at the mention of the name. Mostly out of tune. Graham had crossed the line once again.

"Don't mention *that* woman in my company thank you, it's bad enough having to share you with her so let's leave her out of this if you'd be so kind, and maybe I will put William out my mind."

He attempted to repair the damage once again. He put down his now stale, cold tea and took her hand, leading her outside to the drive-way at the front of her house. As she passed Graham's car she enquired as to the broken wing reaching out a hand and softly touching the damaged paint as she did so. He couldn't or more accurately didn't want to explain the incident with Ottoline and proceeded to dream up a situation pleading sympathy. She accepted it and this it seemed settled down the atmosphere between them.

The three litre engine rumbled into life and it seemed, with it, meant the turning of a fresh page and all that was written on the previous page had instantly been forgotten between the two of them. The miles were eaten up at an alarming rate, even for Graham's energetic driving, as images of his father's motor racing victories flitted into his mind. Green fields rushed past in a hazy blur, trees and hedges shot past as the scenery blended and blurred green in to a rush of speed. Skies were blue, delicately charmed by lazy white puffs of cloud floating aimlessly about the tranquil earth. Newton Lake glinted in the midday sun as the summer remained as warm as he had desired it, seasoned now with a promising new light and some relentless and vigorous flavours.

Graham had always looked for the summer and the warmth that it brought. It seemed that the temperate skies that surrounded them had started to push his belief that he could attain it. The sea front was as busy as usual, people wandering and meandering here and there, dotted about the scene, basking in the fine sea air and radiant strands of sunlight that surely invigorating them all. Many strolled hand in hand reflecting love and affection to their partner, feeling entirely at home with the concept of life.

It certainly was peaceful, totally so, were it not for the calling, swooping gulls and the washing ocean wave, white and crashing and then soothingly soft and melting into the smooth pebbles on the beach. Its rhythm was timeless and its beauty as elegant for Graham as it was for all men. Further out, the sea laid calm, deep set blue, soft to the eye, romantic and serene to the mind. Light sea air rose and lifted flags on the pavilion, cooling brilliantly warm rays of summer sun. Playful children heaped sand into castles and threw coloured shells and pebbles into the vast expanse of water before them.

Walking side by side seemed sublime and as Graham reached for Sally's small hand and placed it in his, the feeling continued to blossom as the pace slowed to one almost of romance. Seabirds, guillemots and razorbills rose and dived excitedly, chasing the fishing boats cutting the white peeks as they went about their hurried yet comfortable business across the horizon. Nets were laid out across the waves to catch next morning's fish when fishermen would haul and hoist them aboard the sides of the quaint wooden boats as they floated about the blue sea before them.

Ladies and gentlemen wandered along the wooden pier, looking out across an ocean as vast as the sky above it. Her skin was as soft and as clear as the blue sky, her emotions as varied as the waves, her affection an endless warming sun above. His lungs filled with the exhilarating salty sea air as he looked at the prize that he proudly presented as his own on the promenade.

Foaming peaks crashing against the sculpted legs of the iron pier made the sea look tame, defiant against its power. But nature would find a way, it always did; it took the land and shaped the stone, curved the caves and smoothed the shore, destroyed the ships and smashed up the boats. Whatever had been constructed by whomever for whatever reason would one day be humbled by its raging power and masterful strength. Maybe not in a day, a year or even in a hundred years, but the sea always had the last laugh.

At night, unwatched, it sneaked up in secret and ravaged the coast, pillaged the castles built on the beaches, cut into the bleeding land. Like a thief it came and like a thief it slipped away. Sleeping harbour men never realised the villain, never understood the robber in their neighbourhood. The winds that blew, the sun that shone, the sea that crashed all in daytime seemed of little occurrence; yet at night; when all is still, their unmerciful ways wrestled the earth, man and all his beliefs, before sinking again to daytime stillness and smugness, watching, just lurking and mocking.

He loved this affection that she showed him, somehow she made it seem different, somehow more legitimate. The news that William would be arriving tomorrow and that Sally had not made their relationship clear before then, had cut him like he had scarcely known. He knew he was cheating on Ottoline and had been doing so from the beginning, he also knew she was doing it to William. Each fed off the other for their social status. As soon as Graham got a bad name for cheating she would leave him he felt. He couldn't afford for this to happen yet could never stay loyal to someone he neither cared for nor respected, in other words, Ottoline.

It was made by society for society and in time would be broken by society. It had taken six months of parties and furtiveness to realise that Ottoline neither cared or respected him either and would soon enough issue his marching orders to him.

He knew too he was cheating on Sally, who in reality didn't know the social game he played and would be the victim, no matter what the outcome. It hurt Graham to know that Sally would get hurt, yet never could he find a way to escape; the knowledge that Sally was cheating on him hurt him more than that.

The house was painted white plaster throughout, from its sleek fluid exterior curves and art deco intricacies to its plain and simple rooms and corridors inside. The apartment at St. James' House seemed cool and strangely detached from the feelings he had inside and the warmth of the day outside the large glass front to the building. The times they shared in the redecorated bedroom were again a welcome break from his worries and again they made the times with Ottoline seem as false as they really were.

It was the closest to love that he had ever known, yet still the dream seemed understandable and as if it had been already decided that it were not for him. Still it was not long before he melted into almost complete comfort and relaxation anyway, with a girl that could instantly relax his troubles with her delicate female touch. They touched, cuddled and kissed for some time. Sally felt easy in her relinquishment of her body and mind and Graham once more, feeling he needed intimacy, gave it and took what came to him with pleasurable indulgence.

At six the couple ate at 'The Watch' on Percy Street, that was one of their favourite places to go to. The restaurant was a small family business that Graham frequented regularly; with its black wooden beams and painted white walls. Freshly caught shrimp and mackerel were the order of the day and both fully enjoyed the meal, leaving the restaurant after a smoke at seven o'clock.

Graham loved the sea and its pulsating charm and with fine food, and a good looking woman that he had only recently made love to, he was again of the belief that he had found the summer. Drunk on lustful thought and sexual satisfaction, Graham took his black leather shoe to the silver peddle and drove the couple back to Sally's home, once again at speed. Graham conversed with Mr Wentingham, who seemed more inclined to accept the changing times than his own father and it was a pleasing afternoon and evening for the threesome.

After many more Martini's, games of tidily-winks and further conversation, Graham left into the cooling night-time breeze and drove home, back to Albert Street. Graham was inebriated and in rampant controlling mood as he made his way home. He just loved that feeling and wanted to indulge to excess so he arranged a repeat visit with Sally on the evening of the next day.

Evening came and was greeted by a visit to Albert Street by Sally, clutching yet another hand written letter. She looked worn out and tired but she kissed his cheek as he opened the door, beaming with delight as she entered. A little frown appeared on her white face as she spoke of recent events, addressing Graham with her usual polite speech.

It transpired that William had not made it on Sunday as he had promised but instead would be arriving on the half past four train the day after. She paused for a while as she carefully selected her vocabulary. Graham thought about criticising the man for not keeping his word, but thought better than to say it. What Sally said next was a total surprise to Graham and certainly caught him off guard. She seemed excited in her speech and with a flurry of arm movements and expression began.

"I want you to meet him. He is really nice you know, you'll like him, he's just like you..."

Graham knew he would hate the man.

"Do you honestly think that would be a really good idea, I mean it's not good enough for you having a secret affair and leaving me but you now want me to meet him?" Her reply was instantaneous.

"What do you mean *I've* got a secret affair? So have you...it's me!"

Graham stood with a blank expression etched on his face, defenceless, Ottoline was carefully devious and always on the attack; Sally always used the simple truth, both were as effective. It was Sally's turn this time to smooth out the cracks ,so attempted to change the subject slightly.

"Look I'm having a Greek and Egyptian themed party tomorrow night at eight o'clock; I'd love you to come and..." Graham was not going to accept what she had to say. Not in the slightest.

"...meet him? Was it?" He interjected rapidly.

"Yes, I'd like you to; you will come wont you? Graham?"

That was how it ended, Sally fully intended for them all to sit and talk despite Graham's temperament. Graham just couldn't see it. He had no doubt that this William, whoever he was, wouldn't either. He bid her goodbye and sat down to contemplate the matter over a glass of Scotch, or several as the evening wore on. It angered him to know that Sally thought so little of him or that she was so naive to think that Graham would accept what she had proposed for him to do.

On a journey to the petrol filling station his attitude changed greatly by a chance meeting with Florence Morrell, getting her little black Austin filled at the same time. Getting out of the car he walked over to her side window armed with a false smile and a pre-rehearsed comment on the dance that they attended last week. Words on more interesting subjects ,as ever when women were concerned, eluded him.

"Oh...hello!" he said, with as much false surprise as he could muster.

"You enjoyed the dance then did you? You seemed to be doing so..."

His words seemed to tail off in the engine noise of a passing vehicle. He found lying easy. Florence looked up out of the open window as if she were thinking of a reason why the man should bother to speak to her and made sure she answered distantly.

"Some may have said so, perhaps."

He remained stuck for words; he wanted to ask her something, anything but all his thoughts seemed to have been left back at Albert Road. She sat patiently waiting and removed her cloth cap with a surplus of style; feeling her black hair with her spindly fingers, looking at the presently disabled man before her. As nothing was apparently coming she reached out and paid the filler with a crisp note before taking the change. Suddenly he had a brainwave.

"I'm going to Sally Wentingham's Greek and Egyptian party tonight, I wondered if I could take you along...if you're not busy that is?"

He stumbled through the words but it seemed to have the desired result in the end. A small yet intriguing smile appeared on her pale and full lips as she casually blinked her eyes for no particular reason before replying in her usual calm manner, yet never looking him in the eye. If she had, then she knew that she ran the possibility of giving in to his charm or folding at that glint in his eye. She was much too stubborn for any situation to be easy and lived to make things difficult for whoever she met. Reality said that she had already agreed and that Graham had also, they both would have agreed to anything that she had suggested.

"I might not be engaged tonight, if you don't have anything else to do that is," she said before looking up and seemingly collecting a thought from the heavens.

"She's not...then...erm...Ottoline not going then?

Florence had picked up on a possible rift between Ottoline and Graham and despite it being her friend she was certainly ready to take advantage of the situation when it did arrive, she certainly had all the hallmarks of Ottoline that was for sure. A curious smirk took over from the smile that the black haired prim and tidy woman held on her face as she mildly nodded to the nine o'clock pick up at her house before smirking once again.

She appeared, from her words and demeanour, to be humouring him more than anything or at least that was what she wanted to portray. Graham knew this but carried on with the idea anyway. Graham was taking a large and wholly uncalculated risk by employing Florence as his date over Ottoline whom society had agreed for him to be with. Why he was doing this was a mystery even to him, as any fool could have predicted; news of the event would in time reach Ottoline's attention.

He somehow liked Florence and was tired of Miss Barker; if he were ever to leave her then Miss Florence Morrell would be one of the few real replacements. In all reality this was as unlikely as a second war before the end of the decade. Florence neither took a fancy to Graham nor did she see an 'arrangement' or any arrangements as appropriate, it didn't look likely. It was true that she knew of his affection for her and most probably that their date would be their only ever formal encounter.

She loved to flirt and fool about as did Graham, if only to add another to her enviable list of suitors, to amaze and surprise guests at parties with. Certainly Graham Wright would be a big catch. Graham could not see this, he'd only just realised that Ottoline had been playing him for seven months and that she had never even been close to loving him. Most recently still he'd only just realised that he had never loved her either, confusing love with lust, novelty, desire and pure spectacle.

Despite never revealing it to anyone, he knew that the time with Ottoline was over and a new start would have to be made. For now he bid her farewell and watched as the tyres of her shiny new black car threw up clouds of sand and dust in a chocking cloak as she pulled energetically away, back down Bennett Road and right into Derbyshire Street. The grey haired and oil stained garage man paused his business of attending to the re-fuelling of Graham's car at the pump that Florence had just vacated.

Graham's insides tingled with pleasure, warmth and delight when he recalled the incident only a moment before. He too paid the stout attendant who proceeded to point out the lovely day for the fourth time whilst absent mindedly working the nuts of a car wheel with an oiled spanner. Graham hadn't any desire to chat and his three polite attempts to excuse himself from the conversation had seemingly failed.

Graham waited a moment before launching into a dismissive comment or outburst whilst the man stopped for a while and fingered his dirty grey beard thinking aloud. The thought obviously never came to anything and instead commented on the car's wing.

Graham gave his reply with usual stubborn shortness and inpatient manner. He was getting closer to anger. "Well, I let the woman drive her you see, and, ha! Well you know women drivers as well as I do, hopeless! I mean, straight into the gate post!"

The man looked concerned and nodded his head in agreement before managing half a smile, as the topic of hapless women drivers was one close to his heart.

"Looks an expensive one I'll tell you! Hey? Women, Women! I ask you? First the vote then degrees, even bloody jobs and that and now bleeding well driving about all over the place, I ask you? A danger to us all I'm telling you."

Graham passed judgement as he was still looking to get out of the conversation very quickly. The check shirted, oiled man in front of him continued much to Graham's annoyance.

"I bet they start living on their own soon, think so much of themselves don't they? I bet men aren't good enough for them now I ask you."

Ten minutes later, Graham suddenly managed to pull himself away and was well relieved. Graham had so much and he appeared so complete, and to the outsider there could have been nothing else that he could have wanted in life. There was one thing that he was yet to have, the one thing that he'd always realised that he was without yet, like a star that glinted above him, it seemed close but always remained out of his stretching reach however hard he tried.

Desperately he'd searched, each time failed and yet still in his heart he dreamed of a time when he could have and hold it, give and receive love. He never could have admitted that as it would have harmed his own image but he still felt it inside. All the society games that he remained wrapped up in were just past-times and with little hope of quenching his relentless thirst for sustained acceptance. He had so much to live up to; expectation was high with the media, higher still with his father and overwhelmingly brimming with himself.

He had only ever lived in the shadow of greatness and often mistaken the spectacle of the glittering dance and sparkling glasses of Champagne to be the glint of success and the bubble of life's victories. Most of his troubles he kept to himself and fortunes when he experienced them, he publicly wore around his neck to impress fickle faceless souls with at parties. They always had been impressed by it and that was why he continued doing it.

Only Elizabeth Howard, his good friend of years past, knew the depth of these feelings that ran within him. He loved to talk on the subject with her, and it seemed that with her he could be himself, with less need to impress. He wished he could talk more freely and more often to her. Elizabeth was a girl that he had grown up with, playing as children amongst neighbouring manicured rose gardens and lush green tennis lawns over perceived hot summer days whilst their parents sipped Pimm's number one and lemonade on the wooden veranda.

The summers of the past were always warmer, always more vibrant and carefree, he had forever been looking for those lost summer days and deluded himself that the next was just around the corner. Reality said that whilst he had the opportunity to experience them he never had the ability to recognise that he had even found them.

He dressed alone as usual in his study bedroom, paying meticulous detail to his appearance intending to make as good as possible an impression on his date as he could; intending to show Sally and any other of his doubters just what they were missing. The black bow-tie on white shirt finished off his wonderfully trim appearance as he brushed his thick black hair back in the mirror with new oil and a flourish of detail.

He felt extremely on edge, nervous and even a little apprehensive of the night ahead. He knew nothing of how it would be, he had no idea or even perception of what would be in store: except that he intended to make Florence Morrell his and make all others wound up in jealous rage. It suddenly dawned on him, why only now he wasn't sure but the reality was quite clear. He finally realised the risk he was taking, cheating on Ottoline as he was, so openly and so publicly, but he seemed to have been drawn to it.

He decided after much thought that for another start, a new opportunity it was worth it. With Sally, he knew she would return to him, even if Ottoline found out about Florence. Even if Sally decided upon William, how could she not return to his charms and thrilling personality? He would always have that to fall back on.

The car started first time as usual and Graham took a slow drive around the block to waste time as he was at least twenty minutes early. His nerves crept up and down his back, tingling and pulsating, more for every second he waited. Time eventually came upon him and he rang the door. She appeared at the door, swiftly kissed him, stepped out and shut the door behind her.

The journey was again filled with an uncomfortable silence, one that neither could break. Graham could think of nothing at all to say, Florence didn't feel it was necessary. Graham was glad to reach Sally's house whereby the occasion itself could perhaps provide cause for some conversation between them to emerge. At least he hoped that it would, the whole evening and a lot more was at stake if it didn't.

The butler showed them to one of the rooms at the back, in which the gathered people uttered many mutterings as was usually the case when Wright entered a party. Many were surprised to see Miss Morrell with Wright and not the much more frequently talked about Miss Barker who had not yet; or as Graham hoped would not be attending. It was doubtful that she would have been invited, knowing Sally's lack of appreciation for her, but this had never stopped her in the past.

The seconds ticked over on the clock as Graham searched for imaginative topics to talk on and amaze Florence who stood, back to the wall, strange, false smirk upon her face as was her usual guise.

"Not much happening yet..." he started with.

"No." Graham had to try harder. "I do like your costume by the way." After another few seconds of silence, Florence finally joined the conversation.

"Thank you, I see yours isn't exactly imaginative," she scoffed.

"The shop had none to hire!" Graham jovially responded but Florence was never moved and looked even less interested than usual.

"Oh I see, how interesting," she replied whilst looking to her side at things that were far more interesting to her. Conversation faltered on like this for some time, Florence determined to have a bad time and to make sure Graham did also; Graham trying hard to do otherwise but being unable. He suddenly hit upon an idea; he enquired if Florence wanted air, away from the stiflingly hot party, and to Graham's surprise and delight she said she did.

He led her outside holding her hand as he did so with a view to kissing her outside away from the hubbub of the party atmosphere and indeed the party makers. Once outside he didn't bother to ask and suffer the rejection but instead he made an attempt to kiss her. Florence was equal to the rather futile attempt and she made sure he settled for a mild peck on her cheek instead and spiritedly walked back into the house, Graham following in hot pursuit like a naughty child that had been told to follow.

Once inside he met Sally who greeted him with open arms and with a brilliant smile and bubbling excitement that told him how pleased she was to see him, apparently not witnessing the previous incident. There was no kiss of course, just as there was no affair. Their business was obviously not public knowledge and both parties wanted to keep it that way, especially as it was in Sally's house at her party.

As many as forty guests dotted the house, hiding in corners behind large bushy green plants in decorative pots, in alcoves and along the halls; chatting, drinking, and smoking the evening away with abandon as the Charleston played out loud on the new stylophone. A few gathered in the lounge where Graham and Florence among others were invited to take part in a word association game by the host who was apparently still oblivious to the fact that Graham had not come alone or at least not with Ottoline. The game created laughs and much social interaction that all involved seemed to enjoy. Florence failed to raise much of smile but Graham launched himself into the game, impressing all with his knowledge and personality.

It was a party unlike any he had ever been to; it wasn't a riotous dance for the bright young things, nor was it a formal dinner dance for the olds; but somehow a combination of them both. This could be clearly seen by the guests themselves, those approaching fifty and sixty remained as enthralled at the goings on as those at twenty and thirty were. A cubist painting hung in the hall accompanied by a water coloured seascape of Brighton in the summer sunshine.

On the table lay short stories by Scott Fitzgerald, on the shelves; books by Woolfe, Forster, Sitwell and Elliot's 'The Wasteland' accompanied 'Traditional Ways and Means' and 'The World and Empire'. There really was something for everyone in the house. Sally seemed to know exactly how to please all of the people, all of the time; with the exception of Florence of course.

Out on the terrace, Flappers ate crisps and sipped brightly coloured alcoholic cocktails and gentlemen casually flicked yo-yos and talked on America, Mary Pickford, Charlie Chaplin and Rudolph Valentino. Inside, in the backroom, couples waltzed and conversed on King and country. Somehow this inflammable combination had been concocted without as much as a spark between any of the guests.

Each time there was a break in the games and entertainment, Graham made it his business to supply Florence with copious dry martinis; and two hours after their arrival both were in riotous mood, quite spoiling a well run affair. Conversation therefore between Graham and Florence became more and more liquid as did their consumption of alcohol and a second attempt at 'air' between them resulted in success for Graham's evening's ambition.

The balcony was crowded but it seemed that the couple didn't much care. Graham certainly wasn't a gentleman about it, he didn't seem to be concerned much about that either. Florence had reached the point that she could have been with anyone and still wouldn't have cared at all. The kiss was dull and passionless, done for the sake of it, because he wanted it to happen, it was forced and wholly over the top. Sally's reappearance during the event took her abruptly back, not realising that the Ottoline 'thing', as Graham called it, was ever in danger or that Graham was such a man.

It clearly hurt instantly for her to see him kissing someone else, yet another woman; it was a bitter pill to take. As she sped out of the room, Graham was sure that he could sense a whimper and even tears and he followed her out in hot pursuit. Florence conveniently melted into the background as was her highly perfected ability to camouflage into any situation that would keep her whole.

Sally, now in a torrent of real tears, ran out through the other door and only stopped when his heavy hand appeared on her slender shoulder. He knew she would accept whatever she would say, he had no choice, and his actions had once again backfired upon him. Graham had been broken down and brought to the lowest level. She brushed the tears from her left eye and looked down to the floor for her prompt to what she should say. The pause between conception of thought and its utterance was filled with utmost shame for Graham, despair for Sally.

He really had hurt her, finally he realised this; it had taken yet another moment of foolishness that had ruined all his chances but at least he now had begun to realise what was fake and what was not. Graham was going through emotions that he had never expected to have to deal with and he could offer no words to explain or to deny what had occurred with him that evening. In fact he said absolutely nothing.

It was Sally who spoke. Despite her anger she spoke with composure.

"You really take *some* beating Graham; I'm not going to say anything, that's your business, but let's just say it's time you met *my* William."

The affair was over with Sally he knew that much and unlike the other women that he had pushed into his life and then carelessly thrown out again, he felt for her, an unnatural feeling of regret and shame hung over him. Sally didn't cause a scene or over-zealously flutter her eyelashes; neither did she raise her voice or fling a reddening slap to his white clean-shaven face. This for Graham was what made all the difference and accentuated the fact that she was different to the others that he had known. Furthermore it made the fact that he hurt her even more awakening.

Now he realised that he had lost at least part of what he had been searching for before he had even known that he had found it. Sally looked up at Graham and he found it hard to look her in the eye or even tear his gaze from the floor just beneath his feet to meet her half way. Graham grew up a little that evening and took his punishment more like a man than he had ever done before and listened intently to whatever Sally would say next.

She had placed great emphasis on the fact that the William she had spoken about was 'my' William and, with that, the affair with Graham had been written off and cast in stone and in history. She said nothing as she pointed Graham to the hall. Graham followed the direction of the outstretched arm and walked ,like the condemned man, to meet even more truths in the next room.

A smallish man, glasses, dark haired and smartly dressed looked at him with almost forgiving eyes. He spoke, knowing nothing of the situation and only that Graham was a man that carried weight and was admired by his lover. He spoke politely and with an exciting tone of voice, bubbling with interest and expectation.

"I guess your Graham Wright then…I heard all about you." Graham dodged eye contact the best that he could and spoke his short reply in a reserved tone.

"...Who hasn't?" Graham said quietly and reservedly.

"Words do carry, even to Hollywood you know." The men looked up and caught each other's eye for a brief moment. It was Graham that broke the stare; he was clearly finding the meeting of the men difficult.

"Tell me, have you ever considered a career in films Mr. Wright? I work with a man called Swift I reckon he'd say you'd be a sure-fire hit in the States, you'd be all the rage…"

Graham cut the speech short with an abrupt comment, wishing he could immediately get out of the situation and away from the mess that he had created for himself.

"I'm not sure I'd be what you are looking for," he said dismissively. Graham tried again to end the conversation.

"I have to be somewhere now, just had a wire from my father, so I'll be going: a pleasure to meet you though William." He stuttered through his words almost chocking on them as he did so. He didn't let William reply and instead they shook hands; William looked deep into eyes that were desperately trying to hide.

Wright turned and briefly and lightly touched Sally on her bare shoulder before solemnly walking out onto the lawn. The stars shone brightly above him, the new moon crescent hung watching him. Graham never outwardly showed negative emotions but had anyone seen him at that moment it would have been impossible for them not to see a man in depression.

He felt alone, desperately alone, as if he had just become the only person alive. He felt cold, the breeze cutting into his wounds, yet he remained out there with his memories, thoughts and regrets for a long while. The lawn was empty yet was filled with regret. He heard the laughter from inside that he was no longer part of, other than the centre of a million jokes. The stars seemed lost amongst the clouds that night and yet somehow each seemed so close, but the stark, almost violent truth was that always they remained one arms stretch from possession.

A falling star could sometimes be captured, if not feasted upon, yet whatever the content; the result always idly left fragments adrift, hanging, mocking amid a timeless and infinite galaxy of lost emotion. How he wished for this moment to be able to reach up and seize one, two or a whole constellation if that was what it took. To hold, kindle and care for; to recall and remember vividly what always seemed to fall short. He knew it could never be what his emotive mind searched always in the belief that this time would be different.

For each time it was the same repetition of a tale he knew far too well. The more he delved helplessly into the well of blind excitement, the more his heart came away bloodied, beaten and black, knowing how the moment had been, yet never reaching the closeness he desired. He became aware of the presence of another person but acted in no way different to what he was doing, falling to recognise the presence. He wished it was Sally, he wished it was still last night.

When eventually he did turn around he was more than surprised to see a partly undressed Greek god before him. It was in fact his friend of old, James Lorenzo, who despite the way Graham had been feeling managed to cheer him to see his understanding face illuminated under the shining silver moon.

"I thought you'd like some company," he sighed in part chuckle.

"Still got those same problems then?" His light coloured hair flicked up in the wind and his brown eyes looked at him full of honesty and truth, he continued.

"Remember that business with Freda Newark? He looked at Graham and he knew exactly what he was about to say. "That was exactly the same, you got through that all right, and it's still the same."

James continued with his home truths: "You thought that she was your world for at least a while, yet she drifted away and you soon forgot her...don't you think that Sally will just be..."

Graham cut his friend off abruptly; he had had enough of the truths and wanted to give his opinion. He blasted his old friend with both barrels.

"You're wrong, Sally is...well she's...she's different she's not the same as those others... I've lost it all this time."

Graham stopped and stood vacant in expression and still in stature before listening carefully, putting his emotions aside it seemed. Suddenly he turned around and looked his friend in the eye, his face changing to a smile as the couple shook hands and embraced as old friends do. He realised that what he was saying just wasn't reality.

"You can't find love with everyone, and you can't just have women; it's something that is either going to be there or not...it's a kind of chemistry I think, some elements look great, some just explode."

Graham thought of saying some critical comment of his friend to mind his own business and if he were so great why was he not married. His friend's words were true and he was not exactly in the best possible position to answer back. Still he remained staring into the open garden and occasionally looking up at the sky as he took in deep breaths of the night air.

"Look, I shouldn't think it means a lot right now and if you think you loved Sally, Florence or Ottoline I'm not going to argue; but this William does love her and they have got a history. It had been going on for ages before you stepped into the ring, you might think so but you can't push that away." He looked the other way for a brief moment before adding a further comment whilst laughing to himself.

"No Graham, not even you!" These were not the words that Graham had ever wanted to hear and it was their realism that aggravated him most. Again a stony science prevailed to which James suggested they leave on. It remained with them throughout the car journey home and wasn't until the two were out of the car that it ended and they faced each other in Graham's dimly lit porchway. It was Graham who spoke in desperation really as the tension of thought in his head had clearly taken an aggressive hold over him.

"So? What do I do then?" He sounded quite aggravated and continued.

"I've lost Sally, Florence I guess I never had, and I guarantee Ottoline will know everything by the morning."

He could give no immediate answer and felt deeply for his clumsy irrational friend as he always had the habit of being. After a sigh and a further pause of consideration he offered his response.

"Maybe you're looking for the wrong girl, the wrong places, what you're showing people isn't the Graham Wright I knew, back at Eton. They all love your moves, your partying and your charm, oh yeah they love it. But your also kind, sensitive and you love women, it's about time you looked at yourself, your priorities and stopped letting these shallow women walk all over you."

Graham was somewhat shocked at this truthful response. James was always honest and up front with his words and he found it hard to be otherwise and of course with the best intentions all the way.

"Is there anyone else?" James asked as he continued to probe and offer his advice; Graham shrugged his shoulders, looked to the floor and frowned like a naughty schoolboy wanting to explain his actions but not quite being able to. James continued.

"I mean, people you know well, none of your usual well-to-do lot or your fickle friends, people whose characters you already know? Well?"

Graham again looked surprised at his friend as he anticipated some remark to cool it for a while or that love didn't matter, or to change his life, or get one for that matter. Hesitantly he thought it over in his mind as he would chew toffee in his mouth; trying not to think of any of his usual acquaintances; he surprised himself over just who he could name.

He wasn't entirely sure that he wanted any women at that moment as the breeze lifted his finely tailored jacket and ended the conversation without reaching a conclusion. Graham looked again to the night sky and decided that he could find no answer there either and drove himself back home feeling glum, empty and angry with himself all the way there.

His father remained fixed in the old world and its stuffy conventions of high bound rules, slow waltzing, tight whale bone corsets and stiffly starched dinner dances. Graham drifted into nights of drunkenness, abandon, gaiety, sex and frivolity. The new world blamed the Great War, foreign immigrants, lower class unemployment and all the problems of society on this old timer attitude. The old world blamed the same problems on the new world via irresponsible, immature and immoral behaviour. The new world was never satisfied with what it had whilst the old persistently attempted to return to a moment in time that perhaps never even existed.

One fought the other each day to the death, neither seemed to have got it right. Music changed, speech changed, arts and literature constantly, dancing changed and it was with this flux that these two people and the two worlds collided till something shook. Graham's father was concerned that his son did not follow in his footsteps however as a solicitor in a successful practice and therefore a man of means and stature he did well in society in the traditional sense.

Graham's father had always wanted his only son to follow him into the army and serve king and country and would have done anything he could to ensure that the future he planned for his son went ahead. Graham could not see a worse waste of men than the twisted iron, mud filled shell craters from rampant carnage and the spilt human blood of the Great War that seemed to have brought nothing but shame on all that had taken part in it; his father included.

He knew having studied at exclusive age old Eton school and at Cambridge University and being from a wealthy family that much had been expected of him. He hadn't let anyone down either; firstly achieving academically and then moving to a splendid career as an office manager and then a solicitor. His standing as a well respected professional clashed explosively with his lifestyle as a party animal, womaniser and slave to the night scene, but it was only what all his acquaintances were doing.

Graham had regularly been in the newspapers for the hedonistic parties that he had hosted and for those that he riotously attended at others'. His dates by association always seemed to get their photograph, or at least an inch or two of print. Many who read the papers from the older generation must have despised his antics and questioned why a young upstart should even have been in the newspapers at their perfectly polished breakfast tables. Professionals wondered how he managed to represent blue chip clients and hold down his job in one of the most respected solicitors in the city.

They knew that standards in society were being eroded by the young and the things that they had lived by and cherished had been disregarded and pushed aside. The Charleston hurt their eyes, young conversation damaged their ears and the way that women carried on with a lifestyle that allowed them to be so immoral, angered them intensely.

Graham was still feeling some tenderness from the wounds that he had received from the party the other night. Sally was the last person that he wanted to be with at that moment but strangely he felt compelled to go to her house and speak with her. Having failed to call on Sally on Friday morning, Graham decided that after some work he would put together some courage, call on her and then apologise before lunch.

He spent the morning, as usual, in the office arguing the point with trivial people on several various but tedious matters and clock watched until after two o'clock when he was sure that his absence would not be missed; as was usually the case.

He found the work boring mostly but suffered it because that was his job, any excuse for him to get out of work he would take, however much he angered the senior partners. He urgently drove to Sally's apartment with an uneasy sinking feeling in his belly and he tentatively knocked on the door and rang the bell.

He waited for a few moments but there was no reply. He knocked again and then banged on it, this time more positively.

Strangely, it was Sally that answered the door and she gingerly made in a roundabout way, a suggestion that he should come in, looking to the floor as she did so. They walked into the ground floor reception room and she immediately sat down on the hard Chesterfield suite and stretched back looking as uncomfortable in her face as her body must have been on that hard leather seat. Graham waited. Sally waited and yet nobody spoke. Graham had called to visit her so Sally was not going to be the first to speak as she continued to look blankly around walls that she must have stared at many times before.

Before anyone had spoken she happened to glance out of the window at the beautiful gardens that unfolded beyond them into the distance. A coloured man in wide brimmed hat stood at the side of the beautiful blooms on a rhododendron bush pruning out the dead or woody stems. The gardens that seemed endless were filled with glorious strands of summer sunlight that drifted and floated across the colourful grounds that softly swayed in the light breeze carefully tended by the man in the hat.

It was just another sunny day outside of the windows of the house and not dissimilar to any other summer's day but she seemed to have noticed something amazingly compelling on the other side of the glass and gave her full attention to that rather than to Graham. Graham's attentions were not on the flowers and birds in the lushly vibrant, green summer garden but on getting out the words that he'd been rehearsing in his mind for several days and waited for some fiery response.

"Sally, I think that we should leave our little thing behind us."

Her reply was nothing other than to comment, "Perhaps it ending was a good thing after all." She then seemed to drift off into the silence and tranquillity of the garden.

He thought much more of her now that she was out of his grasp than he had done before the events of last Thursday after hurting her so. Every persistent second that passed he thought more and more of how foolish he was; twice telling her how much he regretted losing her and how much he hopelessly 'liked' her.

She became quite moved at his uncharacteristic explanation of his heart. Graham found it quite difficult to explain his emotions and found it quite uneasy to even think about. He left her crying over something that he had said or maybe had failed to say and made his way back to the office where he encountered the senior partner in a rage at his absence and his missing of an important meeting with a local company.

He was in no mood to be kind and fired a few rounds of abuse at him and then subsequently anyone that came near him for the next hour. He continued to blast out his anger on anyone or anything within his reach. After slamming a few drawers shut and kicking a waste paper bin across his office he decided he had better things to do. He walked out of the office at a quarter to four and off into the centre of town with no care at all for his workload or his job in the slightest. He was much too angry for work on that day anyhow. The fires of Hell still burnt inside him and he could see no way that those flames would expire soon.

This however was soon to change with a chance meeting with Elizabeth. The two old friends noticed each other walking on opposite sides of the road, each seeing the other for a second before realising who they were looking at. Elizabeth looked pretty but busily thinking about something. Graham looked angry and in conflict with himself; it was a wonder that he even saw her with the red mist that clouded his vision.

Graham perked up immediately on seeing her and crossed the road to be by her side. Instantly he told his friend how he'd honestly been missing her and relished the opportunity to talk. His openness must have taken her aback as Graham was never one of those to come forward with his emotions. Within only moments she'd managed to extinguish much of the fire that he held within him. Time passed quickly, deep in conversation as they had not seen each other for over three months. They could always converse freely and on so many subjects that it was always a delight for both to meet and express themselves. This was indeed the only person that Graham ever opened up to and each time for him was a relief.

They sat on a wooden bench in the dappled sunlight and mellow tree shade of Victoria Park and casually talked on Graham's problems, hoping she could provide a woman's perspective on the situation, or at least a little hope. She felt for him as she always did but she could offer no further advice than what James had already said, but they parted in good heart, warmer than when they had met.

Graham seemed to understand now, both James and Elizabeth had said the same thing but he knew that with her he was a different man and although it was only ever for a short time he really relished the opportunity to start to be himself, even if he had only just begun to realise that the real him even existed.

He was awoken from a drowsy afternoon sleep by his servant, knocking politely on his bedroom door. He called out abruptly as to his business. He wasn't particularly a warm person when woken up. The reply that came back revealed that Miss Sally Wentingham was in the hall waiting to see him.

Having not seen Graham for at least five minutes since she had arrived as she nervously paced the floor, she moved into the lounge and sat nervously there instead. She reclined on the soft enveloping cloth covered suite waiting for Graham's appearance, which after another five minutes eventually came.

Upstairs Graham walked up and down the old oak floorboards of his room as he put on his smooth suede jacket, wondering why she had called round to the house after their supposed tear jerking final encounter. Always in his mind he knew that there was hope in all that he did, his love interest was no different.

He arrived downstairs to a polite yet nervously immature smile that seemed to beckon him towards her. Even so he made sure that he would be in command of the conversation, asserting his authority in his first and every breath. Looking her in the eye and moving towards her he began speaking, he decided not to take any prisoners. He grabbed at the moment and launched into attack mode.

"Look, if it's another apology you're wanting then I think you should leave, once was quite enough." She looked down to the floor, turning her delicate shoulder to face Graham as she did so, as if to take the brunt of the words that he flung at her.

She took the statement from Graham without reply and ingested it before sitting up clutching a soft cushion as she did so then gripping it tight with her sharp finger nails. Uncharacteristically and with a sudden urgency she began to speak, flinging the red cushion to the floor as she did so. "Graham I was wrong about you, I really do like you and I want you to come back, I've told William my feelings about you..."

A rare moment of clarity and common sense came over Graham at that moment. He tried to shrug it off but began to reaffirm his case. "...Sally, I really don't think that would be wise, I really think that we shouldn't..."

She cut him off once again. He'd never seen her with such utter fire and certainty in her voice, such emotion and conviction. Her emotions seemed to be flammable as the fire that was the ardent red of her hair. Graham became immediately and utterly confused, strangely he somehow liked it; she enjoyed the sudden change that she had created herself.

Graham, when confronted with any female demanding to be with him, would normally have lapped up the opportunity and taken it without thought or care. Now that he had the chance he stumbled in his mind as to just what he should do. He knew that there was a bigger picture that he had been interfering with and that he had been defeated once before already. He knew that he should be letting go but somehow he knew he couldn't. It was just not him.

"Graham, take me back: I'll be yours, all yours, forever. Graham, we've been at odds before and we've worked it out each time in the end." She looked up and moved towards him softly grasping his hand before placing the other on his cheek. "Just the two of us Graham, surely you want me? Graham do you want me?"

She sat down and again looked to the floor whilst waiting for sentence to be judged on and her fate to be decided by Graham. Only five minutes before he couldn't have believed such a revelation, but here it was in the plainest truth. James's words concerning Sally suddenly crowded his mind as he pondered the new situation he found himself in.

Here was Sally, a girl he liked for many new reasons, asking him to take her into his arms and into his heart. Ottoline and Florence had conveniently left the scene with haste; he perceived the answer to his persistent loneliness lay before him. The fact that Ottoline had now gone made the situation fall into place for Sally and it was clear that she had realised this sometime ago. Graham knew this as well and on numerous occasions before, he would have ruthlessly taken her away like a small helpless mouse in the relentless clawed grip of a bird of prey.

Now he stopped for a moment, thinking, concluding to himself that, yes the occasion maybe was right but a cold and surrendering thought would pass over him making him think perhaps otherwise. The thought of his self-conscience and his duty to honesty and for the purpose of heightening his dream and true love between Sally and William had held him somehow. He honestly wanted to tell her that she should stay away from him, yet the thought of reviving his persistent dreams and biting back at his increasing number of critics seemed too foolish to miss. He was greedy and usually took what he could get; this time was going to be no different.

He knew he shouldn't have disobeyed his head as he always did but he knew that again his weakness would grab him and force him to do it. He reached down to her with his hand and delicately lifted her to her feet. They kissed when Graham put his lips onto, into and all around hers, this time with greater degrees of loving feeling and expression than they had ever done before.

Graham knew what he was doing was wrong, yet folding with passion, richly embraced with warmth and sensuality he felt unable to do the right thing just as was always the case. For that moment he held in his arms a rare and beautiful thing. A sweet and free girl, wholly confused and totally naive but ready to love whoever would love her in return. Graham for the sake of his own satisfaction took her over and used her for his own cruel gain.

He spent a week with her doing a whole medley of things including the obligatory parties and the occasional game of summer tennis, archery and badminton. Perhaps he knew the edge he was living on and how lucky he felt to have her back with him. Sally never mentioned William, whilst Graham's ever biting conscience made sure he never entered a conversation.

Still the boned figure of the politically well practiced Ottoline refused to even look at him as did the calculatingly smug faced Florence who did her best to make the events of the seventeenth seem far more of a spectacle that they really were. Somehow the relationship between Graham and Sally, although filled with some expression and a desperate desire to prove their decision to be with the other right, was never touched by the warmth of the summer.

Maybe the times they shared seemed intense; perhaps touched even with a little heart and soul but still both Graham's deep-set and only recently discovered conscience and James's sobering words rang an alarm bell in his mind and a cold chill down his back. However much Graham tried to force their suitability as a couple, Sally slipped, slowly and surely away from Graham's ever loosening grasp towards the end of the second month as gradually doubts of her supposed devotion to him became evidently absent. William, for the first time made headway in her thoughts and for a rare moment in his life, Graham had decided to put someone else's life above his own.

Graham continued to visit her, perhaps still in very vain belief that something between the two was right but it seemed to be less and less frequent that he could even find reason. People in the clubs and parties that they went too had even suggested that Graham had become like a 'lost puppy' and that his hopeless public affection for Sally was very much misspent. Sally's mind had been swayed and over the next few weeks Sally and William seemed more and more of a couple than Graham and she had or could ever have been. For Sally, Graham seemed more and more like a fleeting moment from the past and the third person in an increasingly close crowd.

Sally spent the morning with William over tea in the warmth of the glass orangery at the rear of the house, in amongst the twisted old roots and young green tender foliage of ripening fruit bushes. Graham often spent his mornings doing nothing, there was never anything to do when Sally didn't call and her calling on him was something that was getting increasingly rare; life seemed intolerably lonely without an attractive woman attached to his side. His father paid him little attention other than to scorn every move in his frustration of Graham's attitude towards life, when he wasn't doing that it seemed that Graham was ready to take over.

James paid him a call and asked if he would enjoy a visit to the theatre of Durham Street. This topic however sparked a whole debate and the evening seemed to evaporate into it instead. Always concerned at Graham's welfare he commented on how his apologies to Sally had sparked a whole new situation. Perhaps he knew what the outcome of James's thoughts would be as he waited with calm composition before commenting.

"Graham, didn't we speak on this matter? I may be wrong but I think we decided that you were to leave Sally completely to William and give someone else a chance." They looked up at one another catching each other's eye with their own whilst James continued to pass judgement in his honest and ever realistic perspective on life. "You know yourself that she's still involved with this chap, you honestly don't think you can run onto the scene like some actor and steal her away, did you?"

Graham tried to say something but couldn't manage to say a single word, instead his lips remained slightly parted with his eyes gaping with hollow sincerity that his ways were still right, even if he knew again he was living a lie. "Tomorrow you call Sally, you're going to tell her it's all over, and if you don't, then I will."

Graham Wright stopped, thinking for a brief moment whilst he pondered his friend's instructions, simply nodding in agreement. It was a rare occasion when Graham conceded any belittlement, yet he physically acknowledged it with a slight nod of his immaculately well groomed head.

It was in fact a week later before he called on Sally again, who answered her door as Mrs Herring was ill in bed with what was described as a 'frightful fever'. She seemed to know what was coming and met him with a wholly superficial smile. With a little hesitation and a great deal of apprehension he told her to realise that William and not him was the one to choose. Her face told him that she had already decided.

He left with his heart still fluttering and the power he felt from it impressed upon him the quandary of whether his courageous step was the right one. Whether or not he was ever in love with Sally he couldn't remember but it was highly unlikely; this, even he knew. He may have known it but severally disliked the implication and used an ideal of love to make the episode seem calculated and legitimate. Sally was simply there for him at the right time and to think anything else was reality was just nonsense.

He needed someone to love him, a fact that he knew more than ever. He could pick anyone of a dozen young flappers, like low hanging ripe fruit off a tree and it seemed that his little flirtation with Sally had made him all the more desirable in the ethos of living for the moment of all the bright young people. He'd chosen Ottoline and Florence because they too were in the social game. He'd chosen Sally because she was somehow different and appeared to see more into him than the others had the ability or the wish to.

He'd lost Ottoline for Florence and then lost Florence for Sally whom he now conceded on his friend's advice and on the stranger to him that was his growing conscience. The result was now that he now had nobody to give love to and nobody to love him back. He felt alone, truly alone.

Chapter 2

Graham's father, at sixty years old, was old in comparison with the other drivers that drove for the few teams that made up the new British auto motorsport scene. He was well respected in his driving abilities and had won three of the previous ten meetings, with a string of second and thirds to boot. Bentley cars were pleased to have him as their driver firstly for his previous successes on the race track but in addition as a decorated war hero, it just seemed right for their image.

Wright senior was racing at the end of that week and as always it laid heavy on his mind. Graham enjoyed the motor racing and often boasted of his father's successes at parties, despite not openly giving him much appreciation himself. A few years ago, as young man, he had spent much time watching his father's green racing machine in races and trials and recalled much enjoyment.

He was pleased as ever to stop and talk with Elizabeth when he saw her in town and was grateful for the concern that she always showed him. Elizabeth said she'd heard that his relationship with Sally was over and showed him that perhaps it was for the best. He was especially pleased that she had agreed to come over for a drink and a chat in the evening and agreed to have her picked up at eight and have her returned by midnight; somehow he knew the evening would be more than he'd originally bargained for.

As promised, he arrived at Elizabeth's house just before eight in James's hard topped Ford as Graham's luxury automobile was being repaired at the garage. When he reached the door he rang the bell for attention. Her aging grandfather answered the door and both were pleased to exchange greetings with one another despite the fact that her grandfather probably never heard the reply.

Once back at Graham's spacious ancestral family home the couple participated in an evening of conversation and humour and it seemed as if the hours had drifted away in the warmth of the house's comforting fire whilst the cold wind raged outside. He knew he had a friend that would always be there for him. It seemed however that he had not always been there for her, not that she ever seemed to require any support or advice.

Elizabeth seemed complete in life and content in her mind, two things that Graham had always jealously watched.

By half past eleven, Graham suggested that he should take her back home, if she were to get back home by midnight. Somehow a close never occurred and instead she remained sat on the floor before lying down in front of the roaring hot fire and closing her eyes. Her actions really took him by surprise and for a while he just sat next to her, listening to the tune on the stylophone for insight as to what to do. No advice was forthcoming and instead it was Elizabeth that spoke, her eyes still closed tightly shut.

"I'm tired Graham, I just want to stay here, look it's so much trouble to take me back when I can sleep here, I can can't I?"

He was again surprised somewhat but said that it would be all right and moments later was lying down next to her in sweet comfort and serenity. The hours seemed a peaceful and tranquil time in his life that was full of activity and noise. Half an hour after they had first laid down together, her hand reached out, presumably for his, their palms touched and their fingers folded down over one another's, and still they lay there.

They slept for over four hours before moving so that they were closer, touching, feeling the warmth of one another, melting into one another's emotional affection. Neither could say that they loved the other, neither cared to make love either, but their touches and closeness said more of endearment and fondness than it would if they had gone further.

Graham had never thought of her as anything other than a good friend. This episode of his life meant not a new chapter of love, but a single, important strengthening of their friendship and concern for the other. Graham decided in his mind that he must seek to be more with his friend and push to make her part of his growing account of women.

The next day he returned to the Brighton flat and walked alone for a while outside before retiring inside. The only sounds were the gulls and those of the waves that he could hear all around him. The crowds were gone, the castles un-built and the world looked an entirely different place to be in. Excited eyes looked on only through his own and it was the rain and not the sun that flooded into his feelings. Blackened streets, empty and cold, washed with a rain of strangest serenity and calmness.

Behind coloured curtains and leaded blinds hid the hibernating residents as the world passed by through their windows. Occasional peers from glum washed out faces, frowning at the rain and lights that dotted the bobbing harbour boats, keeping the room inside safe for the night visitor. The beach was cold and wet, mostly covered by the washing waves renewing the smooth sands beneath and the nine o'clock skies were drawing in faster than he had known. The stars again perhaps shone for him, high above the earth trying as hard as he could to relax and relive him.

He loved the society game and flourished on people's admiration and assumptions of his wealth, honour and history. If he were to continue this illusion, he must have the money, the women and fresh things to talk about, no matter how or by whom he got it. Others like Florence and Ottoline or any of the young things would not be tempted by any ordinary man, the face, even though it largely was an act; was essential in maintaining his image of the debonair, sophisticated and charming young man. He was never really sure that this was his dream, yet had never had anything different to alter his mind.

He'd taken Elizabeth back at eleven that morning and the warmth he was feeling after she had gone remained for quite some time, indeed the remainder of the day. It was strange really, for her presence had never done this to him before, yet somehow, even though he knew this wasn't any kind of lead to greater things; the summer seemed a little warmer. It was a whole week later before he saw Elizabeth again, yet he managed to keep himself mostly entertained.

He'd called on society's new heroine, Bonny Pickford and spent one afternoon in her company watching Roman Novarro in 'Ben Hur' at the cinema on Manchester Road. She seemed to enjoy the picture as much as Graham had done despite a few lingering thoughts of Sally entering his mind. The couple's interactions seemed trouble free and quite enjoyable, yet hardly burning embers. With a brief spell of warm sun, he presumed a game of tennis on the court on the back lawn could serve to fix some further reason for them to be together and equally to enquire if she would go with him to the club on Friday night, if nothing else it was another opportunity for them to get drunk and reckless.

The tennis game was enjoyable, as were the drinks and the sun. More importantly Graham saw a real keenness for Graham in Bonny's attitude, missing from their first encounter, appeared to have returned. Even up to two days later the young things still sang his praises continually to her friends who equally remained devoted to his laid back style, his charms and his elegant green eyes. It would be the fifth time he would have visited the club in two months, and the fourth woman to accompany him. Despite being a regular patron of the Embassy Club, she had not taken a man before, although this in itself gave little concern as it *was* Graham Wright. He had been seen with many a girl in the past, that was for sure.

Already visibly slightly drunk, she appeared wearing a loose silk black blouse and short skirt, clutching an expensive and stylish black evening bag in her right hand. The black sequins that made up another brand new dress sparkled in the headlamps of James's car as it drove around the corner, Graham at the wheel. Her short black bobbed hair had obviously taken much preparation and a high degree of grooming. Her whole appearance was set off by a cheeky twenty-one year old smile that seemed moist and fresh.

Their difference in ages was almost eight years, a difference only a few years ago that would have caused outrage, but few other than the olds really cared. Bonny certainly didn't, her three big screen appearances, two in 1925 and a year later in 1926 had given her a mild degree of fame and a surprising level of licence to get away with things other girls of her age could not, something that she had always used to her advantage.

It pleased her to inform others that she was dating Graham Wright. It pleased Graham to hear of his association with a film star. How much of a 'star' she was in reality seemed to have got out of all proportion. Perhaps he knew that she wasn't all that people made her out to be. Graham didn't mind the differences in ages either, as his determination to build a relationship had blacked out all that could be called bad.

They found the club packed to the rafters again with smiling, happy people; drunk on song, alcohol, cocaine filled, imported Coca Cola and dance, dressed from head to toe in shallow evening disguises. They all hid from their poorer memories, from the truth and from the future, Graham among them and that's where he'd been all his life. Some knew, some didn't, some tried and some just didn't care. But it was here, in their lifetime that they existed and in their lifetime that they always wanted to stay, however long they could keep the party going for.

The party raged like a wild crazed animal in their minds, growing from careless conversation and frivolous acts, it was like a mad, vivid and excited passion. Where the well-to-do could savour more of their lush lives and dream themselves alive. Before: war and depression, now for those with money of course: there was no excuse *not* to party. In the future the big bright balloon would surely burst; they had no choice other than to live to the full what they briefly had. Life was just one long party for all of society's rich young elite. Few of the 'haves' needed to work for a living or cared or knew about the unemployment of the 'have nots.'

The have nots were split in opinion between those that were horrified by the antics of the bright young people and the other half that were fascinated by them as the first ever celebrities.

Graham and Bonny Pickford were such people. She was young, pretty and energetic in conversation and thought, but somehow just too false for many. Graham seemed to try just too hard to make it work for his own comfort. Whenever close she seemed distant, whenever far she seemed a reflection of what Graham knew he must do without. Somehow she too realised that she were not for him, yet they would keep the charade up right up until the last half inch of stale Martini had been decadently swilled away.

It seemed whatever he did and however he did it, the result was always the same. Yet another night spent sobering up from a yet drunken dream that rapidly melted and faded from view. He was always the same, the people around him also. The sun and moon still shone, the winds still blew and somehow he just had to continue.

Strolling home back to his home on Albert Road, he whistled a melody that had been floating around in his head for some while, and looked again at the omnipotent stars for some clue on his predicament. He thought of all those he knew, who played the same game yet always came out with more than him. He could never tell why or how, perhaps this was where the problem lay; if he changed himself he could change the whole situation. In reality though there was little chance of that.

He decided to take a walk in the park as the day was quite a fine one and was somewhat surprised to see Ottoline walking her elegant and finely trimmed poodles in the opposite direction. He continued walking evidently oblivious to her presence, deciding on the spot in the path where they would meet. He attempted to look startled and stepped back in false surprise at her apparent sudden appearance.

She was as forward as ever and gave a rather curious smile as they met. It seemed as if what had happened with Florence, with Sally and now a one off date with Bonny Pickford had made him infinitely more desirable, if none the wiser. Even he was surprised that his latest label was that of the 'equitable gentleman'. For a full half an hour they sat and chatted as old friends might have done; if they had been that at anytime of course. Before long they were holding hands again, and agreed a trip to the theatre the evening after.

They departed from each other's company in new spirits, created as the two souls had collided in waves of miss spent emotion, rippling through the park. They had already drunk from several of the many golden chalices that life had provided, inevitably, the wrong ones, now they haplessly chose another.

He had again the pleasure of meeting up with Elizabeth the next morning whilst buying another new tuxedo suit in the recently opened 'Archibolds' the department store; she seemed a little uneasy in her speech. She somehow made an offer to ask him to the theatre as friends; to which Graham tactfully excused himself from realising his prior engagement with Ottoline. She looked defeated and deflated instantly; quickly he changed the topic of conversation. Graham realised that his response had been misinterpreted by the sweet thing that stood in front of him.

"No, listen Elizabeth, I'm doing something tonight, it's not that I didn't want to go out with you anywhere...tomorrow?" She still looked a little aggrieved and agreed to six o'clock, a change quickly visible appeared on her round and expressive face.

He met Ottoline on the corner of Darlington Road as agreed and walked with her towards the department store. He purchased expensive French scents and finely dusted Belgian chocolates and paid for entry by half past the hour. The theatre was an elegant affair, with elaborate engraving on the walls and glinting vivid colours of decoration on the pillars that supported the upper tiers so grandly. The debonair people that nestled in amongst its grandeur quietly sat and waited for the performance to start, occasionally entering into light conversation.

The stage was always a place he'd dreamed of being, yet like his other dreams, they remained fragmented somewhere around only in his thoughts. The darkened theatre must have seen hundreds of actors, all playing their roles amid a larger stage. Each would have been a star, and still each would have been nothing but grains of sand across an infinite beach.

It was during the second interval that he began to put an explanation to what Elizabeth had really meant outside in the crisp air. It seemed odd that she would mean something like that; but his ego said why shouldn't she? Many desired to be with him, why not her? She was a friend, increasingly so, felt much emotion: maybe he was wrong, he'd been wrong before, that was no mistake, maybe she'd also been smitten.

Ottoline nudged his elbow on the arm rest, breaking his thoughts away from Elizabeth and informed him and the rest of the audience that she was wildly enjoying the performance. The scent she wore felt a little thick in his throat, whilst her dead furs lay limp and lifeless around her neck. She spoke at ten to the dozen, her eyes flitting between the curtains of the stage and the doors where the audience were returning, rambling the whole time.

The smoke from their combined choking cigarettes billowed upwards towards the blackened ceiling above, whilst Ottoline nattered on human nature, people with bad dress sense, and the appalling lower classes. Graham ingested them all and patiently waited for the third bell.

The cool evening air was getting colder as they kissed half heartedly on the balcony of Ottoline's apartment as the ten o'clock moon absent-mindedly left trails of light upon them. Again he stayed the night, he somehow felt compelled to do so.

He thought how the evening maybe should have been spent with Elizabeth. He didn't want to waste this chance in case he'd figured Elizabeth out wrong Ottoline was always an easier yet far less satisfying option.

He departed at ten o'clock the next morning and strolled into town with the intention of purchasing a new gold watch. After much selection he purchased one and began to walk home. He was surprised when Elizabeth grabbed him from behind in a playful manner. It was a little out of place but not out of character; both were as always pleased to meet the other. She enquired as to the theatre in the evening and once more admitted to her missing of his company. She tentatively asked him where he was going and how he was feeling and again how she was concerned at his present position.

He tried his best to avoid this particular matter of conversation and asked her to his party a week later, she accepted and smiled with the sweetest of smiles at his offer. The film was a romantic, well written showing that the audience gulped down energetically. Elizabeth's speech was light and thoughtful and her manner not aggressive as Ottoline's had been. The film ended and the seemingly endless credits rolled as the lights came on and people began leaving the house.

"I enjoyed that Graham, thank you." She lightly kissed his cheek to which he once again smiled in his inexplicable way. Graham's jubilation was not immediately suspended as he could feel himself being watched with a less than cultured gaze. Florence Morrell stood a few rows up, staring at him as if he had completed some deadly sin. A suited man turned to join her in eagle eyed observations of scandal, it was Fred Potterson. He walked down to Graham's side and spoke on his pleasure that Elizabeth and he had apparently 'sorted something out'.

Graham smugly smiled and chuckled back to Potterson whilst playfully patting him on the back as a way almost of congratulating himself. Elizabeth looked shocked at Graham's acceptance of the man's suggestion that they were together, she was clearly not amused. Florence continued to stare with burning eyes towards him; he knew Ottoline would hear her fictional tales by the morning. The kiss would sound as near as illegality as she could make it. Florence disappeared with Potterson leaving in hot pursuit, leaving the two figures alone in the blackened picture house. "It's Ottoline again, isn't it? You know exactly what happens, what will always happen." He said nothing but looked away instead and wished he were somewhere else. He felt ashamed to be himself and even more so now he had injured his friend with his foolishness. "You're lovely; you are, inside: and you deserve so much better, why do you have to be like this?"

She was not going to let this rest whilst the iron was hot and attacked again. "Why Graham? Why? One day when you grow up, something special may happen, till then..." She didn't finish the sentence but he knew just what it would have been. The two left together but shortly afterwards parted quickly. Elizabeth was furious and Graham realised that again he'd misread the situation and possibly wrecked a very good friendship.

He spent Thursday ordering the marquees and food for a party on Saturday night. Delivery boys were already arriving with cases of the finest champagne from his business acquaintance in Bordeaux, France and long tables for the already freshly mown, green lawn outside. Although a whole day away; many of the preparations had already been completed. It was going to be a most joyous time and he waited in expectation for the excitement and happiness to commence. It had to.

He would be marketing himself as man and as a spectacle. His parties were renowned for the manic and reckless behaviour of the guests that he invited or those that just arrived invited or not. This would be no different. Graham was happy, wealthy and had women waiting in every corner for their chance to be with him, he was ready to prove that all the gossip about him was right. Back inside the house Graham spent the early afternoon playing cards and gambling away small fortunes and drinking Long Island iced teas with a group of society hangers on. An hour or so after the group had departed a serious looking black suited gentleman was invited into the reception room by the butler and was asked to wait for Graham. After the usual prolonged period of absence, Graham arrived and received his guest. Graham didn't know the man but was instantly taken aback with just how serious looking the man was.

"Cheer up old man, what you so serious about? I'm having a party tomorrow, why not come along; it might just cheer you up hey?" Graham let out a hearty laugh to accompany his suggestion. The man was not at all moved by Graham's jovial tone or his joking and did not offer comment, instead he simply handed Graham a business card and then removed his black hat, placing it on the side cabinet. Graham read that he man was from Entwistle, Lord and James solicitors.

"Mr Wright. I have some very serious news for you I'm afraid. You better just sit down sir." That was certainly not what Graham was expecting and so did as he was requested and sat down and listened to the news that the man had to say. It transpired that Graham's father, whilst coming in to the pits during a test run before the weekend's race meeting, had not braked in time and had driven into a gate. The top of the gate had seemingly hit Graham's father on the head causing his death.

In that moment it was just like all the air he had within him had been forcibly sucked from his lungs.

He couldn't speak. All the optimism and life had been ripped from his brain and scattered on the floor in front of him. He couldn't move. Graham's face, demeanour and whole life seemed to flash right before his eyes; he withered and shrank as he struggled to ingest the news. Despite being at odds with his father quite often, Graham felt severely bad on hearing the news. Immediately he ran upstairs and became physically sick across the expensive wool carpet that covered his bedroom floor on digesting the news of his father's death.

When had cleaned himself up and returned downstairs the man started to reveal the details of his father's will. Within half an hour he had left and Graham was left on his own with his thoughts, reflections of his life with his father and a folded last testament. He felt desolate and lonely suddenly and realised that he was on his own. The money, the house and all the estate's affairs were concluded.

Graham sat alone and tried hard to recall what the last conversation he had with his father had been about and yet try as he did he couldn't even recall if it were on friendly or hostile ground. He presumed it to have been hostile one. Graham wondered if he had been to blame in any way and despite his often uneasy silence with his father he felt so very attached to him at that moment. He put in that second all ideas of being emotionally apart from his father behind him and felt for the first time in a long while, immensely alone.

Graham had always hated his conscience and the nagging voices in his head that told him when and how he was wrong: they were uneasy bedfellows. Now in this moment of sensitivity they snarled, snapped and raged at him. Why hadn't he been the better man? Why did he not follow his family's ideas of success? Why was he who he was? The pain was wrapped up in a bitter and jagged pill that he had to swallow. Of not even knowing what his father had actually thought of him.

So often at odds with his father and yet despite not being anything to do with his father's accident he blamed himself for the whole incident somehow and sobbed into the brushed velvet of the chair that he now slumped in. Graham was always likely so show wild emotion or raging feelings in the form of anger when put on edge and this time was no different. Rising to his feet he picked up the nearest item to hand and hurled it across the room. The bronze figurine of a prancing horse flew across the room and struck the grandly sized mirror on the wall, smashing it into a hundred pieces that fell to the ground by the Italian marbled fireplace. He was not feeling in any kind of rational mood and was never a man to face up to his failings so he poured himself a large scotch, a large scotch that turned into a bottle and then two, anything to hide away the pain of his loss. He woke up next morning, still dressed in his suit, lying on the floor of his living room covered in beads of crystal glass, whisky stains and all around his disturbed and smashed furniture. It was afternoon when he woke with his head on fire and his bloodshot eyes shut tightly with dry sleep.

Over the next hour Graham's sorry face has changed little but through numerous cups of coffee, bottles of iced Coca Cola and a couple of glasses of scotch, his mental state was at least a little better. Just after one o'clock, he realised that nothing had changed, he did still have the death of his father at large and he did still feel violently alone. Outside, the sun shone and the garden looked radiant in the summer glow but his angered and bruised heart were not bothered whatever the weather was like or however the garden looked.

Later in the day, a telegram arrived from Bentley expressing their concern and offered their respects. Graham was glad to receive it but remained angered and in his mind somehow blamed them for his death. A Sergeant Major in full smart drab khaki army green knocked on the door some two hours later and duplicated the sentiments of the now numerous telegrams that now lay scattered on the dining-room table and floor regarding his father's death. Graham listened to the sergeant for what seemed like an eternity as he reminisced on his time working with his father and his thanks at his role during the Great War.

It was well into the afternoon when Graham had looked through the windows across his expansively green mown lawns and garden and noticed the white clothed tables ready for food and glasses and the music stands ready prepared for sheet music for the band. Graham realised that the party that he had planned for that evening had already been precisely prepared. It seemed that nobody had told the people that were busy getting the grounds and house ready for the party that Graham's father had passed away. Maybe they knew, maybe the mutterings and social chit chat had summarised that it really didn't matter. Perhaps a party for the bright young things was more important than the loss of the host's father.

Graham decided that the party would go on. The party guests, invited or otherwise began arriving about twenty past seven, the evening ,he was glad, remained under a warm sun, the blue temperate skies were removed from those vivid feelings of a month ago or of Graham's feelings prior to the party. The vast tables before him bore food of a hundred varieties, a fizzing glass of Champagne bubbled excitedly in front of him.

He'd made sure his was the finest tuxedo of them all and made sure to greet every guest of any standing as they arrived as if he needed to maintain his profile despite his loss. Bonny Pickford had helped purchase the suit the morning before and he had helped her to obtain a new evening dress from 'Blanchards' tailors on Mayfair.

Ottoline and Florence arrived predictably together, this time with James O'Bere and Geoffrey Parker, neither spoke as they entered. Sally arrived arm in arm with William and by ten past eight at least sixty guests could have been counted through the gates; if Graham or anyone else had been counting of course. Five minutes later, Miss Bonny Pickford arrived. Something sparkled in her eyes that night, their dark centres glinted a strange truthfulness he'd not seen in her before. They somehow washed over him, pouring instantly the wealth he'd lost over his aching body revitalising and invigorating him.

Once inside Bonny tentatively sipped the glass of Champagne that bubbled in her delicate and intricate hand as the other party guests ghosted the lawns behind her. Inside the black entertainer, Thomas Wilmot, entertained on the piano to some lively tune whilst outside the band played just as feverishly to a new tune that appeared to be all the rage. Bonny took his arm and enquired who his date was for the evening in the cheeky way that she was known for. She knew that she would be his date and that was indeed the whole reason she had spent an age getting ready and taken the taxi and turned up at the entrance gates.

Her dark eyes looked up towards him as a little puppy may have done to a small child. He always had a thing for a girl's eyes; he believed that they could reveal much of the person that they were inside. He knew her as outgoing and even a little wild at heart, perhaps a little too wild sometimes; but tonight he saw a warmer, more tender, face. He looked up and down her face and body with excited gaze and it was with a gasp in his lungs and an obvious smile that he warmly and greedily imagined holding her closely. His gaze rested on her soft and inviting pink lips. He carefully watched as her lips moved as she spoke and he knew that he wanted to kiss them. Graham decided that he would not mention his father's death or that he would be anything other than the riotous, womanising drunk that he always was.

The next half an hour was spent greeting faceless and probably uninvited guests and welcoming them to his grand reception. Bonny was well and truly into Graham by this point, playfully acting as if they were lovers, she could see that gradually he was rapidly falling into her. For a while, many of the guests were surprised, yet soon learnt that he had indeed chosen Miss Pickford to be this evening's date. He had known her before and somehow always believed that the friendship they had could always be bettered, though he'd never given it much thought. She'd playfully kiss him or sit on his knees with her arms around him whilst never meaning anything but fun. Tonight, this continued, yet somehow it seemed more legitimate and more directly intense, he was definitely more receptive to it as well.

He was always one for a young, pretty face and despite reasonable principles he could always be found letting a young thing have their way with him, often with little resistance. She was never delicate nor considered as caring as Sally or Elizabeth would have been viewed. She lived for the moment, always did, more than Graham and made it her rule never to give time to sentiment. Tonight her eyes sparkled with all the caring and heartfelt emotion that on the surface would seem to be absent. He had not seen it before much either; but tonight his suspicions of her other self seemed to have been confirmed.

She blossomed for him like a sweet and delicate flower that evening. She always possessed eternal life and he'd never seen anyone that smiled more over less or made him feel so much with so little. He dotted between the guests for most of the evening and was especially pleased to speak with James who was attending with Miss Rose Blanchard. Most of the guests were in a state of drunkenness by half past ten, some more so than others; Graham remained drunk but only so that he was, and appeared, merry.

His excitable date continued to consume coloured cocktails and Champagne, dance and sing and their fondness for the other continued to flourish. Still her eyes sparkled around a delicate and trim figure as her dark brown hair waved and flowed in a sensual and excited manor. Her movements were flirtatious and her mind was defiantly on what she wanted. The flow of life that passed between them was intense and warming, especially after so much of the recent months' troubles for Graham. He chose not to remember that his father had recently died.

There was plenty of dancing throughout the night and the whole party seemed to go with a smashing swing, and Graham had made sure his reputation prevailed to the end. Party goers had labelled him as a 'new romantic' whatever that was viewed to be. For him she was caring and loving, he was that way with her also. Whether the game they played together would be for more than just the night he could not tell, he felt entirely at her disposal.

He felt so strong with her in her arms, so filled with sensual power and fulfilment yet in the same breath so weak, as if she had cast a spell over him. She could have made him do anything she desired that night and he would have folded and utterly fell to her influence. Of the guests that knew of his father's death, only a couple cared to mention it. The majority of guests either didn't care or didn't want to know. Graham wanted to keep it that way. Hiding the pain was always easier than swallowing it, smiling and carrying on. Many of the guests had departed by one o'clock and the manicured lawns were his and hers alone, to do whatever they dared to do. She reached out with her hand for his and folded her fingers down upon his, resting the coupled hands by their sides. They strolled across the moonlit lawns under the endless ribbons of tiny stars and passed the few remaining guests in a waltz across the green grass. He stopped for a moment and took a sweet breath of fresh air, filled and tenderly touched by the warmth of summer. They stood in awesome splendour at the romance and captivation that they were experiencing. She turned to him and smiled, her wondrous light once again across him. Her eyes still sparkled and still purveyed some kind of superior force into green eyes that must have gleamed emerald desire and appreciation in return.

She stood, just watching his eyes; he stood just watching her's as they tasted the truth between them with expectantly waiting mouths. Together they stood under that knowing moon revealing only to each other the real people they wanted to be at that time. Both of them knew it was only for the other that they shone at that time, proving to themselves what the two of them really wanted and not perhaps what they needed.

In reality he knew very little of the pale, white skinned girl that stood before him. She knew very little of the man that now showed his vast sensitivity towards her, a feast for a soul that had shown so little of previously. He knew she had searched far and wide for someone she could love...and had never found it. He knew that he wasn't the one to love her but whilst there was a chance for high emotion he would greedily take it.

The breeze seemed cool and refreshed, a seemingly endless river of emotion on which they were carried and fluttered like leaves on water, softly, under a night's sky they stopped and gazed into the other's eyes. "We were good tonight." She spoke in soft whispering reserved tones. "We make an excellent team don't we?"

He didn't remember anything else she said but it really didn't matter. Her words drifted through his mind for hours after she had uttered them, captivating and possessing him somehow and he continued to recall her words for some time. By half past one in the morning, they remained the only two figures at the party, but it was a party that still raged and lived to the grand spectacle he had wished it would turn out to be; a party that both would always remember. They danced, there quietly on the lawns to the sweetest music, the grass still crisp to their bare feet and the music remained still fresh in her mind.

He sheltered in the arms of heaven, away from the animosity of daily proceedings. His sweet surrender was immense, here he could feel the whole of creation was once again righteous and once more had been captured by a prison that was his emotion. He held her close, just as he had longed to do with someone for so long. He could feel every move she made, she seemed even more beautiful now, the image was now so clear under the bright silver moonlight. They whispered to each other soft nothings that they had seldom spoken before. Bonny asked him to make love to her.

Her warm glow was exhilarating, her soft skin radiant with passion and thrilling ecstasy. Her hair seemed to gleam with intense glory as he felt the delicate strands through his fingers, whilst the stars shone high above like angels watching over them high above their heads, keeping them safe for one special encounter. It was their special moment; fleeting perhaps, but it remained theirs and they would be living for the sublime. The light and lifting ceaseless calm breeze blew her hair in motions that epitomised all the energy and life within her. How he would savour this moment, just as he knew she would. His life seemed so meaningless to that point when confronted by it all.

By three o'clock, she had fallen asleep on his lap, curled like a playful kitten, soft and gentle to touch, warm and comforting to hold. He sat; gazing at the stars wondering how he, despite always coming close, could never claim that anything he ever did was real or could give him satisfaction. He lay by her side, just watching her body delicately rising and falling with each breath that she made as she silently slept. Her skin was so light and tranquil to touch as he softly stroked her bare arms and legs as she slept, whilst her eyes remained closed and held inside them all her thoughts, were they of him? He couldn't tell. He couldn't sleep and instead decided to watch for the sunlight of Saturday morning creep over the trees at the bottom of the grounds. He looked forward with anticipation to see it rising higher and higher, getting fuller all the while until it would break apart and flood in through the branches like water through a burst dam, sweeping aside all who stood in its path. He realised that the evening had not been complete and he knew that he had to do something about it. But what did he need to make it complete?

Graham knew and it would be Graham that would selfishly strive to get it by waking her and making love to her. She awoke when he slowly tugged at her arm and rolled her onto her back. Her little eyes opened and looked at his as he stood in front of her removing his shirt as he did so. Graham was not a bad man and not one that would have ever just pushed a woman into giving him his requirements but this was a man on the edge. A man that had suffered his father's death, denied the whole thing and was slowly breaking down with the weight of his emotion and missing dreams crushing down on his shoulders.

He didn't ask her, not that she needed to be asked of course as she openly gave herself to his persistence. After twenty minutes the couple parted. Bonny slept again in the swinging chair whilst Graham grabbed the remaining dregs of liquor from a dozen bottles and glasses that lay about the garden from the now absent party goers.

Thoroughly emotionally tired, drunk and now physically satisfied Graham fell asleep on the chairs in the living room half drunk still and the other half sleep deprived. When he woke up, he found that the sky was deep set blue with only a few puffed clouds in between as the birds flitted and glided about the tranquil earth before him. It wasn't until at least eleven o'clock before she woke. The day was warm and fresh, he felt strong and content. It was about then that he remembered his father's death and all of the lost summer days. Suddenly it all meant nothing.

She left for home half an hour later on the day that was in fact Graham's birthday. He needed no cards or best wishes, no presents wrapped in thin disguises, no streamers to celebrate a life or sweet sickly cake and food to eat. All he wanted at that time had laid before his eyes as his mind feasted on the wealth and celebration of life. Her card said `thank you`, her eyes and their time together had said much more.

James and Elizabeth also sent cards of birthday wishes and condolences as did many others and the day remain joyous for his birthday and he wanted to ensure he didn't remember that his father was dead. Elizabeth called at midday and wished him yet another happy birthday, giving him the opportunity to ask where she had been on the night of the party. It transpired that she had indeed attended arriving shortly after ten. She had seen him with Bonny and decided to keep well away.

Graham had not prepared himself for such a reply and clearly was unable to comment on the remark. Again she said how much she'd been thinking of him and by the tone of her voice, Graham detected more than a hint of sadness and he thought even a slight evidence of jealousy. Seeing him acting as he was with Miss Pickford had hurt her clearly, yet she respected him and courageously felt only for his happiness, deciding it unwise to intervene. She did nothing to put the party into the conversation yet remained on the subject of Bonny whom she had talked to the day earlier.

She informed Graham, still sobering up from Thursday evening that Bonny viewed him as nothing more than a friend and casual date. Graham was immediately struck with a rush of adrenaline as he gulped down and almost choked on the news. He trusted Elizabeth and finally could see something happening to her despite not knowing exactly what. He thanked her for her frank revelations yet showed only a moderate degree of interest used to minimalise any further damage on his friend. He knew that in reality she was only a respite from the pain of his father's death and that she meant no more to him than he apparently did to her.

He knew however that he could not say no to a good thing and desired to see her again, until he had feasted all he could and then would once more pass onto another shambolic period of false and hopeless emotion with someone else. He knew from the things Bonny had said at the party that she were accompanying her older sister to the casino that evening. This he felt would be a perfect indication and test of Bonny's attitude towards him and a test of any further openings for more of what he had already sampled of her with such gusto. If nothing else he would surely be creating another society stir in the process.

He spent a life-time, as ever, getting ready in his best suit and tie and really looked the part. He called on James and invited him to attend with Rose: he gladly accepted and the couple were at Graham's house by eight. Rose sat quietly looking prim and proper with James keenly promoting his best friend to her in the back seat but she seemed to have little to say. As they drove, Graham occasionally muttered polite agreements and smiled a little. As always he fell silent when James did this: Graham found compliment nearly as hard to handle as criticism, despite living off it to achieve all he ever did.

The hall had intricately wonderful decoration in cream and gold colours, pillars effortlessly supporting the ceiling; casually emerging from the green foliage beneath it. As usual the tables were packed with people eager to flutter their wages, inheritances and loans away. Graham spent rapidly in a whirl of gaming chips and promises, again appearing to thrill the crowds with spectacle and wealth. Graham had just racked in a pile of winnings from the roulette table and as he was scooping up the pieces when she appeared. There she stood in the entrance hall, catching his eye with a cheeky wink and swayed over to him. His heart still fluttered in wild excitement and anticipation, he hoped he would be winning for the second time that night.

She let out a curious smile that seemed to want to become more, yet somehow was restrained by something inside her head. She asked of his well being and commented on his smartness of dress. He asked her similar fumbling questions and made comment on her new tightly supported and revealing dress in return. Conversation was dry from both parties. Her sister called her away into another room and it seemed that she were glad of this if only to excuse herself from his company.

They kept meeting throughout the evening, conversation getting slightly warmer with each meeting and he'd mostly forgotten James and Rose who mingled together into the background. By ten o'clock Graham was pleased that he and Bonny were spending most of their time together. They talked in circles, each desperately somehow avoiding what the other wanted them to say. Neither wanted to be the first to say it and it was up to James who had, as usual ,been observing to make some sense of the situation. She was a typical woman of the twenties, trim knowledgeable and bubbling with confidence and quite prepared to take any man's position if the need arose. She finally blew, and asked Graham if he thought they should become much closer, something more than friends. Graham gladly accepted, soaking up the power that he wielded for that moment, even going so far as to stall the reply and tease a little.

He felt hugely wealthy that night with the prize that he held in his arms. She seemed again to melt into him and for the first time they both felt entirely at home with the concept of being with each other publicly. In another room, music played and drinks were being served for gold status members, all of which attracted Graham and his new girlfriend into it. Young girls followed Graham and gentlemen followed his date, all desperate to be seen near them, if only to dream or make them look a little more interesting.

She swayed carelessly to the rhythm and soul of the music as his eyes remained fixed to her shimmering light. His spirit hung like the fascinating lights above his head, drawing in and encapsulating the romantic splendour of the occasion. Her skin gently fragranced with all the rich, ever living scents of summer, filling his lungs with exotic warmth and feeling. Her movement thrilled him with passion and intent for profound reason. All she did, it shook and vibrated his mind, possessing him for a moment of intensely sublime. Graham woke and explosively remembered that his father was dead. It was an instantly sobering thought. It was something that had been forced so far from his mind that he even questioned whether it was the truth as it all seemed so surreal, hot and confused. The night soon however dwindled away in the early morning hours as light gave way to the stubborn darkness. The day was marked with silence and lament and closed with quiet sleep alone in that grand and entirely empty house.

Chapter 3

Next morning, when the light returned to the earth with a slither of summer sunshine, the large house on the opposite side of the road had kept their curtains shut as a mark of respect for Graham's father who would be buried that morning as was the age old tradition. Graham woke and dressed alone. After breakfast he waited in the long entrance hall with its herringbone oak blocked flooring for the relatives, close friends, stoutly overdressed, over pompous army contacts and rich well wishers that would travel with him to the church.

The day would be one of reflection and remorse as the black skies above them swirled and clogged up together overhead, he knew that there would be no sign of the lost summer that day, he didn't see how there ever could be. Slowly the funeral carriages and their well disciplined horses arrived and circled the entrance to the family home. Graham led the way down the steps towards the lead car whilst the others followed slightly behind taking care not to catch his lowered gaze.

The Reverend William Wainfleet read out the expectedly elongated eulogy and various people stood to offer words of reflection on Graham's father in lengthy prayer and in song. There were many people inside the small church, many faces Graham knew, many more he didn't but all came united in respect for a good and honest gentleman, race car pioneer and

Great War hero. Graham hadn't heard most of the proceedings as he stood gazing into space, feeling or saying nothing. Apart from the aftermath of pain and grief from the sudden news of the death on that initial day Graham had done his best to put even the thought out of his mind. The fact was he didn't know how to behave at his father's funeral. Cry, look distraught, act melancholy or a combination of the three. There was surely no way that could be determined as the right way. Socially at the time he would be expected to look sombre and 'carry on' as was the way and he didn't like it anyhow. Graham's party, an evening at the casino splashed with liberal doses of cash, sex and liquor had subdued the pain for a while but now at the church, in amongst the most sober and sombre of moods it all seemed to hit him; suddenly he realised that his life was no longer the same. Groups of well wishers came back to the house for food, drink and reflection yet few stayed long as Graham was sat alone in another room searching through years of lost emotion and unfulfilled fond feelings towards his father. It took him a long while to establish a fond feeling for his father at all. He did find a few brief feelings but they quickly ebbed away. James and others let themselves out leaving Graham physically and mentally withdrawn and alone. The house was as silent and empty as Graham was and once again it took several large glasses of whisky, bourbon, cognac and aperitifs to begin to console himself in his grief and his attempts to believe that he was upset that his father was no longer with him. Bonny Pickford never arrived.

It was time to draw a line and leave everything that he knew behind him, for a break away from his life. Graham packed his own bags and took the car out onto the main road out of London heading north-west. Graham drove and drove, eating up the miles of distance at great speed. Eventually after most of the day and six stops for fuel and rest he arrived at a small guest house in mid Wales booking himself in for a few nights. Graham knew he was running from the problem but didn't hesitate to do it. Bonny had left the area to visit her sick mother and conveniently had not sent a letter or telegram since the party before his father's funeral and he assumed that the relationship that they had shared had now also expired. Loveless, lifeless and alone Graham was sick of the life that he led and despised the way he lived it. To be alone now was all he could do it seemed.

The rolling Welsh moorland provided a wonderful setting as the cascading grasses excited with the light breeze mingled poetically with the wild heather and windswept trees. He walked silently across the hills, engulfed in greenery and all the summer colours he loved so much. Clear, crisp waters of the sparkling silver streams flowed freely between fern and hawthorn between vale and hillside. The distant bird song was so practiced, clear and precisely echoed summer mornings. Twisting, turning, swooping and diving, the larks called on the wind, high amongst the clouds of white. The sun was unusually strong for a summer that had only spasmodically been warm as the mighty trees watched him float towards a style and on towards a lake, deep set, hidden amongst the hills and harvesting a vast array of glorious life

Water always created a time for wonder. All were captivated by its strange possessive spell, it was as timeless as the stars, as infinite as the sky yet unique and part of all who ever witnessed it. To draw out from within us all our emotions, Sadness, happiness, loneliness, hope and wonder. For some, the relaxation of the peaceful lake; for some the tranquil babbling of the rippling stream; for others the beauty of the washing ocean wave. Others looked at its power and destructive tones. Some just revelled in awe at its mystery. But for all it was something.

Life and all its hidden meanings seemed so remote and yet were so immediate, but still so happy and fulfilled as Graham gazed with hazy vision across the waters. Graham looked down from rocks high above the river below and for a split second considered throwing himself over to meet his certain death. He decided that he was not strong enough a man even to do that. Graham returned to London two weeks later feeling no better in his mind than when he had left. After lunch and another few glasses of whisky to ease his troubled spirits, he called into work and picked up paperwork from a case that he had started two months before but had never finished. Graham found that there was still too much on his mind to be at work and so he returned home; only to find that there was a letter waiting for him on the door mat. The letter was from Bonny.

Bonny would not be returning to him. Bonny had decided that Graham had not been right for her and now he must face life, once again, alone. Graham read the words and immediately dropped the paper, watching it flutter down and settle softly on the ground. Graham decided at that moment that he would return to the casino that he had been to with Bonny and try and give a sudden and new perspective to his suffering mind. Graham had done nothing but drink and waste himself over the previous two months and the letter had been yet another shattering shot in the arm.

On the verge of blind drunkenness, Graham stumbled into a taxi and after a short ride arrived at the gilt-edged casino rooms and approached the reception room, emerging amongst people hiding with their shallow evening faces. Graham pushed aside an attendant as he stumbled past the cloakroom and on into the main hall and to the roulette tables.

He cared not where the ball landed or even if his number had been selected by lady luck. All he cared for was the drink and the flourish of notes and promissory cheques that he flashed around with gay abandon. Graham lustfully approached young flappers, leering over them and throwing lewd sexual comment with careless gusto. Late into the evening, Graham relentlessly played and pitifully lost, firstly at roulette then poker and even wagered on the outcome of backgammon and billiards.

He spent money and drank vast amounts of alcohol to the point that he had flitted away three months wages. After a short battle he fell off the chair that he had been clinging to for some time before slumping in a drunken mess on the floor. A man close to Graham's side reached out a hand and dragged him up to his feet, a measure that Graham took exception to as he flung his arms wildly around striking the man in the side of the head.

In a pool of blood the man lay as Graham staggered out of the building and onto the street as a camera flashed in his face. Graham Wright would be making the newspapers again but this time for losing money and losing his morals.

It was a sorry and broken man that fell down steps and stumbled across the attractive cobble stones as he attempted to make his way home. The rain-soaked Graham had given up looking for his home or even just a place to sleep as he slumped himself across the entrance to the library on Cross Street. Graham closed his blood shot eyes after vomiting down his chest and then to complete the evening of disgrace; he passed out on the street.

Sometime in the early morning light, Graham was woken by a policeman poking him hard in the ribs with a black wooden truncheon. Gradually he rose to his feet grasping on to the iron railings that ran down the sides of the steps as an aid. His head span wildly and his eyes struggled to focus on anything and the questions and shoving from the policeman did nothing to help him. He felt sick and disgusted with himself but he was in no position to hide from the fact that he was drunk, covered in vomit and looked like he should be in an institution somewhere.

The morning's paper was placed at Graham's side as he woke up clean, bathed and dressed in ironed soft night-clothes in his own bed. Graham's servant had not been paid for over a month but had returned in the course of loyalty and respect for his master in yet another hour of need. Graham thanked him sincerely and shook his hand; he knew somehow that he would not be returning to his aid again.

Graham's money, respect, comfortable life and mental satisfaction had been slowly dissolved over the previous two months and although the same man, was in fact just a slim shadow of the person that he had been before his father's death. Too many Martini's and frequent nights of wild excess had beaten a once proud man to his limits. His father's death had stretched his mind relentlessly with a pulsing, numbing hardness that he had not been able to handle. He had been depressed for years but now it seemed darker and more intense, either way he found it difficult to handle.

A broken man and one that needed help to start to repair him, looked like life had begun to give up on him and that he were the failure that he had always tried his best to push aside. Graham smartened himself up and walked from his house to the shops on the main road after lunch-time. The walk was bracing, with a swift wind that had blown up rushing through branches and ruffling the flag on the church.

Graham still felt delicate as he walked through town as his mind carelessly threw up snippets and flashes of last night's events forcing him to mentally wince and submit to even more self regret. The shopkeeper in the grocery store was busy sweeping the slabs at the front of his store as Graham passed. The man looked up and huffed as Graham passed by, suddenly finding reason to go back inside. Graham without his car, his wealth, servant and job not only had nothing to do and it seemed that he had no inclination to anything either. He still had some money in an account and he intended to use it tomorrow night to impress the ladies back at the Embassy Club.

Graham had rested on Sunday night and after a bottle of scotch fell in bed and passed out. Graham woke up part way through the afternoon and made his way downstairs. Lying on the ground by the front door was a letter addressed to him from his company, terminating his contract and further spreading the strife that he found himself in. He knew that it would come and knew that he had come to the end of the road in so many ways, this being just one of them.

Graham telephoned his man in Brighton and sold the flat that had been built for him for a quick sale price in order to fund his lifestyle now that he had so little to live on. Graham had only had the flat for five months and despite some great times there he told himself that it was only bricks and mortar. With what little cash Graham had, he intended to fuel his raging lifestyle and knew that despite the downward fall he intended to make the best of every moment that he could get. He was a party animal and had made his life based on the good stuff, on women, late evenings and the pursuit of the sublime. He wasn't going to let this be any exception to the rule.

There was still a long while before money from his father's estate would be available to him so with the remainder of his money Graham paid a visit to the Garage on Empire Road and purchased a new car and stopped off at the jewellers on the way back to acquire necklaces, brooches and trinkets for dates with women that he hoped to impress in the very near future. He intended to use fancy Belgian chocolates and expensive scents from France as a vehicle to lash his affections on unsuspecting Flappers and regain his status as a trend-setting Romeo of London as once he was.

Graham got ready in his bedroom, dressing in a smart black suit and red silk bow tie and sipping another whisky as he did so. He pressed his own crisp white shirt as all of his staff had now departed having not been paid for two months. Graham forced a smile at the mirror and yet the man that he saw looking back at him seemed to change his expression to that of a frown. It was then at that moment that Graham truly realised that he didn't much like the person that he saw. He had begun to see through his own disguise.

Graham's burning summer heart had started a descent into the cold depths of despair as it entered winter. Graham perhaps knew that he was living his life in the wrong way but had no idea how else he should be doing it. After his father had died and pushed previously unknown regret and remorse into his mind; the emotions that he found had been strong ones and ones that he had found difficult to handle in his mind.

At that moment Graham Wright felt wretchedly poor and entirely alone. The demons that he waged war against in his head were his and his alone, the fight he seemed to be losing as the heart he needed to fight had been lost a long time ago. His heart pounded and his brain raged and tore at him with claw and tooth as he struggled to make sense of his life and to deal with his feelings. He had thoughts now he was alone, thoughts that he had never noticed before. Why was this? Why was he doing that? Who would do the other? Everything posed questions now, usually questions that he couldn't answer and if he could they would end in self loathing and regret. Graham drank to find answers and to calm the torrent of emotions that shook him. The emotions nearly always lingered, the regret and the depression were put off at least for a while but would always compound as they did so and then catch him unawares at the most inopportune moment.

As his weakest they would rear up and grab him, shake him and throw his heart and mind to the floor. Graham didn't like the reflection before him in the mirror yet found it hard to tear himself away from its unwelcome but fascinating image. He managed to pull away and continued to get ready as he knew that that night there was a chance, a real chance that his life would improve and he would do all that he could to make it so.

He felt a little drunk as he started his new car and although it was just a small, standard, black hard topped Ford he felt glad to feel the engine vibrating through the steering wheel and the power at the depression of his right foot. Graham arrived at the club at 7pm and there was many a face that he knew there, already dancing and throwing themselves about the dance floor. There was an air of surprise from the majority of the guests to see Graham Wright enter the club and walk past them without saying a word.

His head was held high and his face still held its warm and comforting smile as he purposely strode past them in his new handmade leather shoes. Last time they had seen him he had been slumped across the steps of the library in a drunken mess with vomit and alcohol running down his chest, now as if risen from the dead, he arrived looking elegantly smart and sophisticated and ready to entertain and thrill.

Graham knew that Bonny was not there and was in fact miles away, yet he spent the whole evening imagining that she was dancing or at a table ready once again to be with him. The evening seemed so right for their chance meeting and surely inevitable embrace. The warm summer evening blew through the open windows and lifted the curtains, playfully blowing them around. Outside on the street happy, busy, people walked past going about their business blissfully unaware that Graham Wright would soon be looking at breaking point as his tortured mind and heart began to crumble.

Bonny was the closest thing that Graham had ever experienced to love and had been one of the only periods in his life that had even slightly touched the sublime if only for a brief while. Bonny's departure had been a massive blow to him when he had already been down and he had been desperate to at least have the opportunity to find the sublime again. Graham was talked about all evening with everyone having an opinion on his life and the way that he was living it. He ceaselessly chatted to flappers, drank copiously and danced like a crazy fool. It was then he saw Elizabeth. He was honesty delighted to see her and strode across the club to reach her.

In Graham's past she had only ever been a friend, a guide and someone to count on when the chips were down. With nothing else to grasp on to with his flailing heartfelt arms, it seemed that, in his mind anyway, she was the answer to his hopeless prayers. He latched onto Elizabeth as if she were the only woman in the world and flirted around her, offering her the sparkly and fancy things that he had mindlessly bought that morning. Elizabeth was not impressed to say the least, in fact despite not saying so, she felt extremely put out. Her friend that had been with her for years now thought nothing else of her other than Graham's next piece of meat.

Women of all types and sizes drank, danced and enjoyed themselves at their convenience. Many looked at Graham and were impressed at what they saw. Many wished that they had the confidence to speak with him or that he would casually pass by them and say the kind of things that young ladies wish to hear but would never admit. Others hoped that he would stay well clear of them and yet some remained intrigued as to what the comforting smile, fine looks and infamous reputation was all about.

Graham put himself about that night, talking to as many people as he could and especially amongst the female portion of the guests. Graham decorated flappers with fake praise and sweet nothings in order to get reaction and just a little peace of mind. The rapid jazz music played and the people danced and drank themselves happy. People talked and smiled and enjoyed themselves but Graham felt on the outside. The music was loud and people found that they could do whatever they wanted in order to enjoy themselves. Graham couldn't enjoy himself; he felt that there was always something holding him back and some reason why he shouldn't feel involved.

Graham slumped in a chair next to Elizabeth, leaned over and kissed her soft pink lips before she had a chance to defend herself or speak to him. Elizabeth was taken aback and further aggrieved with her friend and company. The evening from then on consisted almost entirely of Graham rapidly getting drunk, trying to kiss her and talking relentlessly about the situation with Bonny. Elizabeth was extremely put off by his behaviour and did her best to keep his voice and alcohol levels down to a minimum, to protect both of their sakes.

She said and drank little and looked shamefully at her friend as he desperately and repeatedly tried to ask her to be his 'thing'. She whole heartedly regretted being a 'thing' and made it quite clear that she were neither a 'Twenty's girl' or Bonny for that matter. Graham slumping drunk in a chair, got up and immediately tripped over a chair and struggled to regain a standing position. Elizabeth knew that it was too late to save anything from the evening and felt that she had to help out her friend; however badly he had treated her.

She escorted him back to his house via the Ford, as he was in no fit state to drive despite the fact she had only ever driven once herself. She whispered in his ear that maybe he should wake up to himself in the morning. Graham immediately fell asleep in the car. Graham found himself naked in his own bed and awoke both disgustingly angry with himself and how he had treated his time old friend and also with a large headache and sickness as had been the case for many weeks. He now thought distastefully of Bonny and this image remained in his mind the entire journey to Elizabeth's house. She greeted him with almost a laugh as he stumbled drunk through his cumbersome vocabulary and through the door and arrived at some kind of apology. She saw through his false sobriety and accepted what he eventually said and told him about the night was best forgotten if that was possible.

Graham had however discovered that Bonny still carried much weight in his mind. He had to see her again. He absolutely had to. He needed to satisfy his mind and his heart; he needed to find something that could change his life. Graham read the post that morning and discovered a letter in a plain white envelope with writing that he knew but didn't know where from. On opening the letter Graham was thrilled to hear that Bonny was returning to the area after all and would desperately love to see him at the earliest opportunity. Graham's heart suddenly jumped with rich excitement and pure emotion as he recalled the feelings that he had when they were together and he desperately wanted them to return to him. A revived optimism appeared to take his thoughts now and with this he would push to reveal his former self.

The week went by slowly, as most days were spent alone in the pursuance of old friends and acquaintances of his late fathers' in order to catch up and to resolve issues relating to his estate or in menial cleaning or tiding of his house. Whatever happened that week meant nothing to him, as Graham was only concerned with Bonny's arrival in a few days. Grocer's boys left their bikes on the wall and called for settlement of Graham's account, as did milkmen and newsagents, all eager to obtain Graham's money.

The night before the day that Graham had been waiting for arrived and with pulsating chest and flitting, fluttering mind he settled down in an attempt to sleep and then wake up ready to set eyes on Bonny once again. He couldn't sleep of course; it seemed that each hour he would wake up, throw his pillow and bed clothes around and then attempt to settle down once more. Still he restlessly shuffled, twitched and overheated and still he strayed away from sleep.

Morning came and Graham Wright opened his eyes after limited sleep to see that the day had begun to reveal a brilliant red dawn and a soft breeze that lifted the slightly yellowing green leaves on the trees and lightly touched his cheek. After shaving and washing, Graham made his way out and walked to the station. Graham was pulsating inside and ready for anything that could happen. He knew that times had been bad and that his life had reached the depths of alcohol abuse and regret. He knew that his mind was against him and that only love with the returning Bonny would do. Graham was buzzing and ready for anything. The slightest thing that he saw was of major importance and nothing would get in his way in the pursuit of the happiness that he used to know.

The station clock was two minutes slow but the 16.34 was on time. Spots of rains started to appear on the elegant cantilevered glass roof high above the people below, as the blue skies turned to a washed out grey. Graham was happy, ready to accept any explanation that Bonny would give him and even the rain or recent difficulties could not dampen his spirits that afternoon. The train eventually appeared, charged into the station then slowed to a stop blowing clouds of steam over the people on the iron bridge crossing the tracks, then shrilly whistling as it did so. No sooner had the platform had become present, the wooden doors shot open as businessmen burst off the train and onto the platform where they scurried off down steps and out into the sprawl of the city. He waited. The clock ticked and rattled around the glass folds of Paddington station roof, flags fluttered noisily as the stream built up to heavy smog around his eyes and still he waited.

A figure finally appeared at a window and waved frantically. It was Bonny and with speed he ran to the door and reached out for her cumbersome case that appeared to get stuck in the doorway. She stepped down with his hand and then looked expressively at the man before her who looked in a similar way back. Her white face set off by eyes that glinted despite the steam and smoke. They stood for a moment wondering what the other would do to break the stubborn air between them. It was Graham who spoke first, commenting on the lateness of the train and how busy people were these days.

They walked, occasionally finding gaps in the smoke in which to slip short sentences, spasmodically looking at the others face as if carefully examining a minor change in its appearance. They were still exactly the same of course; it seemed that the absence had disputed this fact. Speech was uneasy; neither could or would say anything of any relevance to the other. Graham took her hand and led her to the restaurant at the station entrance. The two brown leather cases followed via porters that huffed and puffed their load up steps and through groups of passengers to the luggage room.

The couple sat down at a window table and enjoyed tea and biscuits together as words began to become easier. Graham made no reference to his troubled days or his father's death and subsequent funeral, and ensured that conversation stayed on recollection of their glory days together and how he had enjoyed parties and the good times. Bonny seemed to be relaxed, happy and overjoyed to be back in London and back with Graham. She had little to say but Graham remained unconcerned and just happy to have her back near his side. Her return would make sure that the entire party scene sat up and took notice that his problems were over.

For him it was a line in the sand and chance to once more have the opportunity for happiness. Back at home, Graham once more dressed alone and to impress. Finally he had a legitimate date and one that he had a history with. Graham would press this to the end in order to reach the sublime feelings that he always seemed to fall short of. He had grasped and hopelessly flung his arms but never had be touched more than the smallest part of the summer; now with all effort and chance he started out to grasp the whole thing and indulgently and selfishly gulp it all down as fast as he could.

Graham Wright had brought along all the sparkle and glitz that he could manage by buying the jewellery, the scents, the chocolate and his reassuring smile and soft glinting eyes. The couple had arranged to meet at the roundhouse restaurant at eight and Graham had been foolish to believe that his date would be on time. No woman of the time would ever appear to arrive on time, it just wasn't done. Bonny after all was fashionable and young and as a film star she knew all about being fashionably late.

Graham sat alone, waiting at a table whilst sipping a Long Island iced-tea just waiting for his date. Graham was nervous and clock watched for half an hour before jumping to his feet and walking to the door. He paced back to the table and repeated the nervous and pointless exercise four times before he heard the door shut above the sound of the clinking of glasses on tables and the clattering of plates. Turning to face the door, she entered and walked towards him at the table. His girl had returned, and what a return it was, wearing a sequined silk, black dress that swayed and stirred with each footstep. Bonny Pickford almost looked like a Hollywood actress as she broke the concentration of the diners as she passed them by. Her bobbed brown hair and broad practiced smile set off her appearance of a girl that knew where she was and what she wanted in her life.

She waited for Graham to push her chair in as she sat down at the table. Graham sat opposite her and smiled warmly towards her reaching out his hands to touch hers. Their fingers enfolded each others' as the couple looked into each other's eyes. It was just as it had been the last time he had looked into her eyes and he felt his stomach clench with even the vaguest potential of love. The meal was good but neither really paid it a thought as they had each other to think about and look at. Conversation was rapid and rampantly raced from one topic to another spending little time on anything that could provoke thought or option for deeper discussion. Graham didn't care, for it looked as if things for him were again going the way he way he wanted them. Shiny things glittered and smiles on people's faces grew to fill the frame of photographs. Dresses swished and swayed and soft shoes danced to new and exciting rhythms. He felt that everything had been waged on this night, this challenge and was ready to meet it like a steam locomotive at full speed. Graham presented his new lover, Bonny, with the rings, necklaces and scents, which she accepted gladly and immediately put on to show the world. The couple passed their coats to the cloakroom attendant and immediately kissed in the doorway before entering the club ensuring that as many people as possible had seen them do so.

Graham felt alive for the first time in months to see the faces and the bubbling souls that decorated the already glamorous surroundings of the Mayfair club. People beamed with joy as they partied and gaily danced the night away. Graham stepped boldly across to Bonny and took her hand before throwing her about the dance floor, determined to sip every drop of liquor, dance to every note and make every second count.

He knew that he finally had a date more youthful and beautiful than he was. She was a pretty film star and he was, and had been for a long time, the talk of London and the entire party scene that was how it went they needed each other. He had his downs recently and battled the wars in his mind. Now he fancied having his ups as well. Graham Wright loved the scandal but had received far too much of it for his comfort recently; he knew that there was more for him and had temporarily forgotten the facts of his sometimes sorry life. The band played furiously all the newest and loudest sounds and people kissed and cuddled unashamedly under the powerful electric lights as the warm night revealed a whole new night-time world.

Share prices, wealth and opportunity were on a rapid rise, with the empire and new world providing investment and excitement to all those privileged enough to be able to exploit it. Heavy machinery riveted in Newcastle upon Tyne thundered along in north western cotton mills with power from black diamonds, hand dug from the hard mines of honest Welsh miners and the sweat of entire families producing goods for export all over the world. Suited men invested money in American and world business as the consumer-led market brought them everything from cars and carpet cleaners to yoyos and postcards. It seemed that for one moment the world was on the up and to likes of Graham Wright and the other bright young things it was an open opportunity to take, take and then take some more.

Even the way that people behaved was new and exciting. The things they did had never been done before and the more they helplessly ate from the temptations on the sumptuously lavish table, the more they came back for more. They ate without etiquette and got fat and lazy as they did so. Sometimes they would become sick but still they stuffed it down, always asking for more. They would continue to eat until all the good food had gone and only sour and bitter mouthfuls were left. Until then all they could do was eat, nobody knew when the food would go off or become exhausted and most didn't think it ever could.

Graham and Bonny were two of them and together they shared all the food they could eagerly grab. Inside the club, Graham spoke to all the faces that he knew, regulars of the party scene and rich young things that made up the new bubbling Britain.

The whole party was an opportunity for Graham to show off his date and show the world that he was back to his best and ready to take on the world. Nobody mentioned his drinking or his late father, neither did anybody care that he had been lonely and in despair. Instead, people asked him about Bonny and about money and all the places that young people should be seen. Before long Graham had consumed a large amount of wine and Champagne and began the riotous behaviour that had made his name. On a table he danced and jumped around, with his jokes and witty lines he entertained all. With Bonny he publicly petted, fussed and displayed affection to show the world that he was still well suited to love.

He chatted to one of his father's colleagues from Bentley whom he agreed to meet in the morning to talk over a possible permanent position at the company or garage in some capacity or other. For the rest of the evening he pulsated with a new urgency that he had not felt for a long time. Graham loved himself for that moment, even surprising himself after months of self-loathing and mental collapse. Because of that he continued to drink and socialise his way around the tables of rich and happy people all night managing to slip his young and pretty date into any conversation that he could. Bonny smiled when required to do so and looked exciting, practically on demand. She was devastatingly beautiful and could turn even the most devout monogamist's head as she glided past them swaying her delicate hips as she did so.

Bonny Pickford would probably never act in films again but in reality she really didn't need to. Her young and fresh smile warmly lit a room and awoke the scenes as she took hold of the imagination and pushed the luxury and lush feelings for new and exciting flavours to the front of your mind. She had the ability to take the control from a man's mind and weaken him and yet enriched him then with a single flash of her eyes. Graham was lucky that she had been the one that had taken a gamble on him, on a depressed soul that had been down on his luck.

She had been spotted in films and made a name for herself but the act that she played was as insincere and false as anything Graham had to offer and that for the moment made them exactly and excitingly right for each other. The couple had been spotted on many occasions together both before and after their break up and the match of convenience had also been one of universal acceptance from the fickle socialites of the time. They had been seen, kissed and even shown feeling to one another but Graham and Bonny had never taken any further steps to become closer. Graham was sure that he wanted to spend a night with her, many in fact, yet was not going to push the question until she was happy with the concept as he couldn't afford for her to go.

Graham was unsure as to whether his date had ever made love to a man before him. The way that she presented herself in public would suggest that she had not or even that she wouldn't either. In his mind however and behind closed doors knowing her as he now did, there was little or no chance that she hadn't. Bonny Pickford could reach into a man's mind and pull from it a raging lust that even he didn't know he had. Her eyes glinted and sparkled on the cloudiest day and made a man suddenly and inexplicably want all the things that he never knew that he wanted before.

Graham's smile was broad and comforting; solid and reassuring. Bonny loved that and returned it with a welcoming and special gaze that could hold anyone in its path for a moment or even for a lifetime. Each time she looked into eyes he selfishly imagined making love to her again and fulfilling countless previously unsatisfied urges. Now was no different and he ripped out the cork of yet another magnum of vintage Bollinger RD champagne and drank its contents vigorously.

Tonight Graham wanted to be the night that his fantasies were realised with Bonny and nothing except maybe Bonny herself would get in his way. Bonny whispered into his ear on the commencement of the next song, Graham bent his ear to hear what she had to say. "Come on its time to do a bit… let us dance and show them all how close we are." Graham was more than happy to oblige and in taking her hand consented to enter a slow number for the eyes of all around the club. Just before they entered the dance floor she spoke again. "The lies have worked so far haven't they?"

Had Graham's idea of happiness been just a sham and a twist of his fruitful and raging mind? And had Bonny been playing with that thought? Were they close or were they indeed lies? He had no idea. Rather than dwelling on it, he was pulled on to the dance floor and began to dance closely to his date. All his thoughts and concerns were relinquished as the third dance began and Bonny started kissing him and gazing into his eyes as only *she* could. Within an hour the party and the guests that must have still been revelling and raging in drunken excess, but Graham and Bonny were on their way back to Graham's apartment in the new Ford. The two people elegantly walked across the gravel drive as a couple towards Graham's door in full view of the perfect moon that illuminated them high above in the dark night sky.

In Graham's bedroom they petted and showed affection to the other becoming closer and closer as they did so. Graham remained concerned regarding the words that Bonny had whispered to him before during the dance. Were they a couple? Was the whole thing a lie? Graham shrugged the idea that Bonny was in any way not fully into Graham to the back of his mind and set about tonight's conquest that was to be pure and indulgent self pleasure. In the greatest of pleasures Graham welcomed the young lady into his room and immediately set about her in his usual ingenuous way. Graham was a man ready for the ladies, ready to impress and the focus of many a young lady's desire and even sexual fantasy. At that moment, despite his confidence as a person and his power to impress all, he suddenly felt inadequate and wholly uncertain as to what he should be doing. Graham Wright, despite knowing all and being in complete control of all that, ventured near his bedroom; on this occasion felt unsure and not at ease to do as he wanted.

The couple, over a few more glasses of Champagne and some records on Graham's gramophone sank into comfort and relaxation and eventually melted into the other. As two became one, the idea they shouldn't be a couple disappeared; in fact the whole idea that two people shouldn't be making love despite their tenuous relationship was not even an issue. The couple undressed and ready for the other, nakedly kissing and cuddling whilst making love and pushing the feeling of new and exciting feelings to the front of their minds. Skin rested on skin, just as emotion seemed to rest within emotions as the facade of love continued between them. Were they a couple or were they as

Bonny had said just living out the fact that they were showing the world how close that they could be.

They entertained the other and it was clear that she was indeed not a shy summer flower at all and that her rampant heart and lust was a loud and unsatisfied as Graham's was. They made love as if it would be the only chance they ever would get as the clock ground its way round to four o'clock in the morning; they didn't care however and why should they? They were living the dream.

The new day saw Graham wake to an empty bed. A great white shaft of brilliant morning sunshine forced its way through the curtains and into the room as he sat up dazed, ready to face the world. Closing his eyes again temporarily he suddenly remembered Bonny and her rampant naked sex of the night before, he felt in complete comfort and alive to the fact that perhaps recent troubles were over but he felt embarrassed to see her clothed somehow. At breakfast Graham ate with Bonny in the orangery at the rear of the house overlooking the green dew soaked lawns and summerhouse. The summer sun was awake and buoyant in revealing itself to the waiting world. Graham shared scrambled eggs, more expensively imported Champagne and bacon with his girl as he read through the news that the morning papers had to offer.

Graham knew that at that moment his troubles were over and that he had pushed, fought and battled his way through his mental and alcohol based problems to share his body and his weakest moments with Miss Bonny Pickford. Graham had little to say to Bonny that day and she had little to say to him in return as a result. Graham felt uneasy that that they were speaking face to face over breakfast just hours after having sex with the other in a most restless but intimate way.

Chapter 4

It was eleven o'clock in the morning and Graham had a meeting with George Wilde at Bentley in an hour. Hurriedly he dressed and got ready to meet a man that could potentially provide a new income and a new life for an aimless man. He said goodbye to Bonny but did not kiss her on his exit; his mind was on the meeting ahead. The trip took half an hour as Graham arrived just on time, presenting himself at the gates with five minutes to spare.

Mr George Wilde was keen to introduce himself as the controller of racing and was acting on the instructions of Mr Woolfe Barnato the man in charge of the company, who was a financial banker. At the first moment after initial contact was confirmed, George Wilde mentioned the sad loss of Graham's late Father at the track four months previously. It was a subject that Graham didn't want to talk about, and didn't.

The two men formally conversed and talked their way through the position on offer. The position was not anything to do with the office or with money but instead, surprisingly, it was for the job of race driver for the team in this most fledgling but exciting of hobbies. The pay was high and the risks were higher, Graham's father had been testament to that. Even a week before, Graham had not even considered the possibility that he could be continuing where his father had left off and the whole idea initially seemed preposterous.

The men shook hands in agreement and Graham submitted to being at the track at eleven that Saturday. Birds sang and the soft green trees that surrounded the track rustled as the wind delicately lifted and blew through them. Suddenly Graham's heart stuttered and spasmodically stopped as a green V8 Bentley came to his attention in the open fronted garage; the same car that his father had been killed driving in. It was an immense pull of his emotions as he digested the concept in his mind but he knew that what he was intending on doing was right. Graham hoped that he would get satisfaction from his new career and a chance to set his life to one that he could begin to control. Bentley got for their time and money, a well known name and son to the man that had given them great success of these formative years of motor racing. Bentley had started well and had topped all other teams over the world two years previously by winning the Le Mans 24 hour endurance race.

Bentley got, in addition, a man with much driving experience in a time when few owned, had driven or even seen cars. The race track was of course a perfect place for the company to show off its cars to the buying public and convince them that their cars were 'the driver's automobile'. Graham would of course fit in well with the image of the playboy, aristocratic 'Bentley boys' label. Bentley's green V8 was amongst the best cars in the world and competed with the expectation of performance in all races it entered. Based on its normal road car, its modifications made the race car a high powered and exciting vehicle to drive. There was a whole 175 brake horse power to handle and with its twin rotor supercharger and overhead cam, the cars could reach a top speed of 94mph.

After almost two months, Graham's father's estate had been settled with all articles and money going predictably to Graham.

Graham's own account and possessions were virtually empty and the windfall could not have come at a better time. Graham's world seemed to have started to come to fruition. Graham had in his mind at one point attributed some degree of blame for his father's death to Bentley, but reality told him that it was not a matter of fact. He kept quiet and listened intently to what George Wilde had to say. Bentley had never replaced Graham's father as their driver and the proposal was that Graham would be that successor. An icy shiver shot down Graham's back as a sudden shot of relentless realism struck him full on. His father had died in the green V8 Bentley at the test track and now in the same car Graham was being asked to drive and complete where his father had left off.

He had to agree, just had to, it seemed fateful and obviously the right thing to do in order to finish his father's business. The wage was good and the idea that he would finally be able to take an opportunity for something worthwhile and a chance at clear blue sky was one that he could not miss. In a week he would be driving for the team, until then he still had Bonny to entertain and a whole life of living to do. He returned to the house and pondered over his bold and powerful decision regarding his future, conscience and mental satisfaction.

He sat quietly in the study in contemplation; restlessly swirling a crystal glass of French Bordeaux as he did so. The deep red liquid swished and slurped around the clear glass in wild motions as he delicately held the stem of the glass loosely in fingers of his right hand. The nose from the wine invigorated his senses as he took gulps of it in between swirls. The palate gave rich flavours of plum, black cherry and blackcurrants but his thoughts were not on the flavours of the wine. Instead his mind ran on overtime, thinking about his meeting at Bentley that morning and yet more regretful feelings surrounding his father and his death. Graham Wright knew that he was doing the right thing and that his life for once in a long time, was going in a direction that he was determining.

He met Bonny that night and was delighted to see her; remaining eager to tell her about the meeting at Bentley and how impressed he was with his life at the moment. She looked at him in her almost Hollywood way then delicately and effortlessly smiled a warm and cheeky pearly white toothed smile to Graham that he reciprocated with his usual self-assured and reassuring grin. Bonny at his side made him the man of the moment as ever and at that evening's dinner dance he regaled and informed all that he was the new face of Bentley. Reaction was split between those that felt his decision was wild and un-respectful of his father and the others that realised that the opportunity was waiting for him and that he was only human in wanting to achieve his goals.

The moon that forcefully lit London's blackened residential streets cast luscious silver shadows across the road that led up the hill towards the capital. Graham stood there face to face with Bonny and realised that he might just be happy. For a rare moment he was indeed satisfied and the life he had only recently led was over, a new one, it seemed had only just started.

His heart tugged at him suddenly at that moment as he reached forward with his mouth, cutting off his partner's speech and lightly engaged Bonny's soft pink lips in a passionate and sublime embrace. They kissed and held each other with intent and it seemed with, at last, some legitimacy. They were again the couple of the evening and the exciting jazz music that filled the air only lifted them higher and then closer together. Trumpets that excitedly screamed and sonorous saxophones that softly sounded the new and vibrant tunes ensured that they held each other close.

Cocktails were gulped and soft, shiny shoes were shuffled about the dark wooden floor in the usual way and Graham Wright knew that this was his life and his lifetime to feel, live and love. Graham was photographed in the arms of his girl and would appear in the pages of one of the newspapers. The headlines would be those that would transport him from party animal and ever failing son of a late national hero to that of serious racing driver and an ambassador for the fledgling but well supported sport. Graham's mind was more satisfied than it had been for a long time and despite the rampantly progressing world that he lived in, he was settled in his thoughts and life for once. The money that he had received from his late father's estate had been a godsend and had settled Graham's finances and his black outlook from too many drunken parties and loose, expensive and insincere women. He had a grand house to live and landscaped grounds to relax and impress in. He had inherited bank accounts with enough cash for him to be able to live a life of alcoholic parties and wild women and a little to impress on the side.

Graham was an intelligent man with degrees in business and law and had always known how to invest and make money. Graham as many of those with money across the world had watched as the new markets and financial power of America had swelled at a massive rate. The markets over the last year had risen by over 50% and Graham, with his new cash, decided to take huge chunks of stock to invest in these markets and would be reaping the rewards financially. Lately he had even invested money on behalf of his friends; they too would be impressed with the results he was sure. The world it seemed had gone crazy and the old world that had been left behind in favour of the new was not missed by any of the young things. The older section of society were however very concerned but happy to make a tidy profit all the same. The rule of Great Britain and its empire was under attack. Since the war ended in 1918 and Germany's empire had been taken two steps back, the empire had started to lose its control over many of the pink parts of the world that it had held for a century.

This had put a fringe of worry and concern on the brows of many of those that were in government and leaders in society. Britain, as they knew it, was eroding and society it seemed was leading it. The bright young things as they named themselves, were changing acceptable society and were spending cash like had never been seen before. Graham Wright was one of them. He felt that his life was more complete than it had been for many years and with the new job, if that was what it could be called, he felt that there was little that could get in his way.

Graham stopped by the track on his way back to the house and slipped in through a convenient and excitingly tempting gap in the gates and walked over towards the garage buildings. Silently parked inside the darkness, were three shinny machine-riveted, fuel filled cars that slept quietly in the shadows waiting, just waiting. Tentatively he reached out a hand and placed it on the smooth metal paintwork and slowly ran it down over the cold surface feeling with each moment a wholly tactile experience. He felt the presence of his father in the machine that he had died in and for a brief moment urgently stopped in contemplation before he broke contact with the car. It was just a second or two before feelings moved onto those of excitement and anticipation at the thought of driving the car and proving his worth to his doubters in two weeks time. Graham left the garage to get back into his own car and resume the journey back to his estate. The first day at the track with his new employer was over two weeks away and until then there was living to be done.

Graham felt that he owed Bonny a visit and had planned a trip to the local lido as it was a warm sunny day. As always, Graham Wright wanted to make an impression and wanted the girl that he was with to compliment him along the way. With this in mind he visited the department store and purchased the latest Brooks Venus bathing suits for them both. After breakfast he drove to her house and presented her with his purchase. She knew of course being part of the flaming youth, that it was *the* bathing suit to have. She expected nothing else really other than the best and satisfied Graham's desire to receive thanks by swiftly kissing his smooth cheek and youthfully bouncing excitedly on the spot. Bonny kept Graham waiting for the usual elongated period whilst she first dressed then undressed and then dressed again in order to ensure that she had chosen the correct outfit and look. Whatever she had chosen Graham knew that it would be enough to compliment his image.

Bathing was of course all the rage and the rapid increase in the number of lidos opening was only just enough to satisfy the demand of the young people that flocked to them on hot sunny days over the summer months. Older people thought that the increasing amounts of flesh on show that came with the rise in outdoor bathing was a thing of concern and just another sign that their long cherished society was losing ground to the that of the riotous new one.

Graham and Bonny weren't afraid to show their flesh in order to impress either and arrived at the changing chalets ready to strip and amaze all. Bonny entered the wooden hut to change and removed the clothes that she had spent an age putting on just an hour before. It was worth it to both Bonny and to Graham as the sweet looking young thing that slowly and emerged from the brightly painted wooden chalet looked every bit as new and improved as Graham had hoped that she would be. Dressed in her new suit, Bonny felt particularly assured, top to toe in the latest attire.

When Graham emerged, he realised that his girlfriend's arrival would be front row viewing as the people already in the pool focused on her rather than him. He looked very well suited to the lido with his new and designer bathing suit, his pronounced muscles on show and his well practiced, white toothed grin emerging from behind the shadows of the blue and white painted wooden hut that he had changed in.

Around the pool were many twenty and thirty somethings that were soaking up the rays of summer sun that forcefully flung themselves over their half naked bodies. The sun casually shone across the water and sparkled in the peaks and troughs of the small waves as it rippled and lapped up across the surface of the lido reflecting the sky blue tiles on the bottom. At that moment, Graham leaped into the water with a satisfying and stylish splash that sent the previously glittering water to split, rush and then push against the four sides of the rectangular pool in rapid movements rippling against the sides and then reverberating back to where they had originated from. Bonny Pickford predictably sauntered slowly towards the solid aluminium steps and after ensuring that the entire populous of the lido had noticed her trim and curvaceous pale white skinned body, gradually lowered herself dressed in her new bathing suit, into the reflective deep water one step at a time ensuring a full audience. Feeling for the bottom with her small bare feet she tentatively waded across to meet the already swimming Graham energetically doing the front crawl towards her.

He stopped, breathlessly rising from under the water to his feet, poignantly raising a hand and then smoothing the water from his hair and backwards across his head. Looking subdued she forced another Hollywood smile on her latest audience and graced them with a pearly white smile that infused security and wealth towards them.

Graham looked at her and immediately kissed her; reaching out his arms and grasping her gently as he did so. She smiled and made sure that as many bathers as possible had seen that moment. Each minute with Graham Wright, the new driver for Bentley and the son of a late war hero, was of benefit to her whether she decided that she would be in love with him that day or not. That day when all was going well she was his and would be so right until they parted.

They playfully splashed and messed about with each other in the warm water below a sunny sky and realised that they may have actually been enjoying themselves. Graham Wright knew that his time at the lido was being well spent and had eagerly eaten up lost ground since his recent problematic life had thrown doubt at him and his life style. He had security now and his mind that still troubled him was much quieter these days in its intensity.

For an hour, Graham and the other young male bathers had to pretend that they hadn't noticed that the flappers had so much of their slim, sleek, sexy bodies on show and that intriguing curves and bumps were in evidence everywhere they happened to look. They did look, of course they did it would have been impolite not to. There were bountiful breasts and shapely buttocks very prominently everywhere for the men to avoid contact with. They were also there to catch the occasional carefully timed glance as well; and they did just that. The ladies also had usually hidden bulges to curiously gaze at on the bodies of the men that sauntered around the pool even though they would never admit it of course.

Sunlight glistened on wet soft skin and on the blue tiles around the pools edge. For now the gentlemen would have to pretend that they were completely uninterested in that type of thing. They would have to avoid staring and to isolate their intentions on the particular lady that they were with or of course all of those that they weren't with. It was the new look, accompanied with an anything goes attitude and the women, despite the usual less feminine clothing that had become indicative of the age, still knew they were women and still had a desire to show that.

The way that the women moved their bodies and the way that they sensuously stroked their wet hair and bodies ensured that they could distract and hold the attentions of any man that they caught in their gaze. The lido was just another opportunity for the youth to show themselves off and to weigh themselves up against suitors and opposition alike. They dried off in the chalets and met up once again at the gates of the white painted deco building. Bonny turned to Graham and sighed; it seemed that she wanted to go home. Graham took her back to her house in the car and with little in the way of conversation she retired inside, leaving Graham alone and once more wondering just where he stood with her and even questioning whether his feelings for her were what they should be.

She could leave him feeling cold and useless with just a turn of the head or an ill-placed comment.

She could leave him with warmth and passionate love for life with a smile or a sweet thought. Either way, Graham Wright could never be truly happy, always in want or persistent skirmish with his ever un-forgiving conscience. In a few hours Graham would begin testing and the thought was heavy on his mind. He restlessly paced the floor around the house trying to settle his nerves. His father looked down at him from the portrait that hung by the door questioning him with his expression, worrying him even with its presence. Graham was still unconvinced that he would be doing the right thing for himself even though he knew that his father would approve. At least he hoped he would have. His mind hadn't been his friend in recent months and it certainly was an unwelcome visitor that evening as it hung around him passing on to him thoughts of concern and doubt. He felt uneasy in his room that night, even after a couple of ice cooled expensive malts and a late night walk around the grounds of the house.

The moonlight over the midnight garden was dim and fought in vain against the powerful electric lights that beamed out like a beacon from the rooms in the house across the lawns and patio. The cooling air was of little comfort to him and even when he returned to his bed he remained restless and failed to sleep much more than an hour in the whole night. Soon enough the alarm clock showed 6am on its fluorescent roman numerals across its round, black faced dial.

Graham rose from his bed and made his way downstairs before eating breakfast, dressing and leaving to get to the track ready for his first time in the green Bentley: thoughts of his father's death still heavily intertwined with those of nervousness and concern. The testing was as much to test the car as it was to test the driver. Bentley and indeed the whole racing community that had been so shocked by the death of his father had got itself in a false frenzy.

All concerned agreed that Graham was the best solution to the hot driver's seat being empty in the green Bentley, but the reasons why, were not entirely rational. The papers agreed with so called experts in reporting that Graham Wright would be an exciting and charismatic driver but had not ever seen evidence that he could actually drive a race car. Graham was the son of their hero and for that reason and that reason alone he had been given the chance, whether he deserved or warranted the chance above others was questionable.

Either way, the solemn yet stately figure of Graham Wright walked over to the Bentley garage and removed his tweed sports jacket, thrusting it with an outstretched arm to a mechanic as he walked inside the dimly lit, wooden building. As he walked towards it, the sunlight rose from behind a cloud and shone into his eyes and with that he saw the car. For a brief second he stopped and tried to assure himself that he was doing the right thing. He couldn't. As he had done the night before he reached out a hand and touched the cold painted metal closing his eyes as he did so. Breathing deeply he looked over his shoulder at the twenty or so mechanics, members of the press and interested partners in Bentley that mingled around the entrance to the garage. It was time.

Graham put on his goggles and replaced his tweed flat cap ensuring that it was in exactly the right position on his head. As he sat on the leather seat he reached out and grabbed the varnished wooden steering wheel with both hands in a firm grasp. And there he sat, just looking at the track before him through the windshield breathing heavily and rapidly gulping air, trying desperately to quell his snarling nerves. Looking down to his shaking fingers he offered his index finger to the ignition button. With one final breath Graham pressed the button before him as the engine roared into life, vibrating and trembling under his seat, black exhaust smoke clouding up all around him.

Spots of rain gathered on his goggles as he pulled on the clutch, slipping the silver gear synchromesh into first gear. The car moved forward and he set off at an alarming rate, the engine roaring with passion and excitement as he left the first corner and onto the long straight. The wind rushed through his greasy hair and over his oily overalls as the suddenly hurried world shot about in a flurry of thrilling emotion before him. Braking hard into the next corner his heart beat harder as the pistons rumbled up and down the hot shafts beneath the green body behind which he sat. Petrol fumes excited his senses further with each rapid gulp of air. The suspension jumped and squeaked as he hurtled out of the straight and then immediately into a tight hairpin a hundred yards in front as the brakes struggled to grip the wheels that they clung to. Back into the next straight, the mechanics clocked seventy-four as he sped past the pit area to wild applause and the synchronised clicking of stop-watches. The car commenced its next lap increasing in pace with every moment. The thought of his late father never entered Graham's head, indeed nothing did. The frantic moment of pulsating adrenalin was enough to hold his thoughts in their place and to ensure that his concentration remained on the track and on nothing else. Was it his sheer determination to be a success for once that was directing him or was he just naturally everything that people in the motoring world hoped he would be? He couldn't be sure and neither could any of the animated and enthralled people that stood and sat around the track watching his efforts.

On the fourth lap, after reaching 83mph, the car indignantly back-fired and Graham helplessly watched as thick black smoke emerged from the smooth silver radiator grill accompanied by a splattering of oil from underneath the engine. Holding onto the brake Graham guided the vehicle to a stop beside the track on the neatly trimmed grass verge. He removed his blackened goggles and walked over to his advancing team of mechanics who eagerly rallied round to discuss the next series of changes that they would be making before further testing. People rushed around him and flashed magnesium bulbs in his face shouting and asking vociferate, inaudible and rapid questions towards him.

For a moment the lights just flashed and the muffled sound fluffed around his ears. A second later he was back in the world of the living and very much aware of his surroundings. He loved the cameras and the interest but realised that this alone was not perhaps what the papers were searching for. Shortly afterwards Graham Wright had admitted that he was: 'going to go to a party and be gaily and wildly blind drunk with women for two days', just to have something to say. He probably would do that anyway but he, being who he was as always went too far in saying so.

The comment was reported amongst most circles of society and frowned upon as a result. The papers would report in bold print not that his testing had been a great success and that if the car had held up better then he would have achieved even more. Instead they reported that he had been disrespectful of his late heroic father in wanting to get drunk with flappers at a party in tribute to the institution that was Bentley. Many ghosts had been left behind and still no thought of his father had passed through his mind. For that night he wanted to remain without the idea of his father or failure in his head and blacked out any suggestion that he had been anything but sensible with his mental ideas to date.

Graham called on Bonny on his way back home and asked her out to the party that he was intending on going to in town. Bonny looked light and easy in the chair that she casually rested in by the window of her living room. Graham glided his way over to her across the cream rug that lay in front of the marble fireside and stood two feet in front of her.

"Hello Graham," she said in a strange voice that he found hard to match to an emotion to. She looked up at him and met him just briefly eye to eye before she rapidly looked down again at the book that she wished to appear to be reading in depth. Graham asked her to the party and she said that she would go but he was unsure as to whether she really could be bothered. She arranged a time and date but she certainly didn't look like she was bothered at all either way.

"Nothing then?" He asked and impatiently tapped his heel on the side of the fire place as if to hurry a response. There was no conversation; in fact not even a word and certainly nothing mentioned about Graham's achievements at the testing. Graham turned his back and left to drive back home, leaving Bonny to do whatever she fancied alone. Elizabeth left him a telegraph just a few hours later and he was delighted to hear from her. The card informed him that she would be returning from a trip away and would be arriving at the station the next day. It continued in the hope that Graham might meet her there so that they may catch up on gossip and the like.

For now though Graham felt he must satisfy an urge and celebrate his great fortune in the testing earlier and drink to his own success. As usual he spent an age getting ready, combing back his thick black hair with oil and shaving his face to a shine. With buffed shoes and yet another tailored jacket he certainly looked every penny of the man he felt he was right then.

Bonny had told him that she would be ready and waiting by half past eight and that they could be at the party by nine. Nervously and frustratingly he waited, pacing back and forth in his inimitable way. He couldn't wait any longer and decided that he had spent too much time clock watching so at quarter to nine he rang the bell and waited for her to answer. She eventually arrived at the door wearing exactly the same clothes that she had been wearing a few hours earlier when he had called the last time and with a stubborn look on her face. It seemed that she had changed her mind and made it quite clear that she would not be going out that night.

Bonny looked like the little girl she still was and illustrated it quite superbly with her immature ranting about whatever came to her mind at that precise time. Graham had begun to grow tired of it and instead of quietly leaving as he knew was right stood his ground and argued the point with her. Arguing with a fully loaded woman was not a good thing to do and his fist banging down on the table triggered the book that she was still reading to be thrown across the room at him, narrowly missing his head. Frustrated and angry he kicked the stranded book across the floor and flung open the door, before marching out to his car, setting off and making his way to the party on his own with rapid pace.

There were many familiar faces at the party and he knew somehow that the evening would produce incident and excitement, it always did with him. He socialised and chatted playing the game that he loved and fought with almost every breath to squeeze in a least one reference to his successful testing at the track that afternoon. Most were either wholly disinterested in that kind of talk or were unable to offer much in the way of response.

There were a few however that he impressed and that filled his ever praise craving mind with comment and congratulation. He knew that it was still early days however and that with only one more testing session before the big race at Brooklands he would have to nail down an even better result to even make it to the race at all.

That didn't put him off though and once more he talked himself up and suddenly a slim chance became a certainty and a qualification to the race became a definite. People did want autographs and pictures with a star, others just wanted to be seen with him. Everything that he was and all that people thought him to be followed its usual cause of rising and boiling up until he burst with abandon and uncontrolled social madness.

The rooms that he strode about in and that others merely mingled in, were grand, proud and wide; nearly as large as those that he had in his own house and only just big enough to hold the egos of those within it inside. A white piano, priceless watercolours and Greek statues stood amongst oak and timeless green leather furniture in a room that wouldn't look out of place thirty years ago in the last throws of Victorian England. Graham wasn't sure he liked it much.

It was in amongst the crowds of charming people that he casually glanced upwards to see a face that he knew well, resting her arm on a book case and trying hard to push a smile to form on her face. He started his sideways glance at her red open shiny shoes and slowly took his eyes upwards climbing higher and higher up to her thighs. Her body he knew well but held his gaze momentarily from reaching her face as he took in the rest of her.

Her slim waist and bony, spindly arms he had once shared much intimate time with and her neck he had been told to kiss on many occasions. The tall figure started to move and walked over to him with large strides, wiggling her flat manly behind as she did so. Now he looked up and saw her features, focusing on them and returning a smile back towards the one that she was forcing to appear on her face.

She stood there in all her false glory and assumed elegance. She casually winked her eye and held an outstretched arm out to him, beckoning him to walk towards her with the motion of her fingers. It was just like the fish getting helplessly caught in the nets and lines in the sea that he had seen on the coast when he owned the flat there. He aimlessly swam towards them and then became trapped. There he would swim, struggle and wriggle to get free but he knew that there was no way out and he would inevitably be hauled aboard and harvested for his meat.

In he came, drawn by a small morsel on a line and he stupidly followed it. He followed it right until a barbed hook presented itself and then pierced his mouth. Without satisfaction he became entwined in her trap as he was flung aboard. There she was. Ottoline in all her plain glory; a face he knew so well. He had left her once the day he realised that she were a fake and damaging to him. Now without Bonny he felt strangely drawn to the comfort of something he used to know. Ottoline was still the silent killer but it was the killer that he had become accustomed to over months of shared emotion.

There he was, right where he had begun, outside that house, on the grey gravel drive looking at that unmerciful woman of severely questionable quality or morals. He had grown so strong apart from her and almost found many of the emotions that he had always wanted to experience with girls and with life. The rollercoaster of his wild life had somehow returned to the entrance booth and instead of getting off as the others did he haplessly took the ride again.

He felt compelled to stay sitting in the car whatever its consequences. Within a minute the taxi car had left and he walked past the gatepost with the shattered remnants of his car still lying on the ground. Just as before, he followed her up the steps and into that cold building. Up via the lift and to her cold and lonely apartment. The night could have been a wonderful one had it been with the right person. Ottoline was not the right person and it was not a wonderful night.

Yes, they shared sexual intercourse and were naked together, but they didn't share love or feeling and certainly didn't share all the things that Graham needed to be a part of. In his strange world at that time he believed he wanted her. Why? Even he couldn't say but in his mind he thought he did and that was how it was going to be. There weren't any of the flappers that he had predicted to the papers that he would be with that evening, there was no scandal but there was in his own mind. He found it hard to control his feelings and this occasion was no different he had confused his desire for feeling loved with wanting lust. For some reason he believed that Ottoline could provide all he was after. Obviously she couldn't and never could have but she wanted him for that moment and she felt safe and comfortable and that was what he believed he needed.

All he remembered of Bonny at that time, at that moment, was their last meeting when she had been so short, so distant and so against him. The recollection of his last meeting with Bonny had made him angry and he banged his fist down on the bedside table next to him, dislodging a glass of water onto the floor. He knew that at that moment in his mind that what he was doing with Ottoline was exactly the right thing. He dressed in a separate room and Graham made his way downstairs on his own and embraced the cold early morning when he opened the hard wooden door as the frigid air rushed in.

He felt glad that he had fulfilled his lustful sexual urges but he felt deeply ripped by the fact that he had turned to Ottoline to satisfy himself. She had used him, just like she always did and would have been sat smugly up in bed at that moment, smoking a cigarette with a false smile etched across her face. It was a dimly lit room yet he could see from the light of the moon, that crept in through a slight gap in the heavy curtains, her skeletal fingers rolling the white paper that surrounded the tobacco and her eyes that watched his every move.

He knew that he had been wrong to have even thought of the possibility of spending intimate time with her and damagingly ill-advised to have even shared a moment with her. His emotions were key to him, and whatever his persona on the outside; inside his heart, those same emotions fought, stabbed and bit him with ferocious attitude. Graham Wright drove himself home and got in a five o'clock in the morning. He knew that in the next few days he would be driving for his employer, Bentley, in his first proper race and the first race of the year.

Graham had been feeling nervous at the very thought of driving in a proper race and on that morning, despite the race being three days away he was physically sick at the thought of it. He was confident in front of crowds and people of position and wealth but with himself, the only one that he could control he had a constant self-loathing and concern for his actions. He slept-in later that day and only rose from his bed after lunch. The world was a crazy, fast paced world for those in that age, with uncertainty around every corner. New fashions and crazes, new feelings and emotions, money and wealth relentlessly bombarded the weak minded and few knew what the outcome would be.

Right now ,at that moment, Graham wanted stability and certainty, but as ever his wandering unmerciful mind would not let him have that. Graham was still furious with himself and with Ottoline for the night before and that had not made his feelings about the race any easier to hold within his chest. Drivers, mechanics and other interested, capped, gentlemen fussed and buzzed around the shiny cars that lay silent and waiting in front of the painted wooden garages in the pit area. Graham entered by the gate at the back of the garage and walked across the grass past men that were busy, eagerly revving car engines and frantically tightening the nuts on the wheals.

Graham felt uneasy and seemed damaged still from his encounter with Ottoline the night before. A few yards ahead of him there was his car sitting quietly waiting for him as he walked towards her. His breath smelt of alcohol and cigarettes and his fingers shook with fear and slight alcohol poisoning as he reached out once again to touch the cold metal before him. A light breeze fluttered between the green leaves on the trees in the distance and flicked up the dust on the track beneath the black tyres and around the shoes of waiting drivers, spectators and pressmen. As he touched the metal and slowly ran his hand down the sides of the bonnet he closed his eyes and slowly took in a deep breath. He touched each and every rivet and screw on her side as he stroked the smooth metal the way that he would have stroked a woman's soft skin on her arm, hand and face.

He felt strangely at ease for that fleeting of moments and realised that within the next ten minutes he would be driving her in a race that could be his making or even downfall. Opening his eyes he walked around to the door and opened it. Climbing inside he sat on the brown leather seat and reached out for the beautifully varnished wheel as he did so. Grasping it he again closed his eyes and tried to steady his mind that restlessly switched from one thought to another, whilst his stomach churned and tumbled within him.

Graham's mechanic strode over towards him with the team manager and eagerly shook his hand, wishing Graham all the best for the race now just a few moments away. The car was pushed to the start line as Graham waited silently inside, blankly looking out of the windshield at the three cars in front of him and the track that led away into the distance. The track was clear and dry, the sky a delicate, water coloured blue swept with a fine white brush that held off any threat of rain. The warm day reminded him of the summer that he had only just found and of the warm days that he had spent dreaming and looking for happiness. Birds flew and softly sung in the green trees around him and the grass slowly wisped and swayed in the delicate breeze.

The flag dropped.

Somehow he had blanked out the entire ten minutes or so and with explosive suddenness he realised it was time to slam down his foot and go as cars shot from behind him and from either side as the cars in front of him took full advantage of his rooky mistake, streaming off the start line and into the first corner. Immediately he was at a disadvantage to the others and at the back of the race as he struggled to compose his mind and turn into the first corner in a bid to somehow catch them as they disappeared off into the first straight. He cornered at forty miles an hour swinging the rear end of the car out as he did so yet keeping contact with the inner edge of the corner to keep his line into the straight. Picking up speed, he reached seventy miles an hour and began to come up on the car in front of him watching it as its tail switched from left to right across the track and back and forth across his field of vision. The front of Graham's car the rear bumper of the car in front scratched together and grated as Graham pulled to the left and then immediately back to the right switching and swopping sides looking for a way to pass. The cars again struck one another, this time allowing the Bentley to pull out to the right. Paint and metal flew as the two cars raced side by side but the superior acceleration of the Bentley allowed Graham to pass him and ensure that he was no longer in last position.

Now he picked up his speed again and pushed the car towards the next two cars in the race that battled and duelled in a bid to secure a better position. The silver Schneider car swung unpredictably to his left and into the blue car to his side sending it off the track and into a fence and grass mound with a deep thud, as compacted mud and metal came together in a sudden stop. Graham's Bentley effortlessly took advantage of the situation slipping past again on the right and began increasing its speed towards the central group of cars that lay three hundred yards ahead of him. The engine rumbled and roared with the cars acceleration and it vibrated through the seat beneath him and throughout his body. Wind rushed passed his ears with each twist and turn as his heart pounded in his chest with every breath.

The race continued in earnest, with Graham's Green machine rapidly coming up on the gaggle of cars in the centre of the field and flitting around the backs of them as if biting them and hounding them to distraction. In the crowd spectators with binoculars watched the battle before, them witnessing the excitement that the new motor racing idea brought with it. Into the second lap and Graham had still not made much headway into the pack of cars that stood before him and glorious victory. If he did win then it was certain to bring back Bonny from the cold and to once again relight the fire that they had shared the warmth of for so long. To him everything rested on this being achieved and all he had to do was to push harder, break later and risk more than anyone else.

He began to think about her for that brief moment and he believed that she was still the answer to his troubled heart. The encounter with Ottoline had been a huge mistake and even he knew that, hopefully the facts would never reveal themselves to Bonny and she would soon be running to take Graham back with tearful exuberance. As if inspired he took an extra yard of ground from the three battling cars before him and swung hard into the driver's side of the one to his left. The metal and wood of the two crunched together as a whole side panel of the car ripped off and hurtled back down the track behind them, audibly crashing and bashing as it did so.

Graham pushed again causing more damage to the car pushing it off to the side and into another car. Silver spokes grated against rubber tyres and two of the three cars span off and into the side of grass verge. A carful yet forceful nudge from Graham's green Bentley saw off the third within a moment as he took fifth place. The nature of racing in these formative years remained unregulated and relied on the vague assumption that gentlemen would behave as gentlemen should do. Graham was a gentleman on some occasions but he knew that underneath that he was a hapless rogue and one that was in love with winning and often with himself.

Graham had cheated in love to get the girl that he wanted, cheated with money to gain wealth and now cheated in his new profession to get both. Graham knew that with a win he would ensure that Bonny would return to him with open arms and the world would again be printing pictures of him and social comment would hold him in the highest regard.

Each time he hit the accelerator the engine roared and galloped forward in huge gulps of speed. The deceleration into a corner was every bit as exhilarating as the acceleration immediately out of it. The back end of the car swung outwards as the front brakes ensured that the front of the car stuck to the inside until the pedal was depressed and gas pumped into the carburettor, the car straightened up as grip was found from the four tyres, forcing the car to burst forward.

A couple of hundred yards ahead of him a car sat at the side of the track motionless but on fire as clouds of smoke and steam rose from it and across the track in front of the chasing Bentley. For a second Graham couldn't see ahead of him as he entered the smoked filled area. It was only blind luck that kept him from crashing into another car or spinning off the track. He held his breath on entry and it was a full five seconds before he could exhale as the battered green car pushed its way forcibly out of the smoke and into clearer track.

Ahead of him was a single car. Looking behind him to check for any tailing cars he noticed the car previously in second place struggling to keep up with him as he exited the smoke. With this he took it that there were just one more car before him and the victory he needed and that was the car directly before him. The engine temperature gauge was almost on red as the needle flicked frantically before him but he had to ignore it if he were going to win, nothing else mattered. Pressing down harder on the accelerator pushed it into the red and in danger of blowing the engine but still he eagerly pursued the remaining car in front of him.

Steam rose from the radiator grill and thick black smoke started to rise from every screw hole and vent and in to the final straight, even the optimistic Graham Wright didn't know if he were going to finish the race at all. Wheel to wheel the two cars battled as they approached the finish and as the two cars crossed the line nobody was sure who exactly had won the race.

Braking hard, Graham drove his Bentley to the side of the track and across the grass before stopping it and closing his eyes, breathing out deeply as he did so. His ears rang from the sound of the engine even though it had stopped but he was sure that he could hear the crowd and applause. People ran towards his battered, dirt ridden car as it smoked and sat there spitting boiling water out across the soft green grass beneath it, now silent but red hot and battle weary.

Nobody was sure whether it was the spectators, the press men, the other drivers or someone else that had decided it, but it seemed that Graham had won the race. Maybe nobody had decided it at all but for all anyone knew Graham had been given the victory he so dearly wanted. Maybe it had been due to his late father and all the public hysteria that had accompanied his death and Graham's rise to fame. It was his father's racing history that was the reason behind Graham being behind the wheel at all.

A beaming, soot covered man rose from the car and started a chain reaction of cheers and shouting from those around him. Removing his goggles and victoriously flinging them into the air. Gallantly he stepped out of the car and began shaking hands and smiling that well practiced and reassuring smile towards the crowd. His ears buzzed and his head felt dizzy and he ached from head to toe. But he was happy and a world away from where he had been and on the road to being where he wanted to be.

Bonny had spent the last few days away at a friend's and was returning by train that day, he knew that he would meet her and on that moment she would return to him all the warmth that she had loaned him over the previous few months. It was all he had thought about and he believed that he wanted. Surely he would be able to convince her that she should return to him. He was a racing hero now and more famous than ever. He smiled to himself as he walked along the High Street and towards the station to meet her.

Whilst passing the newsagents he stopped to read on the back pages of his heroic victory yesterday and this gave him even more impetus that morning in his quest for another victory with Bonny.

Graham thought it high time that he put his success yesterday into the picture, asking Bonny if she had heard the news, with a cold and stubborn face she turned to him grasping his arm and glaring into his eyes. "Graham, I just don't care about the race, I couldn't give a damn about that." She was forceful in her speech and wasn't going to leave it at that. "Don't you see what you have done to me? Don't you see how I am now seen?"

Graham couldn't get what she was taking about at all and looked blankly at her as if she weren't even speaking the same language. Graham was tall in height and standing with his large shoulders and muscular build towered over Bonny Pickford in front of him. Although small in stature and well noted as being timid and quiet, she was everything but that when in a rage. She began snapping and snarling just like a small aggressive dog. Graham knew that the thing that could most upset a woman was the thought of another woman being familiar with their own man. The penny had finally dropped and at that moment he knew that Bonny had heard the news that Graham had been untruthful with her and been once again intimate with Ottoline of all people.

How he cursed that woman and how he disliked her whole being. He could not deny that but he knew also that he had agreed to their intimacy and was every bit to blame as she was. She certainly couldn't tango alone. He wasn't even sure why he had done it at all and certainly didn't know what he should do now. There he was being confronted with the truth and as always it was a dark and unwelcoming visitor to his mind. Bonny was hardly the most moral or tender of girls and yet here right now he saw someone that had been hurt and damaged in a way that any other girl would have been. He watched as the proud English rose before him wilted and withered before his eyes. No amount of water or words could revive her it seemed. He knew better than to even try.

It was Graham who moved first as he felt the cold hand of humility resting on his shoulder; he swallowed hard and shivered a little as the hairs stood up on his neck. Avoiding her, he turned and walked away, heading towards the city at pace. Bonny Pickford stood motionless as she watched a troubled man stride off and away from her looking for somewhere he could avoid the truth for yet another time.

In her mind she was now certain to be the talk of town as yet another girl that Graham had milked and led out to pasture. It was certain that she were more concerned with this potential feeling of social annexing than with how she felt inside. She had decided a month before that Graham no longer featured in the game that she wanted to play and that her feelings for him were nothing more of a comforting thought to retire to now and again. She would in time find other men to satisfy her socially and sexually but until then and until the day that she realised that perhaps feelings of the heart mattered at all, she would go back to how she was before Graham. The woman was little more than a show and nothing more than a false promise. The weak promise managed to reel Graham in towards her. He haplessly gave himself to her in the hope that the part of him that was real in his heart would have a chance to live and grow for a while.

The part of Graham that held his heart and honest emotion had for so long been hidden by the party face and social disguise that eagerly fought for supremacy. It had got to a point that Graham could no longer distinguish between matters of the heart and matters of the mind. He could realise, if ever he stopped to think, that most of what he did and said were nothing more than an act. He needed the confidence of mind to push his real feelings forward in order that he may actually listen to them. He needed the help of a real and honest woman to help him listen to the silent screams for help that his heart were making but what woman would want to do that, indeed what woman would he let do that for him.

Reality in his mind could equal pain and truth, both partners he had pushed out of bed years ago. It were easier to pretend and potentially only ever receive a small taste of emotional satisfaction. If he were real to himself then maybe he could have all the wealth of love and happiness and mental stability that he needed. If he were real to himself he may receive also the pain and crushing emptiness that could come with it. He had for years only ever even seen the one side. Now he began to realise that there were another way, if only he had the strength and character to chase it. With a reassuring smile and wink of the eye he could fix the mind with the superficial and temporary and that had always worked, until now that was. He knew what the right way was to be but could he throw away the proudly false mask he wore in favour of his rarely seen own face behind the disguise?

He didn't know, as he had never let his heart out of the locked case he had flung it into years ago. He never fed it or cared for it and for a long time hoped it would shrivel up and die completely. Yet still in the background despite all the muffling and suppressing that he did, his heart still cried out as it banged noisily in his chest. Despite the war that Graham had been involved in with Bonny just the day before he felt strangely at ease with himself. He felt unusual inside and a little unsure of how he should feel in his mind. An ominous weight had been lifted and yet a dark cloud still seemed to follow him wherever he went. He knew that he would no longer have to live in the hope that Bonny would arrive on the scene, asking him to join her in the last throws of a summer that had never really even got warm for him. He knew too that he had finally put to bed the thought that Ottoline could lead him to temptation once again.

On the other side of his mind he knew that he still had no love in his life and that his rampant heart would contrive to throw itself around the locked cage that his heart was in. Even he knew that if he didn't set it free or at least feed it that it would surely shrivel up and die or bang itself to death as it flung itself against the iron bars that it had been caged in for so long. The coldness that ran down his spine from the feelings that were absent from his heart, made him realise that he had to do something about it. What he had to do he wasn't quite sure. It would probably be blundering and ill advised but he would surely be doing it anyway.

Graham was secure in his wealth it seemed, with his American investments growing steadily in value. The world had moved away from the English markets to those in the USA as the potential of the former colony revealed herself to those who had the money to invest. Graham had made a tidy profit from his investment using a huge proportion of the money that he had received from his inheritance following his father's death to bet and play the stocks and shares of the American market.

Graham had spent the whole day dreaming of his victory in the forthcoming race at Brooklands.

Graham knew that if he could win then his rating in society would soar rapidly. If he failed then he knew that it could plummet just as fast. His recent win had built him up and given him the confidence that he needed in his mind to prepare mentally for the race in the next week. Whether he would take the prize or not he wasn't sure but he knew he would have to do all he could to at least give himself half a chance. Graham wasn't sure why but a strange feeling of humility hung over him that night as he shared a smoke with a new face that evening in the old friend's meeting rooms. The unpretentious wooden door at street level and the grey stone walls showed no sign of what was inside. Down the stone steps, pictures and paintings of famous old gentlemen adorned the walls in frames of the same dark wood that matched the panelling around them. Downstairs an old and heavy mahogany door creaked open on its giant rusty hinges when it was pushed, allowing access to a room that was dark and quiet, clouded with tobacco and filled with musty odour from a hundred years of old gentlemen doing what old gentlemen do in such places.

It was a place to forget things and drink away problems in dark corners and it was a place to find people that you didn't know. It was a venue to share loneliness and lament. These were all things that Graham needed right now and that is just what he got. He failed to remain tentative and quiet as perhaps he should have and casual internal thoughts, that he would have usually expressed only to himself he made verbal representations of to someone he had never met. It was normal that with people he didn't know he had had little hesitation in bringing forward his troubles; those same troubles that with friends he would have securely kept to himself. He felt more comfortable with people he didn't know or care for than those that he did; and that was how it always had been.

He talked about his sadness for his absence of love in his heart. He opened up on his father and how his expectation to meet his legacy had driven his nerves to the edge. The man next to him sinking into the evening and caressing his half drunk glass cared not who were talking to him and certainly wouldn't remember it tomorrow but Graham didn't care.

Graham Wright had so much feeling and power within his heart that he would have always ended up a fool or a king depending on who he were talking to. Whether the sunken man next to him had judged him the former or the later, he didn't know or for that matter, care. He needed just that type of anonymous person at that time to open up to as if he were trying to convince himself that he was not alone in his battle to overcome so many struggles of recent times.

It was maybe the drink that had taken control and loosened his emotions or the continental tobacco products that he had been smoking; but either way his usual stiff exterior had melted away into the soft and humid summer evening. What remained was the face of an honest and proudly weak man and on that occasion he was welcoming in his acceptance of this stranger within. He knew the stranger he thought but it had been a long time since he and his alter ego had got on so well.

Gone for the moment was the abrasive and contentious man he lived to be and he was glad to be rid of him. The guard was dropped and the man that he used to walk and talk with had been left a long way behind with the sunlight that had now faded into the softness of night. A tear welled in his eye and his throat clenched as it gulped down reality in jagged pieces. Graham Wright the society man, the flapper's dream, the race hero and the living toy of celebrity, was nakedly just a man at that moment. He was just an ordinary man at the end of any day.

His heart had never been let free but for fleeing moments and his cold, hard steel exterior could take a million bites and punches before it even became dented let alone damaged. Inside, every hit told, every bite hurt and the pain that he felt, he felt with powerful and shuddering intensity. Each comment, each negative response and each rejection he took personally. He remained the same in the view of the majority, bravely sucking in the truth, polishing his shiny gold buttons and dressing himself in the brightest of red to hide the blood stains.

In reality he bled like all men and he felt the pain like a silver bullet to the heart, his tarnished metal would always fade in the revealing moonlight. Then he had to cling to anything in order to rescue himself. A convincing smile, a practiced line and a swift turn of pace would hide the fact that a stray spear had hit him right in the heart and drawn from him thick and precious dark red blood. It was a feeling that he had wanted to express and yet a feeling that in his whole life he made sure never reached fruition.

He rose from his seat and jumped to his feet. Drunk to the limit and drugged to the extreme he would have been fine. Worse than that, he now battled his feelings and they were things that he had seldom held long enough as friends to be at peace with. Anger welled in his mind as a response to these strangers that had trespassed on his thoughts. Pent up frustration and powerful emotion clouded his vision as he turned to the room of faceless people. Nobody looked, nobody cared. He looked around the room for a smile or a calming voice but nothing was there, nothing at all. Desperation started in his weak mind. Nerves tingled and veins pulsed within him and he knew not why. He looked at the black wood table before him that had provided honest drinks holding service all night and he became depressed by it being there.

Looking to the chair before him he became angry and he picked it up. The chair had angered him and the table mocked him. He wanted to pay it back and for that moment to make a difference to it. Randomly he flung the chair through the smoky air and watched as it crashed through a window to the side of him. Getting up he knew he had taught that chair a lesson but he felt like he needed to express himself more. Walking to the exit, his emotions bubbled to the brim and he made his way outside just after he had turned over the table and roared with misplaced emotion in defiance of it.

The warm and humid air outside wrapped itself around him instantly as he got into his car and he clumsily started the engine. Lights flashed and crowded thoughts crashed around him as he depressed the accelerator and broke into the night in an attempt to break away from his passionate anger. Tears welled in his eyes that had born sufferance for so long. Tearing up the road before him only anger and desperation was within him as speed got ever greater. The car swung around corners and drifted across both sides of the road at ever greater speeds as it mounted the pavement.

Graham could no longer live with the thought of who he was and the failure of being himself and he knew in his mind that he had to do something about it. The chair was not enough. The table was not enough. It was hatred he was sure, hatred only for his position even if he wasn't sure exactly the source. The car with Graham driving it must have a been a horrific sight to a pedestrian crossing the road as it swung around the corners and straight down the centre of the road, throwing up dust clouds as it did so. Graham drove past the park and up the hill before pushing the pedal till it touched the floor.

At nearly 50mph he accelerated to the cars maximum and drove towards the boating lake in the park. Sturdy iron railings crumpled before him as the car hit the boat house, ripping through it like it was made of paper and launched it and the car into the air at rapid pace. The car hit the water, lights down, almost vertically and charged into the dark and still water causing the greatest of splashes and noise. Hitting the water the car, now in many pieces, began to sink to the silt and thick mud that was on the bottom of the lake.

Shortly afterwards, Graham swam across to the muddy bank and lay on the side as if he had been ship wrecked. Despite the cleansing, clearing water, blood poured down his face and down his shirt. He had defiantly shown that chair something and the car too and they had nothing left to say that was for sure. He knew he had defeated them and for the briefest of moments he was again a king. He almost felt satisfied with being himself, if even for just that moment and that was a rare feeling for him.

Graham Wright, the ever well presented gentleman looked anything but as he staggered home drunk, wet and covered from head to toe in mud, blood and ripped clothes. He had lost his left shoe and his infectious smile in the boating lake as he made his way on foot back to his house some three miles west of the park. Tomorrow he would be a better man he was sure. He promised himself just that. But for now he sat amongst the shadows of a lonely room with a single candle lighting the room and fighting the darkness that surrounded him on all sides. The early morning wasn't far away and a bird sat in a tree across the street waiting to commence calling and singing out to Graham the imminent early sunlight of first dawn. When it began to sing, that bird seemed like a friend and his heart lifted somewhat when he heard it. Against the silent world it seemed lush and vibrant and it settled him into a sleep that would hide the night's pain and welcome a new day into being. Waking up in his room he knew again that he was alone and despite the victories of the preceding evening he once again felt like the world was against him. There was dried blood on his pillow and his bed was wet. Graham's clothes lay in a ripped, bloody, wet and muddied pile on the floor by the door to his bedroom.

Chapter 5

It was only a week before the Brooklands final for the year's racing calendar and the one date that he had to make and he just had to win. The papers had promoted him so much that even he didn't know what reality really was any longer. There was little chance for the opposition apparently and all that Graham Wright touched would once again turn to gold. It seemed from what the newspapers reported that all he virtually had to do was turn up to the race to win.

His mind felt nothing other than the exact opposite at that time. He had gone to bed feeling all the things that he had put off for so long. It was sobering, very sobering and he knew that all he ever held dear he hadn't yet achieved. Next morning Bonny didn't call to say they should be in love. Next morning Ottoline didn't call to say that he should be society's new pretender. Next morning he woke feeling himself and he didn't like it, not at all. For the rest of the week he remained drunk, angry and alone. Nobody called him, nobody even sent a telegram and nobody cared except Graham.

The race was that day and he had been told by so called admirers that it was only Graham himself that stood in the way of proving he was the greatest. A great race would apparently mean that he was every bit the race expert that his father was. The only thing he knew was that he was a shadow of who he could be. He and he alone could make it but he and he alone could also break it. A cool head, a temperament of ice and a lucky streak maybe would be enough.

The social scene had trickled away leaving only the man, and without the lift of others he remained a mere mortal, and a highly flawed one at that. He would dig his heels in that was for sure, that was how he was but he knew that when reality struck it was as always him, against the world. He was drunk by ten o'clock in the morning and sick half an hour later. He drank again and was sick again at eleven and by midday he walked through the gate and over to his team of garage mechanics a sobering lonely man. The last time he had been in a race he had thrown his cap into the air and pushed a pressman aside before stepping into his car. This time he took the journey alone and he had forgotten his hat to throw down.

It was a different man that held the wheel from the one that had walked towards the car. The car seemed to own him as it took him into its body. The German, Schmitz, tried to shake his hand. He bluntly refused to shake it in a distinctly unsportsmanlike fashion and defiantly not in an English way. He remained significantly drunk and his stomach whirled and swelled inside him. His red eyes must have given his intoxicated state away. Graham's drunkenness had probably in some way been to hide his raging nerves. Maybe it had not been intentional but perhaps in the back of his mind he realised that he would find the race difficult to handle without it, just like life.

He was sick another time before even starting the engine. The brilliant smooth green paint shone with lustre in the afternoon sun as it crept up behind the tall poplar trees in the distance, peeking through the thin branches. The vomit slithered slowly down the shiny driver's door and onto the black rubber tyres, dripping eventually onto the dirt covered track. Graham's rough, sleepless and unshaven face was covered in beads of sweat before he had even moved to the starting area. Dust clouds from the track billowed up around him and seemed to irritate his throat. His head beat with pain like a drum banging between his skull and his brain pulsating and enraging his mind. He was probably not in any condition to even leave his bed let alone get behind the wheel of a race car and drive a two ton machine in battle against other drivers that really wouldn't be giving him any consideration of his physical or mental state.

The mechanical perfection of the car was in stark contrast to that of the driver that was at its wheel. It roared into life as it was gingerly positioned onto the track. Drivers and mechanics looked at each other with slight little sideways glances, assessing perhaps the well being of their competitors. Looking for cracks maybe or finding a weakness that they could take advantage of. Tougher contenders stared at their rivals in order to reassure themselves of their own superiority. Graham was not a man that normally failed to face an opponent or hide away from a possible skirmish, in fact he was more than likely to instigate it than most men. On this occasion he looked away from the glances and instead concentrated on beating and fighting the duel demons of inebriation and self doubt that raged and battled in his mind. There was a loved man and there was a broken man and they both sat in a car that carried the dreams of the driver and his late father with it. He was perhaps the best driver of any of the men that were preparing to race that day but he was also the most insecure and frightened.

The pedal was depressed and the metal beast shot forward with Graham in it. Just before the first corner he gained control and despite the pressure of alcoholic inebriation managed to enter and exit the corner as if he were a true professional. The sun crept lazily out from behind a glum looking wet cloud and cast a couple of brief flashes of sunlight across the race track, glinting off the windshields of the cars but it was never going to be full sunlight on that day. The leading three cars broke away from the pack early on and entered into the straight, pushing the engines to their maximum at an early stage and raising the pace and tension immediately.

Graham was not one of those three as he again languished behind the leading pack in a group of cars hustling and exchanging paint with each other. Graham felt hot, angry and aggressive as the cool beads of sweat continually formed on his forehead and now ran down his cheek. Engines roared as exhaust smoke filled the air in clouds that rose towards the sky. The race began with the fifteen steel machines bursting into life as their black rubber tires ripped up the dirt as the cars lurched forward. Graham depressed the pedal and jerked into the car in front of him, throwing him back into his seat. He gained composure and pushed the pedal down once again, this time steering around the car and forward into the group of cars that jostled and fought to gain early advantage.

Side by side with another car, Graham again made contact, this time with a sideways shove of the car next to him. The cars grated and rubbed against each other as bits of wood and metal broke off. Graham was angry and he shoved the car into his competitor once again as if to try and get the frustration out of him.

He still couldn't shake off his anger yet he had managed to gain a place and pushed off towards the front of the pack in a hope to gain ground on the leaders. He sprinted in fits and bursts accelerating harder and braking later in each corner, gaining ground on the others all the time. Two laps later Graham was chasing the front four cars. He was swerving and pushing the limits of the car and of himself. Corners got wilder and wilder as the back end continually swerved outwards struggling as it did so to gain grip. In each straight the braking got later and later until he flung the car off the strip and across the grass. He regained control and brought the car back to the track and rejoined the race at speed. Further up the field the four leading cars looked to be closing on the podium positions, Graham looked only to be filling one of the other positions, one that would certainly mean he lost face. He needed to gain speed as he would soon be entering into the famous Brooklands curve and needed to make his extra speed in the straight really count.

He had ridden the wild rollercoaster that rose, twisted and turned as soon as he got on it. It had taken him places that he loved and pretended to be at home with and also to places that he knew he shouldn't be but blindly charged towards regardless. He was a brilliant man, an intelligent and kind man but he had spent virtually the whole of his life being someone he wasn't. He had spent the entirety of his life being what people wanted him to be and never what he actually was. The alcohol and the drugs were the escape route as were the loose women and looser excuses that he clung too. He had, with Bonny, escaped and touched the sublime but it was and would never be the route he needed to take despite it being the easier and immediately rewarding one.

Elizabeth was the closest thing to honesty that he had experienced and he had lunged towards her in several embarrassing moments of desperate clinging concernment. That was never to be a route to take and he knew that. All avenues were closed now that Bonny had gone; now it was down to him and his machine. Could that win her back? He wasn't sure, and in his mind he didn't even know that he wanted her to be won back either. He just wanted love. He had never received it or given it but he knew that it was the route cause and answer to all problems. Graham had more to win and indeed more to lose than perhaps anyone on that day at that time in their life.

He had invested hard in America with his money and partied and given himself to the moment with his heart, soul and wallet. His father stood over all he did on the race track and his rampant emotions clung with every living breath to each and every move he made looking for satisfaction. It all rested on this day, a day like no other and a day that Graham Wright would have to secure as his own. Graham was not one of those three as he again languished behind the leading pack in a group of cars hustling and exchanging paint with each other. Graham felt hot, angry and aggressive as the cool beads of sweat continually formed on his forehead and now running down his cheek.

For a second he checked out of the race as his concentration wandered and it was only a sharp shove from the car to the side of him that woke him from his temporary slumber. He regained composure as he slammed a competitor in the side to regain a place as he pushed forward to make up for his moment of lost concentration.

By the end of the second lap Graham had gained four places and attained fifth position in a race that had held the emotion and imagination of the media and public alike. The race and the royalties that would go with it would be decided on that race track and on that day. Graham wanted them to both be his. His father would have loved to see that happen and would have relished the chance to experience his only son achieving in the same way that he had. He would have refrained from publicly bestowing any affection or praise on his offspring but he would have relished and feasted upon the idea in his private time.

Graham always felt unable to satisfy his father's demand for excellence despite often achieving it. He was always his own worst enemy.

Once again he had temporarily checked out of the race and only returned when a competing car flashed past him in a rush of speed and took the place that was his away from him. He pressed again and tussled once more with the car in front of him, racing up one side and then the other before cutting in at the corner and sliding past it almost with ease. The race was in reach of Graham's grasp as he pushed the engine harder and harder until it rumbled under his seat. The cylinders rose and fell, getting hotter and hotter until they ran the danger of blowing and yet he still he charged harder, faster and stronger. At the car's full speed he closed in on the two remaining cars in front of him.

The sun broke free of the cloud and shone down across the damp track and onto the cars that battled beneath it. The crowd that stood witnessing the event rose to their feet whilst applauding and whooping for joy in appreciation of Graham's progress. Second or third would never be good enough for a man with so much ambition and drive and he would make it his quest to attain first place in order to settle his demons.

With the strong smell of petrol in his nostrils and his knuckles white with tension hard on the wooden steering wheel, he pressed on. It was on the next corner that he made his move ramming hard into the back of the silver car that held second place. The driver looked over his shoulder to see Graham grating and shoving the rear chrome bumper of his car with the giant green Bentley. The crowd had folded in appraisement at his driving skill and energetic enthusiasm just moments before but it seemed that, as was typical with Graham Wright, he now went too far. The French driver looked surprised to even see the car again having clearly thought that it was too far back down the field of cars and now he broke left and right, riding up on edge of the track and onto grass before grasping hard on the wheel and pulling the car back on the mud track. Graham hadn't finished yet as he held back two or three yards before recklessly charging towards his opponent and impetuously striking the car in the rear wing and throwing it off the track.

The silver coloured metal twisted and contorted as it banged into the ground, shards of glass and metal flew off and across the grass as the destroyed wheels and doors detached and embedded themselves into the wall of the garage and into the side of the spectator's area. Graham either didn't care or didn't notice that his competitor had violently and deliberately been thrown off the track and continued on towards the only car and driver left in the race that was ahead of him. He pursued him like a relentless curse, infesting and engulfing him as if it was his last remaining wish to be next to him. The Bentley leapt to the left and then the right increasing velocity all the time until the car was in Graham's sights.

As Graham sped around the corner and up to the garages, it was impossible for him not to notice the crowds of people surrounding the mangled wreck of what used to be a motor car. The Bentley had, by the next corner, reached the car in the prized first place, almost effortlessly easing past it and across the finish line to take its position and win the race.

Graham took the battered and damaged vehicle to the side of the track, took off his goggles and climbed out of it. Sweat and grime covered is face except for two white patches around his eyes where his goggles had been. There were only a few people that came over to him, the total opposite of the masses that had surrounded him in the last race. The crowds that surrounded the tangled metal that Graham had passed when he crossed the line were still there. Graham walked over to the garage to see what the spectacle was. He knew it was the fashion at the time to take photographs of disasters like train crashes and factory explosions and it would have been a perfectly reasonable explanation for this to be no different. Bits of metal, wood and glass littered the grass and one of the doors had embedded itself in the side of the wooden garage wall. First he saw a man's shoe and immediately as he got closer he saw the man from which it came. The man was laid on his back with a grey suited man kneeling at his side. There were mutterings and conversations clearly surrounding the man and it was brutally clear that the driver was dead. As Graham reached his side he saw a gash to his head. The man's eyes were cold and open. His skin was pale and lifeless.

Graham gulped and then swallowed hard as the reality struck him that he may have been responsible for his death. Several of the crowd turned to look at Graham and his face, a face that he wished could have belonged to someone else. Dark, accusing eyes surrounded him and all he could do was to look to the ground as he folded and withered under the intense pressure. A short man, dressed in a tweed suit, approached him and stabbed his rigid outstretched forefinger into Graham's chest. "This is your fault, see that man? Dead, he's dead. You killed him," he continued, with increasing volume and sincerity. "What do you think of that?"

He looked around at the assembled men now surrounding him and raised his hands to them to gain their agreement. "You should be ashamed of yourself. Your father would have been ashamed as well, you're nothing compared to him, nothing." The group gathered closer to Graham and in sympathy with their unofficial spokesman began audible mutterings in criticism of the way that Graham had behaved on the track and the death that he had apparently caused. Graham Wright had experienced much in life and was never normally a man to back away from a challenge or confrontation but he felt unable to offer any response to his accusers and felt the weight of the man lying dead across the grass heavily on his shoulders. He looked to the ground and walked away, a solemn character with the eyes of the many watching him as he did so back towards the High Street and away from the whole turbulent incident.

The next day Graham Wright again made the newspapers but this time is wasn't on the society pages that usually reported his antics and those of his fellow party goers. It was indeed the front page of the newspaper that revealed to the purchasing public, the incidents of the previous day's race and the 'regrettable occurrence' that Graham's Bentley had been involved in. The newspaper elaborated on what it called Graham Wright's 'erratic and forceful driving style' and mentioned his late father, four times. Graham Wright didn't read the newspaper at all that day and avoided conversation with anyone. He visited Elizabeth in the early afternoon and it seemed that she had not heard any other media and personal questioning of him and for that he was glad. She didn't mention it and he assumed that was because either she didn't know what had gone on or that she just decided not to mention it for Graham's sake.

She was a friend after all and Graham could count on two fingers of one hand the amount of those that he had in all reality. Many had shown that they were happy to ride with him the society rollercoaster whilst it was fun but as soon as the track became a little rocky they had conveniently leapt out. The two friends walked down to the river and then along its banks for a good mile or so in the early afternoon, stopping now and then to look at the greenery of the bushes and trees against the silver coloured waters that washed against them as busy boats chugged past sending small wakes in ripples towards the river side and then back into the centre.

The breeze was light but it was enough to turn the temperature to one that made them button up their coats and ensure cold hands were kept in pockets whilst they walked. Elizabeth's long brown hair rose up and flicked across her face and about her shoulders as they walked and her little white cheeks became rosy in the wind's chill. Despite the black woollen coats that they wore, the summer seemed a little cooler and more bracing since the race but the warmth from his friend and her insistence that they must not talk about the things that troubled Graham, ensured that at least the sun still shone above them.

Between them, over the course of their meeting, it was decided that Graham should go away for a while to settle his mind and find something new to focus his raging mind on. A short holiday may help the tide of discontent within him pass out at least for a while and a touch of warmer more full bodied continental sun may sooth his lust for love, life and good times.

Chapter 6

Graham packed his bags and belongings that he was to travel with. There were five snakeskin and tortoiseshell trunks and cases that accumulated in the hallway throughout the afternoon waiting for a taxi driver to pick them up once he had been called. It was just a matter then of buying the tickets in the city, firstly for the train to the port at Southampton and then the boat to somewhere hot. He considered Spain and its islands would be a worthy place as he had heard a lot from various newspaper articles and radio broadcasts and they had all sounded excitingly different from all that he had known. The liner that he was to travel on would be a grand one, he made sure of that and ensured that he had packed suits, tuxedos and all his fine outfits as he was sure that there would be some living to be done whilst on board.

Graham sat in the tall, light brown leather-clad chair that was positioned to take advantage of the afternoon sun. It was a place that his father used to sit to read the newspapers and catch up with correspondence, it was a place that before his father's death, Graham had never sat in. The wait for the taxi cab seemed to take an eternity as it was with mouth drying anticipation that he waited. The cold and windy weather that had been the theme of the day so far, had slowly given way to black and grey clouds that formed over the south side of the river and then spread to gather menacingly over most of the city.

Rain spots started to form and fall from the sky, descending individually towards the earth from above, faster and faster in its velocity before hitting the ground with the smallest insignificant sound of inaudibility. One raindrop became two and two became many. Soon enough the whole sky was full of rain that formed and fell in rapid swathes blown and swirled around by the wind. Rain lashed against the windows of the old house in a way that must have happened a million times before. Rain fell down on the fields and onto the gravel drive and soaked the entire city. The air was filled with the sound of rain for a good quarter of an hour but it did not dampen his spirits.

The taxi arrived in the middle of the rain storm and the driver became drenched to the skin as he struggled in and out of the hallway with the bags and cases for the trip, whilst Graham buttoned up his coat and waited in the dry, patiently watching the taxi driver's efforts through the window. As Graham opened the door from the house the fresh smell that rose up from the soaked green lawn filled his lungs as he waited for the bags to be loaded. Finally all the bags were in the taxi and the driver now presented an open umbrella for Graham to walk under to the taxi door which he shut behind him once he was sat inside.

The taxi reached the main entrance of Paddington station at midday and a smartly dressed, long legged porter took his bags and cases into the waiting area and rushed away with gusto, Graham followed in his own time. The station was packed with people, some restlessly pacing and striding about in a manic hurry to be somewhere urgently. Others were standing or sitting waiting for trains to arrive and take them off for a relaxing lazy week's holiday. Trains hissed and blew steam as they arrived at the platforms their whistles shrieking as the approached. Painted wooden doors swung open before the carriages arrived and people jumped or stepped off onto the platform and away into the city. Eventually Graham's train to Southampton arrived and the bags were loaded into the luggage carriage by a chain of porters with trolleys whilst Graham made his way further down the platform to the first class section where he made himself comfortable at a table.

Graham waited for a full ten minutes as he watched the hustle and bustle of the station amongst the soot and steam through the window of the train. The dried pea in the shiny silver whistle in the guards hand vibrated quickly and a shrill blast was let out as a green flag was waved positively at the other end of the train by a man with a large black moustache. Pressure built up rapidly as the huge iron wheels temporarily span as they tried to grip the rail beneath them and eventually propel the mighty machine forward. The massive metal structure began to move, taking the hundreds of people aboard it to their destinations and to new emotive experiences.

Graham was embarking on his journey to relish and soak up new opportunities and live a little more of the life he craved. Graham Wright was grateful also for the opportunity to run away from the criticism and anger that he had endured since the fateful race that had sealed him as the best and worst of the racing scene. As the train left the station and made its way slowly into the open, it became evident that the rain, that had been such a feature of the afternoon was still falling though less so in intensity, the sky remained grey and overcast. The black iron frame of the train began to gain speed as it reached open countryside until the background faded to a blur in a rush of colour and contrast. Piston rods furiously shifted up and down pushing the huge wheels round with relentless speed as they sped along the tracks ahead and towards the horizon.

The train banked to the right along a tight track and the smoke from the chimney blew into the open window above the seat, causing Graham to get to his feet and slam it shut when the smoke blew in. The smoke was black as the engine burnt extra coal as it pushed up the increased gradient and across the viaduct that span effortlessly over the valley and river below. The viaduct was a fantastically large structure, handmade by hard work, sweat and injury. It had taken over two years of construction to build but the train took just a minute to cross as it powerfully proceeded from the dark sprawl of industrial London to the bright breezy and bracing coast.

The wooden first class carriage was a sumptuous place to be, with silk head rests and thick white and gold curtains with delicate blue and white cubist flowers across them. The oak table between the seats was varnished and polished by meticulous and intensive attention over years of service to well financed gentlemen. The exuberantly bouncy sprung seats were quite upright but comfortably welcoming to tired travellers and Graham was more than content to spend the time travelling to port at Southampton on such a seat. It was a half hour into the journey when the train began to slow down and pull up at the next station. The station was set in a lush green valley and the rain that had fallen on the earth for the last few hours had made it seem all the greener. There was an earthy rich smell in the air that became apparent when the doors opened and passengers clambered aboard.

Waiting on the platform there were children excitedly chatting and squabbling and there were their mothers or nannies dragging them on board. There were gentlemen in suits, deep in contemplation, boarding with newspapers rolled up under their arms and leather briefcases in their hand. The second class compartments were packed by this point, the first class, where Graham sat was less busy but still busier than it usually was. Most of the bench seats had at least one person sat on them and the four or five people that did get onto the train and into the first class carriage began to look for seats and places that they would share the rest of the journey on.

A lanky man dressed in a smart yet bold cream suit and hat to match, approached the seat that Graham was sat on and asked him if the seat next to him was available for him to sit on. The man was very well to do and obviously a very positive and assured gentleman in everything he did. Graham was neither bothered nor otherwise whether he should have company for the journey as he had been engaged in the scenery and in the social spectacle that he had been witnessing over the journey. The train started off gradually after the compulsory shrill whistle and flamboyant flag drop had signalled that all was correct, all passengers were safely on board and the train was ready to build up steam and commence the next stage of the journey.

The tall man before him suddenly broke the silence and introduced himself ,extending his hand to be shaken before he had even spoken. Graham shook the outstretched hand with his usual businesslike firm grip. He introduced himself in grand fashion as William Henry Stewart and revealed that he was a politician making his way from London to France to discuss matters of international relationships, with other similarly pompous people no doubt.

Graham pretended to be excited by the fact that the man was a politician although in reality it meant nothing more to him than if he were in any other job. The black haired man was assured of his opinions being correct as he was about himself and with every breath relentlessly gave comment on everything that was happening on the train, around the train and everywhere else.

Graham suffered his highbrow comments and assertive assumptions of everyone else for quite a while without even an interjection. The comments however became a debate when the man became angered somewhat with one particular topic when he put forward his thoughts on society and how the whole situation of people with money that they didn't deserve to have, would ruin the higher and ruling classes.

Graham of course had money and had until recently been a key member or society and knew more than many of the people on the train on the subject of what money could buy and what it couldn't and certainly more the man in front of him. Graham felt the presence of the bulk of a man before him and felt even a little intimidated by him, something that he certainly didn't usually have a problem with. Graham was glad when the ticket collector came through the divide of the carriages and approached the two men for their tickets.

The man was dressed in a blue uniform that matched that of the porters on the station platforms in London and was finished off with eight small, silver buttons that had been polished so many times that Graham have could almost see his face in them if he had got close enough to one. Tickets were inspected in meticulous detail as they changed hands and were turned over and back a few times with a smooth inspector's thumb feeling out the paper. Something was removed from the man's deep side pocket as the ticket had clearly passed the close scrutiny. The ticket was put again to its landscape position and then punched with a shiny metal instrument that made a small half moon shape in the side of it. The man's equally meticulously manicured moustache seemed to quiver as he did so. No word was uttered but a small sign of satisfaction seemed to be produced from somewhere as the man continued his short journey of the rest of the carriage.

The well dressed and pompously presented politician had by this stage decided to keep quiet and hold his opinions inside and Graham was glad for that. His intentions could now refocus on the rail journey that was rapidly reaching its destination of Southampton docks. The train was at full flight and masterfully ripping through the countryside pushing ever nearer its final station where it would allow the second part of the adventure to continue.

Fifteen minutes later and two station stops the scenery of open and green countryside slowly began to give way to that of grand industrial buildings, grim terraced, blackened, back to back houses and the occasional church or public house. Soon the heavy, soot filled air became evident as the built up sprawl and crowded streets began to encroach the train on either side as the train began to slow down and draw into the station at Southampton. After a whole twenty minutes of silence, William Henry Stewart got to his feet and reached out his hand once again for Graham to shake in order that they may say goodbye and go their separate ways at the docks.

The train finally pulled up at the platform and let the passengers off to go on their business, be it in the city or on a boat to somewhere a whole lot more exotic. The docks were not far from the railway station but Graham Wright organised a taxi to take him and his mass of luggage to his ship that would be waiting to leave for Spain on the hour. Just like outside the house back in London, the taxi driver struggled, huffed and puffed the bags and cases this time out of a taxi rather than into it. Life for a first class passenger was a whole lot easier and more comfortable than it was for someone occupying second class. There were no fussy porters manhandling your baggage if you weren't from a first class carriage and there would be no well sprung seating or table side lamp to ensure your journey was a comfortable one.

Graham had never had to work hard, worry about money or had to struggle to do anything in life really and he had lazily enjoyed all the benefits and luxuries that money could bring. Graham got aboard the taxi and took the short journey from the train station to the docks where the ship would already be waiting to take him to Spain and a whole new world. The taxi drove through the dirty, black docks that buzzed and heaved with life. Hundreds of men hauled thousands of goods in boxes, containers, skips, sacks and bags from one place to another, again and again from sunrise to sunset. Cranes lifted cars, industrial engines, pumps and machinery onto ships. The goods came from all corners of the empire to be shipped and brought ashore to then be put onto trains and canal boats and busily taken to all areas of the country.

The taxi was comfortable and quick and made its way from the smart first class waiting lounge at Southampton station to the cosmopolitan suite onboard the huge liner, 'The Empress' that lay waiting for them. The men either side of the taxi sweated and painfully worked until they were black in their faces and exhausted in their bodies. Whilst Graham would see his midday drift lazily away with a four course meal and champagne, the men that worked the docks would have five minutes to eat dry bread, cheese and drink tepid water before once more resuming their heavy manual tasks and pick up their wages. The wages that they would pick up would be enough to buy their family a meagre meal and maybe a few cigarettes or a beer.

The rain had cleared the skies as the soft breeze cleared away the remaining clouds, blowing them away and across the channel to somewhere else. Graham was glad as he had had enough of dealing with the rain and welcomed the presence of the sun as it rose to become stronger. The summer day revealed itself as the sun gained strength over the next hour, forcing Graham to remove his overcoat and fold it up putting it on the seat next to him as the taxi moved on. The dirty faced men shifting wool and corn in sacks from boat to shore were not as welcoming of the hot sun as it made their task even more arduous. The sweat on their faces trickled down their leathery cheeks and down their bent spines but life continued whatever the weather in its hard and tortuous way.

The taxi continued on to the quayside where it pulled up with a couple of other taxis and cars. After being paid, the taxi driver began shifting Graham's bags once again, this time from his taxi car to several porters' trolleys. The porters then took their trolleys up ramps and disappeared to somewhere deep inside the belly of the vast white liner. The massive steel structure seamed to stretch on for miles. There were four gigantic black and red iron funnels that reached up high above the wooden decks and white painted metal railings. Stretched between the funnels were lines of bunting with flags of all types and colours that fluttered in the light breeze displaying a nautical message to other vessels.

On board were amassed at least four hundred people that stood on the decks around the railings and sat on chairs dotted all across the wooden decks at both ends of the ship as it stood waiting to be towed out of the quayside and into open water. As Graham got out of the taxi he immediately noticed the animated people the length of the ship and the whole side of quayside excitedly talked and busily readied themselves for the journey ahead of them.

Graham dressed in cream suit complete with hat with a thin black rim that reflected back the bright sun that shone onto them from directly above him. With almost a swagger he strode onto the wooden ramp that led to the ship from the quayside. It was only a few minutes after Graham entered the ship that it set off and it was almost as if everyone onboard was waiting just for him. He would have liked to have thought that anyway. Inside the ship Graham was immediately taken to his suite by another porter and his luggage arrived shortly afterwards. The room was decorated in black and gold and was clearly one of the finest examples of art deco exuberance that was on a ship of the time. The whole decadently splendid ship had taken four years to build and its glittering and shiny fixtures and fittings had been grown from a wealth of money carefully invested in its handmade, purpose-built creation. White marble sculptures of horses and gloriously masculine gods flanked the corners of all first class communal areas whilst the lounges and seating areas were entirely decorated in the style of Louis XVI of France.

Having had his clothes and luggage unpacked and put away ,Graham took a stroll around the ship for the first time to see where he would be spending his next week before reaching Spain. Directly outside the door to his suite was a short dark mahogany walled corridor that led to the main staircase rising to the top deck and into the first class area at the front of the ship. Graham had left his woollen coat back in his room as the day was still pleasantly warm and he exited the bottom floors onto the deck into brilliantly bright sunshine.

The varnished Canadian maple decking was beautifully new as was the brilliant white gloss paint on the metal railings around the ship that reflected the sunlight in every direction. The small chugging and smoking tugs that lay further out and only joined by a couple of tightly wound thick ropes pulled the liner out to open water and away from the quayside. After a few minutes wait and a huge excursion of human toil and sweat, the boilers had made enough pressure to set the huge pistons rising and falling to propel the massive vessel forward in its pursuit of the continent and a new undertaking. Graham had never been overseas before but it had always been a dream of his to do just that for the sheer hell of it or at least to be able to talk about it at parties.

The whole experience was a new one for Graham and as he was a troubled and loveless man it was also a great opportunity for him to experience and develop new opportunities, to draw more from life. Graham had overheard from one of the crew that the deck was some 676 long and an incredible 20,000 tonnes. The part that Graham was walking within was dotted with well to do people that strolled about with no particular purpose or aim other than to soak up the flavours from the start of their journey.

The liner passed out into open water and began to push its speed as it belched out smoke from the three towering funnels. Flags at either end of the ship blew wildly with the uptake of more speed, surprising a few well to do ladies whilst a gentleman had his hat blown clean off and across the decking. White lifeboats were suspended down the sides of the ship, each looking like the main vessel in miniature and even supported the ships name on each one. Graham wandered to the back of the ship where over the back a long stream of broken water came from the twin propellers that whirled and rotated with intense speed and awesome power.

Half an hour into the journey the docks of Southampton were long gone in sight and in mind and on all sides of the ship lay miles of grey water that had become quite choppy and turbulent. The massive liner made short work of the rough sea as the pointed metal bows cut through it like it was not even there. Graham had removed his hat and placed it under his arm as he walked down a flight of stairs and into a lounge area where ten or so gentleman smoked cigars and swirled and swigged excessively expensive brandy in large glasses. Conversation was on the subject of foreigners and their place in the British Empire and although not a topic on which Graham was particularly opinionated he became drawn in just by entering the room.

"You sir?" A fat bald man voiced in a drunkenly loud volume as he turned his head to face Graham at the door. "These darkies should know their place hey? They have no right to imagine they should be anything other than servants for the English hey? What sir, do you say, hey?"

Graham wasn't allowed chance to utter a reply as a second fat, equally drunk and loudly spoken man answered for him. "He is clearly a gentleman, what else is he going to say?"

"I want to hear from the young man," replied the first man and repeated his question once again, his bushy black moustache quivering as he did so.

Graham spoke, "We clearly have been given by God the right to govern these people but they do have some things to offer us don't they?"

Graham's reply didn't seem to have been accepted or even listened to as another man got to his feet, jovially raised his glass of brandy and triumphantly said "Well who cares? They make us rich don't they?"

A chorus of raucously exuberant laughter, cheers and hand clapping broke out across the whole room. Graham left the self-congratulating noise at that point and walked out and back to his room another flight of stairs below. Graham rested on his bed falling asleep for a few hours before washing and changing into a black tuxedo suit and red bow tie.

Graham noticed the sound of string music as he climbed the stairs at the end of the corridor at the entrance to the dining room and its sound was quite inviting. He definitely looked the part and felt well with himself and ready to welcome anything that dinner would bring him either in taste, in conversation or in subtle experience. The dining room was as grand a spectacle as the rest of the ship with yet more swathes of wooden panels on either side of the room with commanding white plastered pillars decorated with gold leaf inside the tight cornices.

Everyone in the dining room was dressed in their finest attire and were ready to impress relations, acquaintances and people with status, money and influence. There were certainly many of those and money was a theme across the whole ship. Graham felt quite at home as he walked into the room and immediately took his place amongst a group of young gentlemen who were busy sloshing drinks and chatting about girls.

"John Malcolm, and what do you do?" A lanky man of about twenty turned to face Graham and asked in a high voice holding out his hand as he did so.

Graham met his limp hand shake before introducing himself, "Graham Wright pleased to meet you, I'm in erm, I was the..." He was unsure how to explain about the racing and was in two minds whether or not to mention it at all. He decided to draw on his investments in America instead and reported that he was something in the money markets. The men before him seemed to be happy with that explanation and conversation moved onto the ship and its construction instead. Graham took up a glass of champagne from a silver tray that seemed to float about an inch above a waiter's hand as he circulated around the large room amongst the guests.

Ladies mingled with gentlemen but not in the way that Graham had been used to at his parties, it was all far more sophisticated and maybe even a little boring at this point. People and couples passed him as they walked around, with many smiling or politely asking, 'How do you do?' as they moved on but Graham didn't know a soul there. People knew him though, and one such person approached him from behind a group of ladies and tapped him on the shoulder, coughing quite loudly as he did so. The man was obviously a military man as he stood fully dressed in his green outfit proudly displaying a whole rainbow of coloured ribbons with gold, silver and bronze medals attached to them.

"Major Harold Winterbottom Smedley. I served with your father in Ireland." Once again a hand was held out for Graham to shake, this time a little more firmly than the last offering. He continued. "I was sorry to hear of his passing, he was a great man and you must be very sorry to have lost him."

Graham just nodded his head slightly closing his eyes as he did so before offering reply. "Thank you, I miss him greatly." The Major still holding onto Graham's hand and periodically shaking it again began reeling off his recollections of their tour of service in Ireland and revealed how close they had been to each other, in a strictly professional manner of course. It couldn't really be called a conversation as it was all one way traffic but Graham politely nodded and smiled at the appropriate times with the occasional yes or no being offered when required.

It was nice to find someone that Graham had something in common with but he was glad when people began sitting down and had had chance to move away.

There were ten seats to each large table and Graham sat at the end of it, furthest on the left of the room and was joined by a young couple from Wales and two much older couples from Birmingham and from Lancashire. The final three seats were taken by the Major, a woman that was presumably his long suffering wife and a young woman that he perceived to be their daughter. The daughter sat straight upright in her chair and clearly knew every form of etiquette that a young woman should know and was obviously well practiced in performing it.

Her hair was like the gold colour in the frames of the paintings that hung on the walls. There were a series of tight curls in her hair that attractively fell around her shoulders and down her back as if it were a fountain, cascading water down smooth stone. Her eyes were the deepest green colour but her head very infrequently raised enough for Graham to see from the position that it was in, looking down towards the table in dutiful obedience.

The major stood and faced Graham, introducing firstly his wife Rose and his daughter Catherine. Graham got to his feet and politely shook the hands of the two women, All seemed to be well. Graham was immediately attracted to Catherine's smooth, angular but pretty face and curvaceous body but was somewhat put off by her formality and rather pompous attitude. He figured that she would be too much like hard work for a man like him to be bothered with but even so she was still good to look at whilst he was at dinner. It wasn't too long before the starters arrived and Graham was satisfied when he saw that it was smoked wild salmon despite it being minute in size. The dining room was beautiful in its decoration and the people around him all wore their best and acted in a way so to compliment it.

The Major was boring him and drivelling on about anything and everything he could. The Major's wife and daughter remained silent with the exception of the occasional one word comment on the Major's conversation. The Champagne was sipped rather than slurped as it would have been at most of the parties that Graham normally attended. Speech was light and complimentary rather than contentious and aimed to gain bragging rights. The music was traditional strings and was at a pace that did nothing other than to fade into the background. Graham had already decided that he was bored.

The main course came and went as did other dishes to compliment it and that led into desert, cheese and then port and cigars. The people at the ten or so tables around the room all sat and talked on subjects that didn't really involve thought or conviction as they made new acquaintances through the smoke filled room. Catherine looked up and seeing that nobody was watching her she purposely made contact with Graham's eyes, casually winking as she did so before immediately looking down again at the empty white table cloth in front of her.

It seemed such a strange thing to have seen that Graham wasn't sure that he had actually experienced it. He looked across at her face opposite him, just to check if it had been a trick that his mind had played on him. There was no response this time and he put it down to mistake or maybe the champagne that had begun to weave its disarming effects. Graham had taken enough of the laid back sounds of strings and slow aimless chat and made his way back onto the top decks of the ship that still powerfully made its way through the sea and into the night. The sky was black above him and as it slowly reached down to the horizon it lightened slightly to a pale blue just before it dipped into the black sea beneath it.

Silver stars shone from every corner of the vast sky. The stars were tiny and slight but bright and strong in the night's sky beckoning the ship beneath them to press on to another land and to live all the dreams that could be lived, to the full. There was a breeze that blew across the decks and across Graham's face, it was a sobering one for him. Despite the new adventures that he was already a part of and the pursuit of the summer that had been eluding him for so long he felt for a moment all the things that he had run from him suddenly return.

Graham's neck was tense and his shoulders tight as he stood at the bows of the ship looking out towards the horizon with his hands on the steel railings at the edge of the vast liner. "Mr Wright?" The question came from somewhere behind him but he didn't know from whom it came. It was a woman's voice. He didn't turn around and for just a second he held out in responding to the call. The call came again it was timid and polite and Graham just knew who it was that was uttering it, he just knew it. He turned slowly to face where the sound was coming from and it was indeed who he thought it would have been. He wasn't sure why he thought it would be that particular person. It was getting darker but the bright lights above him shone down onto the decks and revealed the face of Catherine who stood five or six yards behind him waiting in silence for something. That something was clearly Graham Wright.

As he turned to her she smiled a curious small smile that began at the corners of her lips and then spread to the whole of her face. Her lips were inviting and slightly parted in anticipation of saying something perhaps but she said nothing.

She walked a pace forward and then spoke again. "Are you interested in getting to know me better then?" Graham was so surprised that he could not offer any reply other than to 'um' and 'err' before stepping a pace forward to be within arms stretch of her. It was a new situation for him, but one that he knew instinctively how to handle.

Had it been Graham Wright that was doing the chasing then that would have been something that had been done a hundred times before, but it wasn't. This time a very attractive and curious woman of fine proportions and beauty was clearly thrusting her attention towards him. It was this fact that made it all the more exciting for him. He looked into her eyes and for the first time since he had known her was able to see exactly what they were like as for the whole time previous to this they had remained focused on the food and table in front of her.

The two stepped a further foot each towards the other until they were only just parted. Graham drew his breath before replying to her, remaining fixed to her eyes in order to gain the maximum response from his reply. "Well that depends exactly on how you wanted me to get to know you," he answered with a glint in his eye and a wry smile to match. She looked to the side as if a little coy about the response but Graham was sure that it was only a cover for a deep set desire to make the most of what remained of the evening. The image that had been portrayed of her throughout the whole evening was clearly just as cover to mask a bubbling cauldron of desire. Within the heart of the oppressed major's daughter lived a fire of naughtiness and wild emotion that only now she let out to view.

Catherine now smiled and again coolly looked into Graham's eyes as she reached forward with her neck an extra inch before closing her eyes. Graham reached forward in response and their lips touched for a moment or so before reaching lusting arms were brought around each other's waists as the two embraced passionately. The skies were virtually all black now except for the bright starlight above them as the iron ship pushed on through the night. The decks were empty of people as many were resting in the lounge or remained chatting in the smoke filled air of the restaurant.

The crisp air would have been a little bracing perhaps as the breeze blew around the decks and across their faces but the warmth that they shared during their embrace meant that it wasn't even noticed. In fact, at that moment, nothing mattered at all except for what they were doing. They didn't really know why perhaps that the situation had come about at all but whilst it had they were going to make the most of it. It was a good while before their lips and arms unlocked from each other and the two people parted again. They looked at each other, up and down each part of the other's face and then settled again in soft stare towards each other's eyes.

Graham's hand was taken and he was led away towards the stairs that went down three flights and back to the wood panelled corridor where the first class accommodation was situated. Catherine pushed against one of the gloss painted doors and it sprang open to reveal a room that again was panelled in wood and that had several other rooms coming off it. "This way," Catherine forcefully announced as she pulled him towards one of the doors that led from the main room. The two entered the room that was in complete darkness with the exception of a small porthole that let in enough light to make out that the room was a bedroom. The door slammed shut as Graham was thrust violently against it with his back against the gloss painted wood. Catherine quickly kissed his cheek, his neck and then again his lips. His jacket was removed in a wild, flurry of motion. Shirt buttons fell to the ground as his shirt was physically ripped from his body and flung to the floor.

Graham was far more delicate than his female companion as he slipped the slender straps that held Catherine's loose fitting dress off her shoulders. Young women of the time were keen to show that they were free and ready to take control at every occasion. It was not unusual that a girl of the time would be far more provocative than a woman a few years before her. Graham watched as the dress fell to the ground around her feet as he felt his expensive and slight leather belt being tugged off his waist. The fact that the dress slipping to the floor revealed that Catherine had chosen not to wear undergarments was not a surprise. The couple continued to kiss as they pushed each other onto the bed and began what had been started with the first kiss on deck just before.

Only a few words were spoken, however Graham was clearly getting to know Catherine in much more detail and vice versa, she to him. The couple completed what they needed to and the relief that they both felt was immense. For a full hour later the two sat on the edge of the bed smoking and drinking and taking cocaine before parting with little interaction above that in any way. There was no parting kiss or long goodbye as it was clear that what needed to take place had taken place in a way that meant both parties were satisfied enough. Graham returned to his room where within the hour he had removed his sexually ravaged clothes and got into bed to sleep for the night. The night was peaceful and with it satisfaction that came from the evening's excitement with Catherine. The release had been one that he had waited for and needed and he was sure that he wanted that feeling again.

He awoke the next morning feeling fantastic with himself and glad that he had a fulfilling sleep. He could see that the sun was bright in the sky through the small round porthole just above his bed as it floated above the horizon of dark blue foreign sea. Graham opened the small window with a push and immediately he could feel the fresh air against his face as the slight breeze blew in through the open space in the ships bows.

After dressing, Graham made his way back into the main dining room where he was greeted by a waiting line of finely dressed liner crew that opened the grandly exuberant varnished wooden doors for him so that a gentleman could walk through without exerting effort. He didn't look up or utter any reply to their good morning greetings other than to casually raise an eyebrow and instead went inside to take a seat at the same table he had sat at the night before. A pristine, new, white tablecloth had been laid and the silver and gold cutlery sparked perhaps with even more lustre than it had the day before. The uninvited morning sunlight came across the fine cutlery that sparkled across the beautiful virgin white cotton of the table cloth laid so precisely and exact that every table were precisely the same.

In the corner of the room the officious looking khaki covered Major was again very evidently vocal whilst he continually droned on to yet another victim about whatever was on his mind. Graham sat facing the window whilst plates of eggs cooked in many various ways to satisfy even the most discerning of first class customers were brought in to be placed in front of him and other passengers. Eggs were followed by cold meats and pastries, each carefully prepared and dutifully delivered to each table by well disciplined and pristinely presented staff. The seat opposite became occupied whilst Graham was looking down at his plate. As he looked up he was quietly excited yet slightly nervous by the fact that it was Catherine that had taken the place at the table, accompanied by her mother who delicately sat at the place to her left as it was pushed inwards to meet her as she descended.

Graham looked up in order that he may catch her eye to determine the mood that she was in at that time. Graham could not tell how she was feeling just then as her eyes never rose from the place setting that was below her. Occasionally she confirmed or denied a question that was proposed by her mother or a statement made regarding a topical event, but with the exception of this it was as if Catherine and Graham had never met other than at the table. There was certainly no possibility that the two of them had shared a rampantly intimate night together just a few hours before. There was no verbal or physical communication between the two, once again, Graham was not surprised that words were not spoken but the way that Catherine had been the night before previous to their encounter had been no different to the way that she now presented herself at breakfast.

He was unsure if they would meet again in the same way that they had done the night before and even if they were to meet again, he was unsure whether it would be for the right reasons. Graham was sure however that he wanted more of what he had experienced so breathless relentlessness and would press its provider to supply more of the elixir that he craved and presumed he needed. Graham was a complex man at heart and someone that could think a situation out clearly and in every detail before coming to a solution or explication if he wanted to of course. At the end of the day however he was just a man and a man that required the things that men needed to live and feel satisfied and this occasion was no different. It was just physical satisfaction it wasn't emotional or sustainable but it was what he needed.

After the consumption of a beautiful and hearty breakfast, Graham walked out of the dining room, along the corridor and up two flights of stairs onto the deck where he immediately experienced the light breeze and the slight sea spray that was thrown up across his face. Finally he could see land for the first time in two days of looking for it and it was a most welcome of sights. The coast line was green and soft with the top of the land being only a small way above the sea. His education told him that is was the west coast of France near the area of La Rochelle. The sandy beaches, that were clearly visible from the liner that cruised effortlessly past them, were full of children and families at play enjoying a summer's morning. It was thrilling to see them and to finally see the coast and to know that the ship was only two days from the coast of Spain and the end of the first stage of the sea journey. Already the temperature and humidity of the day was so much more than it would have been if Graham had still been in England. It was a comfort to him that at every stage he was getting to a place that was further away from his troubles and closer to a chance to live a little more of his dream.

He wasn't exactly sure just what the dream actually was but he knew that it involved a woman nestled within the high life that he already such a part of. He had seen so many characters within his short life and seen so many women with so much of what he didn't need. There had been, however, some that held all the thrill and excitement that he desired but were real and honest with it; he had just not met them yet.

White gulls called high above the boat calling out to others that there may be fish or some other thing to eat around the boat or at least around the crowded beaches. Happy people on board the white liner came to the railings to look and wave at the smiling people on the shore line who eagerly waved back to them. Graham didn't wave but was happy enough to feel the breeze on his face and to have a hot sun above him, forcing him to remove his jacket and drape it over his arm. He loosened his tie and instantly felt more relaxed.

Catherine stood with others at the railings looking over the side at the new sights that met them. Graham knew that she had noticed him with several slight glances that she gave towards him. Within a few moments she started a meander towards him. She looked at him over her shoulder as she walked past from several yards away to his left. She wore a black dress that started high at her neck and dropped loosely all the way to her feet where it looked as if it were pools around her ankles. She stood tall and proud as she confidently waltzed across the wooden decks as if they were her own. She smiled across to Graham as he stood watching and he was helpless but to smile back. He thought better however than to speak to her or move nearer to her. He wanted to though; he wanted to do it so much. He felt wild, felt lustfully weak and needed her right there and then. It was eleven o'clock in the morning and there was no chance of that but there was chance of furthering his cause with her and possibly allowing him to open a door to exercise more of his desire later on in the day or night. She stopped suddenly, noticing that Graham had not risen to the challenge of suggesting that he wanted her, standing with her back to him five yards away looking in the opposite direction. She had obviously presumed that he would have followed her after the smile in the game that she played.

Graham wasn't sure whether he wanted to play a game but once more he was helpless to do anything else than to follow the prize in front of him like a puppy dog with his master. Slowly he walked in her direction, like a moth to the flame, or maybe a lamb to the slaughter. He walked towards her slowly; waiting and looking around him to see that nobody were watching him but they were far too interested in the scenery around them. She waited for him to arrive at her shoulder before she started walking again towards a small room in the centre of the deck. A quick glance to her left and to her right was all it took to ensure that there was nobody watching her.

She turned the shiny brass doorknob before pushing the door open with her other hand and walking inside. She held the door open with her arm as Graham walked obligingly in behind her. The room was again blackened as there were no visible windows and she wanted it that way, and that was the way that she always liked it to be. Graham wasn't sure that he wanted the darkness to hide his insecurities but it was a comfort that it was blackened in that room.

It felt all the more intensively sexual as it were hidden in the shadows of the darkness but on the other side of that coin it felt away from reality and realism that he wanted. She stood by the wall of that small room and reached for the back of her dress slipping the tiny buttons out of the holes that held it up and letting the material drop to the floor. The extent of the readiness that the woman before him had for dropping her clothing and accepting any man that were in front of her disturbed him. He wanted her because she was in front of him, naked and wanting him.

They were the same reasons that he now didn't want her. Because she was ready to sleep with just anyone for any reason that she fancied. The thought that she wanted him for a bit of recreation and nothing more was a little difficult to accept but by accepting it he realised that this was a girl that he should not be with. He had not been that decisively brave for some time about his feelings and it was a friend that he had lost touch with for too long. He made a sudden pact with his conscience there and then and made his impression felt on the slim naked woman that now laid, legs akimbo, on a large wooden table waiting for him.

He walked towards her and bent at the waist pausing for just a moment before kissing her cheek and then with his right hand softly touched her white slender shoulder. He stood tall once again and with nothing to add verbally he turned and left the darkened room and into the bright sunlight of continental midday. Graham made his way down to the bar and ordered a brace of cocktails and immediately drank them before ordering a couple of long island iced teas with which to while away the hours of the afternoon. He stayed below decks, away from the hot midday sun that shone, hot and orange, in the clear deep set blue sky above the white ship that cut through the sea on the way to the coast of Spain.

Downstairs he was away from the high possibility of an awkward re-acquaintance with Catherine as she would no doubt be furious from the rejection. Graham sat at the bar and smoked a large cigar that was presented to him by the bar keeper from a wooden case with the word 'Cuban' branded on it, "Rolled on a virgin's thigh!" the large, black African barman added as he passed it over the counter, cut off the top and then lit it for Graham, heartily laughing as he did so. Graham saw little that was humorous but the sound of his laughter was something that infectiously made him chuckle and produce a smile. The noxious, black smoke filled the lounge area along with the output of other large, similar. virgin rolled cigars and hung in persistent clouds around the vaulted ceiling distributed from the mouths and nostrils of the various gentlemen. Graham held the cigar in his fingers and occasionally offered it to his lips whilst he thought out the situation that he found himself in following his decision not to sleep with Catherine.

Chapter 7

Catherine seemed to have been blown away by Graham's rejection as he had not seen her for a whole two weeks but he was certainly not bothered with that. He was just waiting to alight from the ship and get onto land in Spain. It wasn't for another two days that the vessel left the west coast of France and got close to the Spanish coast and slowly began to move around the high outcrop of land and into the port of Tarragona. The heat and humidity had been building since the day before as the ship approached the coastline and it was a feeling that Graham welcomed. He had never felt it before and the brightness that came with it was indeed a strange experience for him.

Graham stayed on deck coolly dressed in his cream suit and matching hat whilst resting against the railings at the side of the ship as it slowed near to the coast. Even hot and bothered Graham Wright was the epitome of style, with the clothes perfectly hanging from his large frame whilst the fringe of his hair flicked in the breeze. Before the ship had completely stopped and its mighty engines ceased turning, a pair of smoking tugboats to tow it into the port arrived and came up alongside it.

Graham didn't understand what the local men with their dark hair, bare chests and olive skins were shouting to each other but after a few cigarettes and much hearty hilarity with each other, they started throwing ropes onto the liner. The ropes once fastened to the liner began to tighten and slowly inch by inch the huge vessel that must have been a hundred times the size of the tugs that now pulled it, started to move forward again towards the dock at a controlled and constant rate. It was a good few minutes before the liner got close to docking but many locals had already assembled on the shore line ready to sell locally made lace, arts and crafts to the white faced foreigners that were disembarking from the liner. Finally the ship came to a standstill and was tied up to the dock to prevent it from moving. A bridge was set up and once various official checks and conversations had taken place with port masters and the ship's personnel, passengers began to disembark from the ship.

It struck Graham as he stood there high up on the top deck of the ship that the countryside was not a bit like England. It was dry and burnt with little other than rocks and dirt broken by the site of the occasional poorly nourished tree. He knew now that the lawns and lush greenery of the grounds that surrounded his house in London was something that he enjoyed despite not realising it before. There was no rain and there was no cold. These were replaced instead by humid air, bright skies and thorough warmth throughout; the feeling was a most welcome one.

Graham, with others, eventually made it ashore and made their way up past the locals that spoke in broken fumbled English in order to sell their products to him and the others that passed by them. Everyone seemed to be so different in Graham's eyes; indeed he had never seen someone from another country before apart from at the cinema of course. Seeing their dark eyes and vivid black hair was as stunning as their olive sun tanned skin and the clothes they wore were also a whole new experience for Graham. Whites and vibrant colours were visible everywhere, from the terracotta roof tiles on the white plastered houses to the brilliant golden sun in the fabulous blue sky above them.

There were two taxi cars waiting with their tieless, short sleeved drivers standing and chatting at the side of the road for the liner's passengers in order to whisk them to one of the few local hotels down by the sea front golden beaches. The hotel was much larger than the other buildings around it which were all single and double story buildings. It certainly wasn't as grand as the normal hotels that he was used to but it had charm. Tired after travelling he was sure that a bed was all he needed, whatever it was like and wherever it was located.

Electric fans that clung on to the white painted plastered ceiling above the reception, whirled slowly around transferring the already warm air around the high vaulted ceiling and about the room. Creaking wicker chairs haphazardly placed around the room were occupied by stern faced Englishmen that sat reading books whilst puffing pipes and cigars, just as they would have done in England. Graham felt entirely at ease with his position and was determined to enjoy his holiday and new experiences and that started with the hotel, with the local people, a new country and of course the strange but beautiful hot temperatures. For that evening, however, he decided just to pull a chair up to the wall on the balcony and rest in the early evening sun whilst he watched the sun slowly make its way down until it melted into the soft blue sea. As the sun dipped itself into the sea, it was replaced by a brilliantly silver crescent of the moon that rose majestically above the landscape accompanied by several early sparkling stars.

It was a brilliant scene to look over from the white walls of Graham's balcony and a warm and welcome break from the all the trials and traumas in his life over recent months. It hurt him that he still didn't have a woman to be with, though he wasn't thinking much about that just then. He sat in his white suit just soaking up the atmosphere. He didn't have a drink and he felt that he didn't need to either and that was a rare first for him for recent months anyway. It was clear that the holiday was a break and was just what he needed to make a new start before returning back to England to try and rebuild his life in a new way. After unfolding brand new fine shirts and clothes from his luggage that had been sent up to his room by a porter, Graham took a bath before changing in order to go out for a meal somewhere in the local area.

Graham made his way down to the hotel reception where he encountered a jovial man who made his way clumsily through several obvious English sentences explaining where Graham could eat that evening. Graham was unsure whether he knew exactly what the man was saying but his intentions seemed to be good and he seemed to indicate that around the harbour would be a good place to eat. Graham made his way down the steep steps that lead to the road running parallel to the small fishing harbour. The streets were lit only in places but it was enough for him to see the way that he needed to go. Small electric bulbs shone from inside the various tiny restaurants, taverns and houses that dotted the scene around the harbour walls. The silver moon shone its beams out across the tranquil water as it got caught in the small waves as they lapped up on the shore and against the dark rocks all around the harbour.

The light breeze softly fluttered the yellow and red Spanish flag that flew from the top of one of the white plastered buildings and ran through Graham's hair and across his face. It was still a warm night and it was pleasant to be strolling down by the front. Even though he was on his own he didn't feel like he needed anyone, it was a comfort to be a world away from London and the cold and daily grind. It was more comforting still to know that after so long he was beginning to return to being somewhat near to himself again. Even if that was a stranger to him.

The small businesses were clearly all just family run affairs and were a whole new experience for Graham and it was yet another new opportunity to learn and live this very different lifestyle to the one that he usually led. Graham wasn't dressed with his usual gusto and his expensive clothes stayed in his room, instead he wore a simple cotton shirt and beige, soft, sports jacket that he removed and draped over his arm as he selected the venue that he was to eat at. The place was not richly decorated or illuminated by huge signs and lights and there were no evidence of flappers milling around the outside looking for a date.

The lack of exuberance or lavish design continued inside but that certainly didn't mean that it suffered for charm or rustic appeal as this was clearly in abundance. There was just six or so round, cloth covered, tables across the whole of the place of which four were taken up by couples eating or in deep considered and propitious conversation. The room was mostly green in colour and each corner had a sizable terracotta pot in which grew various plants that clung to the wall and crept up, feeling into corners and across picture frames.

It was just a moment before a tightly buttoned up waiter arrived and stood to Graham's left, waiting to ask him for his drinks order. The man, complete with greased black hair and large bushy eyebrows, asked Graham in Spanish but clearly Graham had no clue as to what he was asking. Eventually, after a moment, he realised this and instead mimed a drink being poured and then consumed with exuberance. The waiter didn't know what his new English visitor was asking for either but seemed to respond to Graham trying the word 'vino' to which the man smiled and then quickly ran away. He returned promptly with a jug of red wine of which a third of a glass was poured and placed in front of Graham on his table.

The aroma of the wine immediately filled his nostrils and he was sure that he could smell plums, black summer fruit and sun ripened cherries. With the wine came a menu that was handed to him as the waiter again quickly went away. Graham understood the menu no more than he did the questions that the waiter has been asking him. It took a conversation between various people in the room and the waiter before they had practically decided for Graham what he should order to eat and the menu was taken from him.

Outside the restaurant ,there was traditional Spanish guitar music that filled the air from a tavern further down the street and the smells that came from the food that was cooking in the kitchen were once again things that he had never experienced before. There was tomato and onion and fresh fish smells and that along with the taste of the deep red wine that he gently sipped was a full-on experience for Graham. Just as he had always done, Graham Wright took on the situation head first; ready to take in as much as he could even if it made him sick along the way. It had often done in the past but now he was away from it all, half way round the world he would still do it but perhaps with a little bit more caution. Graham waited for quite a while before a strange dish of tomato, fish and yellow rice, which was still bubbling furiously in a round cast iron dish appeared and was laid down in front of him. At first the smell took him by surprise and the taste was like nothing he had ever tasted before especially as it was perfectly complimented by the strong flavoured local Rioja that he consumed in copious quantities, as the earthenware jug in front of him was seemingly bottomless.

It was typical for Graham to gulp down anything that was in front of him with little care or appreciation for what it was or how it tasted or looked. This time was different. He seemed far more relaxed and eager to think about and savour the new moments that he was suddenly surrounded by. There was so little else to think about at that time, after all the ups and downs since his father's death and alone in Spain as he was allowed time to think and find some space for himself. He had never enjoyed space and time to think before as there had always been voices that he had not want hear, that hung around him whenever he was alone but for that moment he knew it was right.

The waiter returned to his table and spoke to him in Spanish once again but with a simple raising of his thumb and a smile from Graham he could answer his enquiry as confirmation that his food was indeed very good. There were no flappers or jazz swing, no money being waged or cocktails being served and Graham Wright was all the better for that. He didn't know it yet but he was starting to return to being himself. In most social occasions he wanted to be, and usually was, the centre of attention but right now he most certainly wasn't. It wasn't a problem for him either.

It was after a smoke at the table and another few glasses of wine that Graham's thoughts again returned to that of women and more specifically Bonny, of whom he had not thought for a long time until that moment. It was obvious that she and he were long over with and he could not pretend otherwise. The time that they had been together had been full of parties, money, drink and frivolity. It had also been full of superficial sex and forced emotion. It had been mostly wrong but whilst it lasted it was the best and closest to love and a proper relationship that he had known.

He thought back to those times with affection but nothing more. He had been angry that she had rejected him and he felt sure that his gamble with the racing would be enough to pull her back. It wasn't however ever going to be a going concern and it seemed that whatever he did he was never going to be with her again. He felt that he could still taste her in his mouth and her smell, he was sure, filled his nostrils from time to time. He missed her smiling young lips and her slight frame and for the time that they were together they were considered a good match. He knew it was time to leave any thoughts he had concerning her right in the back of his mind and by moving for a holiday so far away in Spain, had let him escape both the trauma of the racing and the instability of his heart.

He completed his meal with yet another course that he had neither tasted nor even seen before. He wasn't sure even what he was ordering from the smiling, olive, tanned waiter but it was brought over to him anyway and it was surely a triumph in taste. It looked like the evening in the little restaurant would last into the early hours filled with locals that revelled in its simple charms and fayre that oozed warmth and relaxation. It had been a new and unique experience for a man that had rapidly needed a change and a break from normality, if only for a while. The little green interior of the restaurant and the food, right down to the sounds and smells that he had been surrounded by on that first day of his grand trip, he would remember forever after. The dark skies allowed the small shards of bright silver starlight to shine through above him. All he could hear was the waves that softly made their way onto the sandy beaches that were below him. For the first time in a long time in fact as long as he could remember he was relaxed and felt free, despite it being a relatively new feeling, it was definitely one he liked. He had drawn a firm line underneath the past from that point and he realised that things could only get better for him. He had money and experience and he was starting to believe in being himself once again. He felt that he needed a woman still to share his life with and this was an urgent and pressing feeling that he held dear to becoming whom he wanted to be.

He walked back slowly along the sea front in the darkness but surrounded by the warmth of a continental evening that he found most pleasing to be in. His light shirt was all he needed and with a fat stomach and a fuzzy head, he was happy and fulfilled. Those feelings had been friends that he had seldom been around for some time and now they had returned he knew that he wanted them to be his friends forever.

That night he slept better than he had done for years, in comfort for his body and total relaxation for his mind. He woke up when the intense light of the morning broke through the sky-blue curtains and across the rustic wooden room before catching his eye. Within just an hour Graham had received his breakfast and on the balcony he sat and ate it once again with an enjoyment that he had seldom enjoyed. That morning's still warm bread and orange juice freshly squeezed from fruit from the trees that were outside the windows, that he sat above, were on the table. Accompanying them on the white table clothed table were pieces of pale yellow, sliced cheese, dark coloured Serrano ham, nuts and other fruit were in bountiful supply and he indulged gratefully in them.

Graham's two week excursion to Spain was a once in a lifetime opportunity for him at a time when few travelled overseas, especially in such style as he had done. He wanted to make every day count, as time as he knew all too well, would not wait for him. The day was hot, even at breakfast time and it certainly was not something that he had experienced before. With wide brimmed hat firmly on his head and only a short sleeved white shirt open at the neck he made his way from the hotel into town that he perceived to be a few minutes' walk away. The town was a hive of activity with its residents walking around the tight streets from small shop to shop with fresh food in wicker baskets and coloured material bags ready to take home to prepare meals for the family with. The market was busier and noisier still, with offers from the local traders shouted out to tempt passersby to buy their wares.

Both the quaint little shops and the noisy market must have been the same for a hundred years at least and it was a pleasure to find the ways and customs of old times were still popular in an age where such technological and social change had already taken place. A couple of young ladies sat on a wooden bench in the market place in the morning sun, soaking up the rays of sunlight whilst maintaining their cool by lightly fanning themselves with colourful, intricately carved, traditional wooden fans. Graham was immediately taken with their beauty and in particular the thick, long, black hair that lightly flicked up with the air disturbed by the motion of the fans. Nearby the smell of fresh bread took hold of Graham's senses as he passed the shop where it was being made. There were sellers offering fish and meat cut from the fresh carcases of animals that were strung up above their stalls and shop windows. Rabbits and wild game that had been caught that morning accompanied them and each would have offered a fantastic meal for anyone that wanted to buy them.

The fish were of shapes, colours and sizes that he had never ever seen before. Some had teeth and others were slimy and wet. There were some that remained live and swimming in tanks, ready to be chosen by a hungry customer and killed to order. Further into the town historic stone buildings containing government offices, banks and professional businesses stood behind fountains and palm trees. A rectangular piece of rough compacted gravel to the side was causing much interest to a group of local men that seemed to be thoroughly engaged in activity upon it. It seemed like a similar game to crown green bowls but with the throwing of a solid bowl rather than rolling it. The winner was the one that got his bowl closest to the marker at the other end of the gravel.

Graham stood watching the game for some time amongst the locals in the shade of large palm trees that surrounded the competitive but friendly arena. The slight breeze lifted up the leaves of the palm trees and their dry and solid branches made a distinctive rustle as they settled back down again. The favourite seemed to be winning the game and Graham applauded with the other spectators whilst enjoying the increasingly hot sun from the comfort of the shade of the palm trees. Just out of the centre of the town was the harbour and the sea front. The ancient clock perched on the apex of the sandstone town hall called out that it was midday and there was clearly a change in something. The town seemed decidedly quiet with many of the shops having had boards placed on their windows and their doors locked. Stalls were beginning to be emptied by their proprietors and there was starting to be an absence of shoppers from the busy square as Graham walked towards the harbour.

The sun was above him, high in the noon sky and he could truly feel his neck and head burning as a result of its strength. It was certainly a new experience for him and he wondered how locals managed to deal with the sun in their day to day lives. He realised then why the locals had vanished and that they were probably sleeping or resting whilst the sun was at its hottest. Graham carried on regardless, down to the previously busy harbour where the painted fishing boats bobbed and swayed in the light sea water, whilst tethered to the harbour side with their hard worn ropes. Each was unique and dissimilar to the others and each one belonged to its owner that had pride and concern about it. They were working boats that had brought fresh fish and ocean creatures to the market, houses and restaurants for a generation.

Nets were left on the side of harbour to dry in the sun whilst wooden buoys were collected in a group ready to be used again the next time that the ships and boats were taken out to the deeper water of the sea. Graham sat on the wall and looked out across the scene and felt at home with himself, which for a man that had constantly craved excitement and novelty was a strange feeling to have. Graham wandered back to the hotel for lunch at about half past two in the afternoon and sat down in the window of the hotel at a table where he was presented with another exotic dish that pleased his senses and made him extremely full. He spent the afternoon talking to other guests that had arrived on the same ship as he had and reading a book that had been in the hotel reception with its tall ceiling and tired fans that whirled around, wobbling as they did so.

The creaking wicker chairs were off-putting to his relaxation and concentration of the book that has somewhat carried him away. Later in the evening he decided to venture out again to the same restaurant that he had been to the day before. The evening was again warm and pleasing to be walking in, as he walked by the side of the dimly lit washing sea that politely lapped up onto the sands. The leaves of the palm trees rustled as the light breeze blew through them. That night he had once again only spent just a few moments getting ready with a loose jacket and white cotton shirt. It took just a quick comb across his hair and a wash of his face to assure him that he was ready for the night. Graham would have normally taken an eternity to get ready and ensure that his clothes were the finest. He would have combed and styled his hair, splashed aftershave and even brushed his teeth on a normal evening out but tonight he knew that all he needed was himself. In the restaurant the same waiter, as has serviced his needs yesterday met him at the door with a genuine broad and welcoming smile. The smile was accompanied by an outstretched hand, poised and ready for a sturdy handshake. Graham reciprocated his offer of a hand with his and they both felt at ease. Graham was warmly offered the same table as he was sat at the day before and an earthenware jug brimming with the deepest red wine that was immediately poured into a glass for Graham to drink. Within a few moments this hospitable welcome was extended with the provision of another dish, this time of roasted fresh sea bass on a bed of green salad and sautéed Lyonnais potatoes.

Once again the simple cuisine, from a humble family run restaurant in a Spanish coastal town, tasted better that the highest of the high of London restaurants that he had frequented many times before. The restaurant was again packed with locals who were obviously regulars to the restaurant and all of which were curious and interested in the new visitor. They were probably as interested in their foreign guest as Graham Wright was with the locals in the new environment that he found himself in. Around the room he noticed a few people that he had seen the day before, including two young ladies sitting together on a table opposite from Graham who seemed to be talking about the new visitor all evening. Through the mains and the fresh fruit dessert, Graham ate and enjoyed his way through quantities of food that would have been enough for a king. For every moment in his journey to Spain and within it, he had enjoyed the most wonderful of experiences and relished every moment of it.

It was obvious that by the fourth night of his visits to the green painted, wooden restaurant that he was attracting a great deal of attention from his fellow diners who seemed to be the same every time he came down to sample the food. The attention came firstly from the waiter whose smile seemed to grow with every visit and secondly from the two young ladies that sat at the table opposite the window seat that had been made Graham's.

The girls seemed to look similar and could have been sisters but it was clear that one of them was enjoying Graham's presence more than the other, though both were plainly keen to repeatedly see him near to them. Few people spoke to him in the restaurant as speaking English in Spain was not of common occurrence. After over a week, Graham began attempting a few Spanish words, that he had discovered the meaning of, involving food and beverages. On his way out of the restaurant one night he felt a light hand on his shoulder and he turned right away to see who it was.

Graham had in his mind an image of one of the women who was in the restaurant that had been the person that touched him on his shoulder. To his delight it was indeed the person that he had thought it to be and, with that, his heart and stomach gave a little flutter that he enjoyed immensely. The girl was clearly quite shy in her mannerisms and as Graham turned she withered and shrank. He smiled at her and that was enough for her to rise again and look into his eyes. She smiled back as if unable to do otherwise and for a moment the couple looked into each other's eyes. The girl spoke in English the few words that she knew or had learnt over the past week or so.

In broken English she said to her foreign visitor that she liked him and that she found him 'good to be with'. Almost as sudden as it had come about, it ended with playfully touching his hand, laughing and then jogging back down the street where her friend was waiting to hear all about it. Graham enjoyed the attention as he always did, especially as it was a female. He felt glad to have been able to impress someone, especially as he was not trying. It was late and he continued on back to the hotel to sleep but he walked back with a satisfied smile on his face and a spring in his step.

He slept easier than he used to despite the humid temperature causing him to take a little longer to drift off. His thoughts were of peace and relaxation brought from days of new experience, rest, good food and a quieter and easier tempo of life. The soft white cotton sheets were freshly pressed and laid and possessed that crisp morning scent when Graham lay down upon them. The pillow enveloped his head and it wasn't long before he entered a deep sleep.

The morning was again bright and brilliantly warm as he woke up late and ate breakfast on the balcony high up looking over the sea front and harbour.

After walking down to the sea shore, Graham made his way back to the busy market where he took time looking around the stalls before investigating the centuries old church that stood humbly amongst the green of the citrus trees just up the hill from the town square. Graham had never seen orange and lemon trees before and the fruit that they bore looked plump and ripe. He reached up and pulled an orange off the tree from a low branch and walked away with it to the wall that surrounded the church wall. On the wall he sat and peeled it before tucking into its juicy and plump insides with gusto. If ever he saw an orange and happened to eat one in England it would always taste seasoned and leathery. Here the fruit tasted fresh and delicate with fragrant juice and a vibrantly, brilliant, bright orange coloured skin.

Each time he walked into the restaurant the welcome he got would be warmer and from wider and wider sources until the whole restaurant would involve themselves in his entry. Each day he would walk down to the same restaurant where he would be treated to more fine food and drink and within a few more days the girl that had approached him outside the restaurant began to sit at the table next to Graham's. For the first few days of this they didn't converse other than the occasional playful smile and slightly flirtatious eye contact. It was a practice that Graham knew well but its originator, in the form of the girl with long, black hair who couldn't even speak his language, had been something that had taken him by surprise.

After another two weeks, Graham decided to sit next to her. At every opportunity he would speak to her about anything that came into his head, despite him knowing that she probably couldn't understand a word that he said. It revolved around the food or the wine or the beautiful day but he knew that whatever it was about it meant that they were getting closer somehow. By dessert the girl began to speak back to him, in Spanish of course, and in the same way her reciprocation meant that they were sharing common ground together. Despite her topics probably being as mundane as Graham's had been, it resulted in eye contact and even a cheeky smile. It was the same over the coming week and towards the end of it Graham had even attempted a few words in Spanish, to varying degrees of success. Any attempt however good it had been was an attempt that mattered to the girl that sat at his side on a nightly basis.

The same night, after food, wine and sweet afters Graham said his farewells to the people of the restaurant and began his walk back to his hotel along the sea front in the warm but slightly breezy air. He sensed a presence a short distance behind him and he turned to face it and it was exactly the person he wanted to see at that time. In hastily learnt English she spoke his name, to which of course he replied with his customary broad and well felt smile, outstretched arm and open hand. She reached out her hand to his and the two locked fingers and moved slowly in to face each other in close proximity.

They looked into each other's eyes and she spoke to him again in lusciously smooth rolling continental tones. "My name is Aina."

In broken yet beautifully pronounced English she continued to say that she had had a lovely time with him and that she hoped that he had also enjoyed the weeks that they had shared. They had of course been at a distance but a proximity that had been rapidly reducing as the days had matured, to form the meeting that the two were now closely enjoying. There were no more words.

The words that were absent from him were replaced by Graham's broad left hand on her back. Her skin was soft and warmly brown, even in the moonshine of the June evening sky. Her words were replaced by a slender arm on his muscular back as she worked her hand up to the base of his sunburnt, red skinned neck. It was inevitable perhaps that Graham Wright would end this evening with a kiss and he fulfilled his destiny by the end of it, and that wasn't surprising. What was different from his usual flirtations with the opposite sex however, was that there was nothing more, no further touching or fondling and certainly no love making.

The kiss was warm under a temperate sky that held its moon floating in orbit high above them amongst the silver light that beamed down on them from it. There needed to be nothing further to the moment than what they had already achieved and that was indeed proof that Graham had grown from the man he was on the road to becoming the man he wanted to be. He had no Saville Row, London, suit. He had no expensive French scent. He had no patent leather Italian shoes. He had no clever lines to say or expensive Egyptian tobacco to smoke and yet he had gained more tonight than he had achieved in his life to that point. For that moment, although totally brief and entirely unnoticed by anyone, he was king and he was all that he hoped he could be. He had achieved so much just by being himself, not by being his falsely perfect self for so many faultless frivolous days over the past back in England.

They parted with a further kiss and a naughty wink that perhaps suggested more from star-dusted skies in the nearest of futures and they left on that kiss to go their separate ways, for now at least. Graham slept much better that night than he had done for a long time, free of worry and insecurity and full of optimism for a richer life. Having now spent over a month living on the sun soaked Spanish coast, Graham, although satisfied and enriched with his new life, knew of course that it was still temporary and that the ship was already on its way via various other continental coastal towns and cities to the harbour side to pick him back up and take him and others back to the grimly cold and dirty docks at Southampton, England.

Graham woke that morning to a sound that he had not heard since the morning that he had left the coast of England five weeks ago. Large and heavy rain drops had already been falling on the town for ten minutes before he heard the sound of them splashing on the earthen terracotta tiles on the roof above the bedroom that he was in. Graham walked to the window and pulled back the curtains to reveal a view from the roof top window that was a world that was sodden and wet. The sky was no longer the deep-set, cloudless blue that he had seen for so long on every morning that he had woken up since arriving in Spain. Instead it was a white washed blur of colours just like in the skies he had seen in watercolour paintings that hung in the galleries of London town.

The beaches were no longer golden but dark yellow. The white stone cobbled streets were no longer filled with busy people going from place to place and there were no women sat in the sun combing their hair or fanning themselves on wooden benches in the square. In their place, on the vacant streets, were puddles of water that appeared grey and cold, two things that he knew that he certainly didn't miss about England. He did miss however the lush green grass and the excitement of a new world that still raged in every street that he frequented back in London.

Spain was so laid back, so quiet and peaceful and indeed it was a pleasure that he could experience, a world that was so far removed from the falsity of money and fickle fashion and the desire of the powerless to become powerful. Although they were the wrong things to follow, his mind in some parts wanted to immediately return and throw themselves at them with his usual gusto.

The rain grew in intensity until it was almost ferocious in its downfall onto the already saturated earth below. After some twenty minutes the rain seemed to subside almost instantly as the sun came out high above them and set about its work of drying the puddles and returning the Spanish coastal town to its hot and dried up, almost desert-like self again. The grey clouds that caused the rapid precipitation, urgently departed to be replaced hurriedly with brighter and blue skies. When rain fell from the skies of England to the ground below it would of course set in for a day, two days or even a week. Once more a new experience for Graham and one that he wanted to immediately run to Aina and tell her all about his thoughts.

Graham now mended from within, except the absence of a partner of course, was able to see some future for him. He had money from his growing share and bond acquisition in the United States of America.

"All people with money and vision..." he often said to others "...know that America is where the money is." Graham had arranged for a predicted profit of twenty thousand pounds that his house be staked as security on new bonds in emerging American banks and financial institutions. It was a bold move for sure but in money all he had ever been was ready to go with the greatest opportunity to make profit and benefit for his bank account. Graham had managed to make money from doing little. He had trusted advisors that in time returned vast sums from investments in America to him, minus their own arrangement fees of course.

Graham did little that day other than to soak up the rays of sun that beamed down on to the beach where he fell asleep and after a midday lunch at the hotel he filled the day with precious little until eight o'clock. His mind had been wandering all day since his first thought of Aina during the rain storm and he could not wait to be with her from that moment. Time had drawn on to the point that it was the right moment for him to dress for dinner. His heart raced at every thought of his Spanish girl that he anticipated would be thinking of him in the same way.

She had of course been thinking about him all day, waiting in eager anticipation for his arrival and had spent the last hour dressing, washing, preening and making the best of herself so that he would think the most of her at their very important meeting. Her hair was straight and her eyelashes were curled. Her dress was ironed and freshly washed, her heart pounded with anticipation and an urgency to get to the point that she needed to be at. There was nothing other than time that was keeping the two people apart from one another and as that ebbed away their mouths felt dry and their hearts seemed to beat louder, right until the century old town clock struck seven times.

At that audible cue, Graham and Aina left their respective abodes and made their way to the restaurant that had instigated and fed their tentative relationship until this moment, that both parties presumed would be escalated that evening. There was no mistaking it, she had fallen for her foreign fancier and had been smitten by his sensibility and novelty. He had been feasting on her exotic and emotional heart that she had worn on her sleeve and her fascinating aura that had been such a revelation to him.

Graham made his way down the tight coastal path that led from his hotel to the little green restaurant about a third of a mile away. The sea was calm and the sky still blue in the most temperate of special Spanish evenings. Graham knew that his time there in the town was very short and that from now on every minute there counted as special, emotional and physiological. He had grown so much over his time there in a way that would allow him to become more of what he wanted to be.

Reaching the exterior of the restaurant, there was no sign of her and this fact raised his expectation level even further and his chest puffed out in exhalation, attempting to calm his nerves as he waited. It was a full fifteen minutes of pacing up and down the track outside of the restaurant before a figure appeared at the bottom end of the coastal street. The figure slowly drew closer until Graham could see that the woman had black hair and a closely tailored white dress that flowed right down to her feet. It wasn't of course panic but Graham felt unsure of himself with the urgency and reality of the situation growing in intensity as the figure approached. His pace increased right up until the point that he realised that it wasn't Aina at all, to which he suddenly stopped his walk. His embarrassment caused him to kick a stone across the floor like a child having a tantrum might have done. Just as he did so however, Aina appeared from behind him and playfully tapped him on the shoulder, to which he turned quickly to see her face. Her face was natural and bubbling with happiness at the sight of Graham stood before her, just a couple of inches apart from her. He reached his neck over to her and kissed her made-up lips that were slightly parted in anticipation perhaps that he would do just that. Her eyes closed as she melted into the kiss, reaching her hands to place one on his neck and the other tentatively on the small of his back. As their lips parted they hovered an inch away from the others before reengaging for a second time after the briefest of moments.

Graham squeezed her hand lightly as they walked into the restaurant to the usual welcoming smiles and uplifting comment from the manager and the waiter that Graham could now legitimately give some answer to in Spanish. Aina smiled as he replied to them and clearly enjoyed her English date being able to say things, however basic they were, in her native tongue. They sat opposite each other at the same table at which they had met at the start of the summer. The waiter brought over local wine as he had done in the same way each evening that they had eaten there, in a large glazed and seemingly bottomless earthenware jug. A third of a glass of the red liquid was poured and placed in front of Aina and the same was repeated for Graham who sat attentively intent. The taste was as consistent and of course as good as it had been the first time that he had been brought the wine, prepared locally from juicy ripened grapes grown under the hot Mediterranean sun.

It was just after settling on a decision and making the order for the starters, that Graham reached out his hand across the tablecloth to hers, which she gladly accepted by curling her slender fingers over his and meeting his eyes with hers. They spoke little as it really would have just been idle chatter. Instead their affection for one another spoke for itself through what they didn't say, for how they looked at each other and for the natural smiles that portrayed happiness and warmth towards each other. It was a strange but a very welcome felling that Graham Wright was starting to experience within himself and it was unlike any other that he had felt before. His stomach remained tight and his fingers were slightly cold. His heart fluttered irregularly, his breaths remained short and intense, he was only just starting to realise it but perhaps these were the feelings that he had searched the whole summer for. The meal was light as was the conversation between the couple.

Graham then sensed the revelation that he may be falling for the girl opposite him and the starkest truth was that he knew that she were feeling in a similar way towards him. It was a huge feeling for him to comprehend and despite the many emotions that he had experienced in his life to that point, this one was probably the biggest of all.

As the meal finished and they got to their feet to leave the restaurant the manager got up from his seat and walked towards Graham with an out stretched hand and firmly shook it before fully embracing him in a hug. Graham was not used to such shows of public emotion and certainly not amongst men and was quite surprised by the manager's action. He joined in with the waiter that had scuttled up behind the manager seemingly waiting for his turn.

After kissing the hand of his date the two men watched Graham and Aina say their goodbyes and walk out to the cool of the evening and away back down the beach road. It was clear that the entire occupants of the restaurant had been delighted that the couple had got together and were united as an item.

After a few minutes of leisurely walking down the coastal road, Graham, feeling that the moment was right, slowed to a stop directing Aina's face towards his before kissing her with all the swirling passion that he had pumping through his veins at that moment. Finally he realised he had to let go of all that he felt and to melt into the moment with pleasure, passion and with full emotion. Aina held him closely as he did her in an embrace that said so much about the two of them that the world had somehow become instantly a lot warmer because of that moment, because the two of them had found each other.

Graham was not the man that he had been before his arrival in Spain and it was only a new, tanned and more secure man that could have arisen from the ashes that he had found himself in. Graham knew that this would not be forever as time was inevitably slipping away from him and within the week he would be departing back to England. He knew that the relationship that he had struggled to find urgently reached its climax too and that every moment would now count.

As the couple reached the door to Aina's house, Graham had thoughts of continuing the evening, to reach a conclusion that would cement their relationship further. Had this been back in England he would have not have hesitated at all in making his move. Now he had grown, now he had finally reached something that was real he knew that to push the situation further would simply never be right.

Instead the couple kissed again on the steps to the front door and with every fleeting second expressed more than they ever could by talking. They parted without further word but instead with a warm smile that spoke satisfaction and genuine emotion. Graham continued the walk back to his hotel and made his way to his room. Tonight he felt had been as wonderful as he had always dreamt of. Tonight he was the man he had been waiting to be. Graham was woken early the next morning by a banging on his hotel room door and after a second or so coming round from his slumber he got out of bed and walked across to the door to see who was trying to get his attention, grabbing a white cotton robe as he did so. Graham was surprised to see Aina when he opened the door, she immediately walked into his room before shutting the door behind her. "Graham there is something that I wanted."

Graham was unsure what she was referring to and raised his eyebrows before she continued. "I wanted last night, I would like to..." She was clearly struggling for the words to say and looked up at Graham with her big wide eyes searching for words that she knew Graham would understand. Stepping closer she softly grabbed his face and pulled it towards her. Slowly he kissed her lips before she removed her shirt and threw it to the ground in a most unladylike manner.

Graham was surprised to say the least and the look on his face must have been that of a startled rabbit in the headlamps of his car. She reached forward and pulled his robe aside revealing his chest before loosening her dress and slipping it to the floor. Graham's heart raced inside his chest as he moved closer to her before wrapping his arms around her and once more engaging in a closely intimate kiss that ended in Graham's robe being completely removed and the rest of Aina's clothes being dropped to the floor.

The couple fell onto the bed and within moments were making love to each other. The passion from last night's kiss continued into the early morning, the first time that they had made love or even seen each other's naked bodies. Graham had never made love like this before with any woman, with such feeling and unselfish sharing of feeling. Graham had never felt able to relinquish his desire and emotion until this moment, it all felt so natural and so right to him. The release that he explosively felt from his final moment of ecstasy was like nothing he had ever felt before and from the look on Aina's face he knew that the strange, yet wonderfully welcome, feeling was everything that he ever hoped he would experience.

Some time into the morning the couple dressed again and made their way out to the blinding, hot sun filled savannah of the Spanish coastline. Graham and Aina lazed all day on the beach, playfully messing in the sea and making castles from the sand. Graham had always wanted to be somewhere or be doing something but now, with the right company at the right time he wanted to do nothing but spend the precious few hours he had left in Spain with the girl and object of his desires. Graham flashed his cash and a freshly made picnic of cold tapas and open sandwiches had been hurriedly made by the hotel and placed in a wicker hamper for the two young lovers to casually eat between themselves as they lazily sunned themselves on the sandy beach. Spanish omelette, wafer thin Serrano ham and Mancheago cheese were perfectly pitched against cold cava that the couple sipped as they watched the waves lap across the sand towards their bare feet.

For that moment, Graham had the world in his hands and he had spent none of his wealth to achieve it. He had used none of his lines to woo the girl with and he had not drunk a drop of alcohol to enjoy it. The cool of the deep set blue sea lapped up against the parched and thirsty dry rocks and washed liquid life over them whilst the mild breeze reduced the strength of the sun above to a warm and most comforting of Mediterranean afternoons.

The sun picked up the slight peaks and troughs of the sea as it washed up further out towards the horizon and cast sparkles and twinkles of light upon them. Further out, the sea the colour was of the darkest blue, closer to the shore it was as clear as the still spring waters that he had seen in the heart of the Welsh countryside. Swimming around his feet as he paddled were tiny fish that darted here and there in groups in the shallow waters near the beach that cooled his hot feet from the sand that had been heated up by the relentless late summer sun. The couple played and frolicked in the waters.

Now, at the end of October, Graham realised that the year had gone by in a flash and more specifically the summer that Graham had found eventually, had been so much like the roller-coasters at the new Blackpool attractions or those at Coney Island in America that sometimes he had wanted to scream and just get off. Now he was in love with the easy life and in amorous affection with the feeling of relaxation and relinquishment of the heavy burden of responsibility and his conscience. Now he wanted to just cling onto the ride for as long as he possibly could. That morning he had, for the only time in his life, made love with a real someone rather than to his lonely and always over inflated ego. Last night he had let his heart and his emotion out of the cage that he had kept them in and had been free to run around and to finally experience real life.

After the picnic, the couple lay side by side on the sand hand in hand, next to each other just spending what precious time they had left, together. The sun was certainly getting warmer and half way through the day, just after midday, the couple packed up what was left after their lazy picnic and made their way back away from the beach and into the ancient town. There was only one thing that prevented Graham Wright from being the man that he needed to be and the person that he was inside. He had for years denied it and spent all his efforts to avoid it and now he had no reason to run. Graham had not presented his money, worn expensive clothes or shown Aina that he had wealth in his life and that was of course a guarantee that she had not judged him in any way other than the man she saw before him.

Aina had raised an eyebrow at the costs involved in the provision of the fine foods in the hamper that had been prepared so hurriedly by the hotel at Graham's wish but other than that she had started to love him and yet all he was being was himself. The town was starting to quieten down as the locals retreated to their homes to rest or to wile away an hour or two in the shade until the temperature cooled down a little when they would return to their day to day activities. Graham and Aina walked through the market place and into the tree shade of the cobbled churchyard where the couple sat at a bench and began to talk. Graham's early grasp of the Spanish language and the ease that he had embedded his lifestyle and attitude towards it had been immense.

He had learnt so many words in such a short period of time that, although still very basic, it allowed him to converse well with his girl. Where he couldn't find the words or expression she was now able to help out in her newly learnt English, courtesy of Graham. She had never been out of Spain and certainly not to England. Just as Graham had been surprised by the environment that he found when he arrived in Spain, he was sure that Aina would find the same if she were to go to England.

Graham was enjoying telling her all about his home country, from the rain, the industrial sprawl, to the levels in society and of course the greenery of the countryside. She was enthralled at the differences between his and her life and listened intently to anything he had to say. Graham didn't mention the money that he had or the racing. He certainly didn't talk about the duel relationships with women or alcohol that had twisted and pulled his life in so many frantically difficult directions. The conversation moved on to families and Aina began to stumble through a conversation about her family who all lived with her from her grandmother and parents right through to her younger brother. It troubled Graham slightly but much less than it would have done a month or two back to talk about the passing of his father but Aina seemed interested and concerned for him. Graham was not sure whether she really understood all that he was saying about his father and his relationship with him or even the manner in which he had passed away but it felt good to talk about it for once.

The hours of heat from the high midday sun were beginning to pass as the temperature outside of the shade began to drop enough for people to begin returning to the town square. Within the hour Graham noticed horses being ridden or led into the square until there were maybe twenty or so that had been tethered to the black church railings. The congregation of horses was beginning to draw crowds from all over the town until at least a hundred people lined the sides of the square and around the area where the horses were. Men dressed in tweed jackets and country attire held pads of note paper and wallets full of crisp new bank notes and talked whilst they passed up and down amongst the horses looking at every part of them in great detail. Their conversation was intense and obviously surrounded some kind of transaction between the men. A rider rode the first horse across the cobbles at quite a speed, firstly up towards the church and then returning back the opposite way to which the crowd dutifully applauded its return to the holding area.

An auction began with the men in tweed and country wear bartering and exchanging the money from their pockets and wallets, presumably buying and selling the horses. Within a moment the next horse and rider set off up the square to yet more applause and financial bartering for the ownership of the horse. From somewhere within the crowd, plates of olives, sea food and pastries appeared and made their way around the people as light snacks whilst they watched the obviously regular horse auction. It was like nothing that Graham had ever seen before and to experience it was once more part of his redesign as a human being. Graham took Aina in his arms and kissed her. Their lips entwined and when they parted the complete look of satisfaction on her face thrilled Graham. It thrilled him to know that he was the reason that she smiled that she was happy.

Aina invited Graham to her home where he met the family, all of whom seemed delighted to see him yet obviously unable to speak to him much. It impressed all of them when Graham spoke his small sentences in Spanish and did his best to look the perfect partner to their prise possession, Aina. The meal and gathering continued into the early hours with much humour and good heart throughout. It was what he perceived a traditional Spanish family in a setting that felt homely and comforting to be within, even if it wasn't his own. The house was much smaller than his own home back in England, but that didn't bother him, in fact he even began questioning why he had such a large house with only him in it.

The thought passed and instead he relaxed a little more and folded into the evening with Aina's family. When Aina's grandmother retired to her bed and the party began disbanding, Graham said his goodbyes to the other family members and left the white painted house to the sound of clicking insects and the slight rustle of the breeze in the trees. Graham and Aina entered into a tight embrace and Graham's heart fluttered inside his gut and throughout his body at first contact. This strange feeling was getting to be something that he was thoroughly enjoying and the thought that such a small thing could thrill him was exciting in itself. The small fishing town slept now amongst the clear and starry night skies. The white painted houses cooled down after the sun had crept below the horizon and the world seemed a different place.

The wind picked up slightly but neither of the lovers were bothered as they walked hand in hand along the deserted main street to the town square and then down to the beach by the steep stone steps. Without their shoes the sand was cold and wet beneath their feet but they walked on regardless until they reached a small cave in the side of the rocks. Inside was pitch black but the light from the silver moon cast a warm illumination over the inside that allowed Graham to just see Aina's soft cheek as he ran his hand down it.

He turned towards her and kissed her pink lips that remained poised and slightly parted awaiting his to come towards her in sweet anticipation. There were only the sounds that they were making amongst the quiet of the night and the washing of the sea lapping against the rocks just outside the entrance to the cave. It was a special and impromptu moment that they shared, intimately personal and expressively warm, they deserved all the wondrous and exciting bounties they were receiving from that moment in their life time.

It was the most wonderful moment of passionate excitement that Graham had ever shared with anybody for any reason and it was the pinnacle of his time in Spain. Spain, the warmth of the summer, the company and experiences that he had been within for over two and a half months had changed him and at the same time made him. All that had gone on before had been forgotten; all that now lay ahead of him was now much less of a challenge. It remained cloudy and unsure but he was confident that the clouds would eventually lift and his path would be clear. The twenty-four hours following would be the last day and night that he would be spending in Spain and of course the final time that he would spend fleeting moments with his most precious Aina. Graham had ignored the truth that he would imminently be departing from the shores of the laid back smooth Spanish sea coast back to dark, wet, dirty and manically busy London town in England.

The evening and early morning that they had shared had been special in every way and to end it with the devastating news that he was soon to be leaving would have left the most sour of tastes in the mouth of Aina that he never wanted to do. Tomorrow was another day and he would have to tell her tomorrow after he and she had both slept and woken in amongst a new day. The couple returned to the hotel where the two took the stairs to the room that Graham had been residing in for his time in Spain and for the first time they spent the night sleeping next to each other until the morning light.

The two lovers shared a breakfast on the balcony high above the street, watching over the seascape and looking into each other's eyes. It was then that he cleared his tight throat and prepared in his mind the words that he was about to say to his girlfriend. His plans of quietly slipping into the conversation the small fact that he was leaving on the boat tomorrow morning were then instantaneously blown out of the water with what Aina tentatively had to say to him instead. It was a simple three words and yet they were three words in a combination that he had never experienced anyone saying to him before. He somehow knew that they were on their way but when it came it had still knocked him sideways. "Graham, I love you." Those were three simple words that transcended their one simple meaning into almost any language instantly and although uncomplicated in their structure when first they are spoken with the fullest of emotion and sincerity then their effects can be life altering. Graham for once was speechless for a few moments as he chewed over the implications. There weren't any of course other than that he wasn't alone in the strange feelings that he had been experiencing. It was the strangest thing to him for that moment but managed to speak his mind with confidence, sincerity and clarity. Graham's affirmation of his love for her was the culmination of all that he felt and the totality of her affection for him.

It was after the exchange of more kisses and consumption of the hearty breakfast that Graham again made an attempt to talk about his imminent departure. There was no way to make it easy on her, he knew that and so he just had to say what he needed to, there and then. There was a small pause for thought before Aina turned and looked in the opposite direction before tears welled in the corner of her eye. As Graham moved to the side of her, one tear broke free from her eye and he watched it as it slowly rolled down her soft cheek before dripping of her chin to fall solemnly to the floor. She said and acted in no further way but to fling her arms around the bulk of Graham and hold him tightly, her small frame clinging to him as if to attempt to restrain him from leaving there and then. She knew of course that he would be leaving from the second that she had made eye contact with him and witnessed the impressive smile that he could always throw into a situation at any moment. Now the moment had arrived she somehow could hardly believe it.

There were just a few hours before midday when the huge white liner would arrive fresh from England's busy shores and pick up passengers for the return trip. The liner was a spectacle in itself, even in England but in that part of Spain with its rural and quiet pace of life it must have been even more of an impressive sight. The liner, when it arrived would of course dwarf the ships and boats that flitted in and out of the port in style, mass and in financial spectacle. Made from the smoke, sweat and hard labour of the men of Newcastle upon Tyne, the liner was a filled with pride and money.

Graham and Aina made their way to a cafe in the square where they shared cool drinks in the sunshine of the day. They tenderly held each other's hands and looked into the eyes of the other. They said little but the last few hours that they spent would be based entirely on the love that they had worked towards achieving and nothing else mattered. Graham made a pledge that he would return to her. He even went as far as asking Aina if she would come with him back to his home in England. He knew that she wouldn't agree, their lives were so different but he had to try at least. At that moment Graham almost started to talk about his money, his vast house and his high society gaiety. He knew however that these were things that would only highlight the differences in their lives and could have the potential to drive a wedge between them.

By the time the liner appeared on the horizon, towed by two industriously smoking tug boats, Graham and Aina had already kissed and said their goodbyes what seemed like ten times. The journey back was going to be the longest he had ever taken, with the thought of Aina getting to be further and further in distance from him with every inch of sea travelled closer to England and away from Spain. The liner berthed at the same point that it had done when it arrived three months ago but this time, rather than boarding the vessel with optimism and high expectation, he would be boarding it in sorrow and somehow short of his dreams. The contrast with him as a person from leaving England to returning to it was also stark. He had left a broken and heartless individual and returned a fully rounded and emotionally stable man. Gone the constant thoughts of money and spectacle, absent was the man of the moment. Now a man of thought and warmth and of consideration and care, returned to where he a left ready to live again in his world, but as a different and better person.

There was just time to kiss the woman, that he had finally found he was in love with, one more time and to hold her tightly in his arms. Of course, he didn't cry, he was a man after all but for the first time in his life he felt like he wanted to and it was a feeling that he was definitely unsure of. As their tightly united hands parted from each other, Graham knew that it was the change to something. He had waited his whole life and travelled half way around the world to find love and now he was leaving it behind.

Aina shouted with tears flooding down her cheeks, "Graham! I love you."

His heart fluttered and despite being almost inside the ship he ran back down the gang plank and wrapped his arms around her whispering softly into her ear "I love you too Aina, thank you." He looked into her eyes and with the utmost feeling, promised that he would return to her as soon as he could, at that moment he let he go and returned inside the ship. Inside his cabin Graham shut the door and lay on the bed feeling thoroughly sick inside, he presumed that it were sickness from the sudden absence of love that had made him feel so bad. The feeling of longing was immediately too much for him and he hurriedly left his cabin before running upstairs to the top deck of the luxury liner and to the port side where he could see the throng of people on the dockside.

It took a moment or two scanning the assembled crowd of people from high up above them to find the girl that had seemingly changed his world. When he did locate her she wasn't smiling happily or frantically waving but instead she looked dejected and deeply into her own thoughts. Graham called to her excitedly waving as he did so. There were so many people shouting and exchanging good wishes and farewells, whilst waving hats and arms around that it was difficult to make his presence on the top deck known to her. Eventually though she saw him and moved closer to the side of the great hulk of metal to get within ear shot. "Graham!" she shouted whilst looking up at her man dressed in his dark suit and hat as he pushed up against the rails of the liner.

"I'm coming back, I promise," he sincerely replied. He felt slightly sick somehow and fought to maintain his cool amongst the high emotion and midday heat that beat down up on him from all sides. There was a mighty blast from the ships horn that surprised the majority of the people on the ship and on the dockside. A lady dropped the bag that she was carrying and a child ran away crying but the sound indicated that it was time for the liner to depart in the direction of England.

It certainly was a grand affair with a band playing on deck and refreshments of champagne being offered around the first class passengers by smartly dressed waiters. Whatever the waiters had brought around to the passengers would not be able to please Graham, as the taste of his loss was already starting to sour his appetite. Within a few moments the ropes that held the huge liner began to tighten as the two tugs started to pull their cargo away from the dockside and out to progressively deeper and deeper waters. As the liner slowly pulled away it began making more and more pace until it was moving at a speed that by the time it reached open water would be able to move at under its own steam.

The figure of Aina started to get smaller and smaller until it had disappeared into a blur that became part of a beach that then in time became a coast and then vanished into a blue sea. By the time the engines had started turning the massive propeller blades under the surface and the two hard working tugs had drifted back to the docks Graham and Aina were once again truly separated. There was nothing that Graham needed to be on deck for now and so he returned to his cabin where he lay down on the bed feeling fully miserable. She was in effect only a few miles away from him but it seemed a like he was already half way around the world away.

There were so many new emotions running through him, feelings that he had never experienced now began hitting him fully in the face. He felt sick and completely aimless, without order or sense in his mind. this was the way that it was for the next two days really, with Graham doing nothing more than moping around from deck to cabin just biding his time in the day by walking, smoking and consumption of the occasional whiskey. The alcohol just didn't seem to be doing what it should have been doing for him and the feeling of empty loneliness was surrounding all that he did, or didn't do. In the evening Graham made his way down to the ballroom where there was dancing and an eight piece jazz band that played such lively new songs that he couldn't fail to have his spirits lifted a little. There was no edge to his charismatic personality or sparkle to his charming smile that evening and he was quite content to talk with a gentleman on a banquette corner seat rather than flirt with a couple of young ladies that sat at a table a few yards closer to the sprung dance floor.

Graham was far wiser than he had been before he had left for Spain but the satisfaction in himself that he had found, he had paid for perhaps by losing the entertainingly dynamic persona that had happily paraded for all to experience and lap up greedily. He was sure that with Aina he was a better man and now she was no longer with him he wasn't sure how exactly he should behave.

Chapter 7

A man introduced himself as Richard Swift, a manager of a company that produced films. Graham had not heard of any of the films that he mentioned but he was an interesting man with many interesting tales he was sure. Graham didn't speak about himself and that was a rarity in itself when in a social environment but instead he listened to the man in front of him who revealed that he was producing a film that was set in London, about the police service catching a criminal. It was not really a subject that interested him but he continued to listen intently as the world of cinema had always been something that he enjoyed. Richard Swift was a small man, both in height and width; however he was clearly a man who had money, by being forthright and commanding in presence. His voice was booming and almost absurd for the stature of the man that it came from and it brought a smile to his lips whenever he spoke. The film industry was an area that Graham found alluring and his regular trips to the cinema he always enjoyed and it was a pleasure for Graham to listen to him.

Conversation on the cinema reminded him of the time when he was with Bonny and it used to please him that he was associated with a film star. Bonny's films were, in reality, not seen by many but the fact that she had been in the films at all was enough for her and of course Graham by association to ride on. Graham at that point thought about Bonny and his relationship with her. At the time he was of course quite troubled that the two of them had parted as a couple. Thinking back now, he finally realised that his emotion had been wasted and the way that he felt now about Aina and the way he had felt about Bonny were completely different. What he thought was love with any of the girls that he had intimately known was so far from the truth that it made him laugh even to think about it. That was except Aina that he now loved with full licence more and more as time drew on.

The band was a good one, playing some of the latest songs that had been written and it was a good accompaniment to have to keep his mind from wandering from talk of films to her. Graham paused from his conversation with the scruffily attired Richard Swift to go to the bar to purchase a long Island iced tea for himself and a black Russian for his new acquaintance. Walking back to the seats that he and Richard were using, he noticed a table with three girls to his left that were in frantic conversation with each other with much exuberant laughing and joking around. Graham sat down at the table that he vacated before but continued to watch the table of girls repeatedly glance across at him and then back guiltily if they happened to have caught his eye.

Graham was in love, that was for sure but was also still a player at essence and occasionally, for a good feeling, Graham smiled back, to which the ladies all responded with yet more childish giggles and conversation about romantic or intimate suggestion amongst the group. Graham didn't want any romantic or intimate liaisons with any of the three women sat to his left but he didn't mind a little fun, playing with them as he had so much experience of. The girls didn't look the type to be able to summon up enough courage to actually come over to converse with Graham but knowing that put more emphasis on him.

Richard was not in approval of Graham's flirtatious game with the women of the nearby table and talked with even more volume to ensure his points were made, whilst Graham played his game. After a few moments more, Graham excused himself from the conversation and his company and made his way to the lavatories. He passed by the table of girls on the way there smiling in his inimitable way towards them that further fuelled their interest in the tall dark stranger that had filled them up with lustful thought.

On his way back to his seat, he playfully passed them once again, stopping at the side of the table, speaking to them as he did so. "Hello ladies, my name is Graham, Graham Wright. It's just wonderful to see you." He paused for a second before continuing with the game that he played. "You all having a gay time now?" None of them spoke but instead looked embarrassed, looking at each other whilst they blushed. Graham knew that there would be no more from them that evening at least. The liner was due to dock for an afternoon on the coast of France and Graham was looking forward to that but he knew that he was going to have trouble filling in the time in the meantime. The music still lifted his soul and the alcoholic drinks soothed his mind he returned to his seat and continued with his conversation on the film industry with Richard Swift.

After ten o'clock, Graham returned to his cabin and after laying out his clothes on the chest, he took to his bed for sleep until the morning whilst the giant ship ploughed on through the vast vista of deep, cold water. Early in the new day about six o'clock, there was light pouring in through the red, curtained porthole into the bedroom of the cabin, that in time woken

Graham from a well needed sleep. It took him a few moments to come around from his slumber. As he did so he wiped the sleep from his blurry eyes and knocked back a tumbler of water that sat on the cabinet by the bed into his throat.

As he pulled the curtain back the brightest sunlight that concentrated itself through the tiny glass porthole flooded in almost blinding him. For a second he imagined himself back in Spain, waking up in the arms of his love, Aina. He felt sad that he was not there right now but he was glad inside that he had been there and done that. It pleased him much further to realise now that he had found love, found peace in his mind and changed his life for the better. The wooden interior of the suite that he was residing in, was of a polished mahogany brown colour that was devoid of modernity or interest. The chair, dresser and table were also absent of interesting features and instead were covered in intricate carving from the steady hands of aged gentleman with time on their hands. The bed was comfortable and the room had been warm and had all the facilities that a first class passenger could expect.

Graham decided to take a swim in the pool and so took his costume and towel with him onto the deck of the ship that was at the highest point, just underneath the tower that contained the crow's nest. Inside the little space in the crow's nest there was an eagle eyed officer with a smart hat and a pair of leather bound binoculars that he used to watch out for potential hazards and other vessels in the same waters. As Graham arrived on deck he was comforted to again know that the same hot sun that had kept him and Aina warm beat down upon him again. The highly polished and meticulously tended varnished wooden decks were flooded with bright rays of sunlight that hit every part of the ship. The pool was not in any way as large as the lido's that he knew or even the inside ones in fact it was only about thirty foot by ten. Around the pool were striped deck chairs in rows that held some of the passengers on the liner that wished to pass time during the crossing before the stop in France.

However much Graham Wright was in love with Aina Maria Esquer, he could not deny the fact that there were quite a few very beautiful women laying out on the chairs in fabulously expensive swimming costumes sunning themselves to get a natural tan to remind them of their time away. The tans, of course would also play part of the disguise that they presented themselves with at parties and other social gatherings in order to amaze, delight and capture flies with, in their webs. Graham was only a man at the end of the day and the sight of attractive women with quite revealing outfits lay all around him was a difficult thing for him to maintain his calm with. There was a sudden air of excitement and expectation when Graham appeared in the pool area. He wasn't known here as the socialite that he had been but he was a very attractive young man with a tight torso and coolly finished exterior. As he disappeared into the changing booth there was more than one female eye that turned in expectation as to what would come out in a short while.

The door to the white painted wooden changing booth opened with a slight creak and out of it appeared the trim muscular figure of Graham Wright dressed in a tight black swimming suit that revealed more than just his broad shoulders and thighs. There was a murmur amongst the frustrated ladies in appreciation of the appearance of the stranger as he entered into the water from the ladder. Keen to make the impression on his new audience Graham made the most of the moment and launched into the front crawl with some gusto. As he rose from the water on reaching the sides, he raised his head and brushed back his black hair with his fingers pushing the water off whilst styling it as he did so.

Several of the ladies decided to join him in the water splashing and making themselves the centre of everyone's attention. Graham played along with them for a while engaging in small talk and swimming the odd length or two in between for the benefit of himself and his temporary company. Graham wasn't in the pool for more than half an hour before climbing up the sides via the steep metal steps and sitting down on a vacant deck chair and lounging back in the sun to dry.

The sun shone on through to midday and the liner pushed forward, breaking the water before it on the way to France. It would reach the coast of France in a day and Graham was excited about the prospect of visiting another new country and experiencing the wealth of things that he perceived would be found there. The space of time between then and now, he knew would be hard to fill and he was sure that at least some of the moments he would be lost in thought with the continuously more distant Aina.

At lunch time, when guests began meandering into the dining room to be seated by the army of finely dressed crewmen Graham followed suit and sat down at a corner table by the windows that looked out over the ocean. The table was as it had been, in all its pristine white and silver decoration, on the voyage outwards, its cutlery and condiments sparkling in the sunlight. Graham sat down in the large room at a table that had five other seats, it had started to become occupied by other people, none of which he knew or wanted to get to know. A lady in a ridiculously large flowery hat that looked like it was growing in volume and was about to take over the whole room at any moment. To the left of her was a man who was most probably her husband who looked to Graham to be intensely boring. The couple were polite and introduced themselves but Graham politely declined to involve himself in conversation and would concentrate instead on his food when it arrived.

Once the vast majority of the people in the room had taken their seats and settled down then food started to appear from the kitchen via an army of speechless men dressed like penguins that whizzed around the seats delivering the ordered plates of food at speed. Graham had ordered duck liver pate served on French toast, something that he had eaten many times before and indeed it was one of his favourite foods. Glasses of perfectly cooled and lightly sparkling white wine appeared in front of him and the other passengers began pecking through their starters with discerning first class taste.

The fine foods that Graham had eaten in Spain and been a revelation to him and now the starter that he was eating on board the luxury ocean liner was also full of wondrous taste and exquisite presentation. By the time the mains had been served Graham had been brought into a conversation, whether he wanted to be in one or not by the married couple opposite him. "Well Graham...no lady friend hey? She somewhere else on the ship maybe? The husband inquired.

Graham didn't know in what way to respond but decided to give him the truth anyway. "She's not on the ship I'm afraid, in fact she is in an entirely different country right now."

He sighed as he did so, looking to his plate for a warm and sympathetic response. Instead it was the man opposite him that spoke again. "It's a shame Graham, it would have been exquisite to see your wife, yes, pity." Graham evidently had no wife but didn't want to suggest that to the person in front of him. His wife then interjected into the conversation authoritatively. "Fergus, don't presume things...Graham, show me your hand." Graham felt obliged that he had to do just that and showed both his hands above his plate before the woman continued again. "You see Fergus? He's a single man. Courting though hey? Who is the fortunate lady then?"

Graham didn't feel like divulging much more but he was suddenly stricken with pride and satisfaction and he wanted to talk about his girl now that he was asked. Graham talked for sometime about his girlfriend and the fact that they were now increasingly far apart whilst eating his main course of plaice in parsley sauce with sautéed potatoes. It was unusual for him to talk about private things with anyone but there he was opening up to the world on his private relationship with the first woman that he had ever really loved. He felt it, he meant it and he loved doing it. The plaice that was served to him was of course magnificently presented and was so fresh that it must have been caught less than an hour ago. It was however a fish that he had never tasted before and he was keen to eat it unhurriedly and appreciate the flavour with every bite.

At the end of lunch the passengers made their way to destinations all over the vessel to rest or redress in their cabins, to stroll around the decks, rest and recuperate in the bars or to recline in the sunshine on the various deck chairs and iron benches that dotted the liner. Graham took a walk onto the decks and strolled around in perfect comfort with himself. Graham had enjoyed the meal and had relished the opportunity to open up his heart on the subject of Aina, albeit with complete strangers but he felt at ease to talk about her.

It was a further two days before the liner came within sight of the French coastline and it was a very welcome thing for

Graham to see as he was beginning to get bored of the cruise however much luxury or entertainment that was provided for the liner's affluent passengers. Within the hour the ship slowed to a dead stop and was moored to the docks so that its passengers could disembark from the vessel to French territory. Around him were more sights and sounds that fascinated him and for a moment he just stood there watching the scene in front of him. At the side of the square was a cafe that had multi-coloured parasols on pretty square tables. Ten or so people sat chatting and drinking coffee or tucking into pretty iced cakes that sat on china plates. Graham decided to join them and made his way across the square and sat down at a table, before he had even made himself comfortable a waiter had whisked his way over to him and stood looking down his nose and through his round spectacles.

"Oui Monsieur?" he asked.

"Un café," Graham replied.

The waiter audibly confirmed the order to himself before scuttling off into the back of the cafe and started to make the drink.

It was a couple of minutes before the drink arrived and was placed on the table in front of him. Graham was taken aback with just what had been presented to him. The white china cup was tiny whilst the saucer was large and the smell from the freshly brewed drink was immense. The taste was so strong that Graham nearly choked on the liquid that was almost completely black in colour. Graham struggled to enjoy the taste as it was far too strong for his liking but slowly sipped at it over the course of half an hour whilst he casually watched the world go by in front of him in the square.

People were busy shopping for goods and food that they needed for their families in the market place, pretty similarly to the scenes that he had witnessed in Spain and there was an exciting buzz about the place that he enjoyed just watching. The sound of the accordion he could still hear from the other side of the market square and it was indeed very atmospheric. Graham could not understand a word that anyone was saying and, although this was unusual, he found the fact quite charming and different. Graham left money on the small round table after finishing his drink and then left his chair to walk into the market and a have a closer look at what was on sale.

Although he was now alone of course and separate from Aina, he still felt much better equipped to handle life and all that it threw up for him to deal with. He knew that the next day when he re-boarded the Empress liner and began the final journey from France back to England that his world would be entering into yet another phase of his life. There would be many ghosts to deal with that he, for the summer, had entirely forgotten about. The racing incident he knew would be of issue as soon as a member of the press saw him or even if he went near the Bentley garages. If he happened to pass his previous employers then he was sure that he would be wanting to avoid them should he see his previous partners in the solicitors practice. More difficult than all of those things to deal with would be meeting and talking to all the faces that had been so much of his life prior to his trip to Spain. The women that had surrounded him he would find doing the same things that they always had done and he was not sure that they would want to even entertain him in their presence.

There would be Ottoline and Florence with their smug faces hiding round every corner waiting to trap him or at least cause trouble with him. Sally would be, he was sure entirely busy with her relationship with William whilst he practically knew that Bonny would be ensuring that the world knew that he was a bad man and not to be trusted.

Thoughts of his father would also, he was sure, be clouding his mind when he returned home to the house that still held so many feelings both welcome and not so. On the brighter side has couldn't wait to see Jack Lorrenzo, his friend and Elizabeth that he just wanted to hold tightly and tell her all about Aina. Before that however, Graham would be staying the day in France before re-boarding the liner. Even then the best part of three days would be taken in sailing to the docks at Southampton and then a train ride to London.

The wind that Graham and the other passengers had really noticed when they had disembarked from the ship had really started to increase in force until it blew a man's hat clean off his head and the French tricolour flag that clung to a pole in the square. Graham wore a hat that covered his head from the sun and with it the light coloured suit that he had worn when he took the ship from Southampton nearly four months ago. That was before his adventure had even really got underway, before he had found love and before he had left it at the port in Spain.

There was a wind that had risen up by the time the liner had stopped and the passengers had begun to leave it to reach the French coast. It wasn't cold or discomforting at all but it was certainly not as hot at it had been on the ship but Graham was prepared to lap up with interest and enthusiasm all the new sights, smells and experiences that a new country could bring him.

The town looked a little battered and worn after centuries of looking exactly the same but it had winding, meandering cobbled streets that all looked quaintly intriguing and clearly charm in abundance. Immediately ahead of him was the town market with all its fascinating stalls attended by the characters both serving from one side and buying on the other. In the corner of the market square was parked an MG open tourer in brilliant vibrant red, that gleamed at him, its chrome grill sparkling in the sunlight. The sight of the gorgeously sleek and exuberantly styled car took him back for a second to his racing days in the not too distant past as one of the famous Bentley boys and of his giant green vehicle. He loved the feeling that it gave him and he could almost feel the adrenalin pump urgently into his veins and the hairs on the back of his neck systematically jump to attention. He didn't recall however the tragedy on the race track that he had been part of at that time, perhaps it was physiologically blocked by his mind.

The sound of the busy market and the French voices that were part of it were accompanied by an old man in a black flat hat that played an accordion in the corner of the square. He played vigorously to a tune that he had probably played every day for years as he stood there with his eyes closed in concentration, wholly ensuring the music he played was just perfect. Graham held his own hat tightly to his head as he feared that too would soon be blown across the square and under a market stall.

Quite involved in keeping his face out of the wind and his hat on his head, Graham mistakenly walked square into an old woman carrying copious amounts of shopping in hessian bags, knocking her to the side and one of her bags onto the pavement. The bag opened and much of the contents fell out and onto the floor. Oranges rolled along the floor and bunches of carrots lay strewn by their feet. Graham got to the floor in a hurried attempt to pick up the fruit and vegetables that remained on the ground. Graham received a torrent of abuse from the old lady who screamed at him with harsh words that with her French tones was really quite vociferous. Most of the produce was now back in the bag before Graham was hit with a stick of hard French bread around his head. What the wind had failed to do, the old French lady's bread stick completed, knocking his hat onto the floor. With that the lady offered more words of anger, picked up the bag and then walked in the direction of houses that were half way up the hill to his right.

Half way through the day as the hands of the church clock reached nearly midday Graham decided to eat in another cafe that bordered the square and after a small wait was delivered a menu. Having studied French at school he was sure that he could communicate enough not to be troubled. Graham ordered and placed a finger on his desired choice of food and the waiter sidled away. Within ten minutes, some plates of cut spiced meat, olives and slices of bread were brought to him. The meats took his breath away as they seemed far too spicy a food for his mild tastes but the black and green olives he did enjoy. The bread although no longer in stick form having been cut up, he placed pate onto with a small flat knife and whilst he enjoyed the taste, he decided that he had seen quite enough French sticks for one day at least!

After the food had been eaten Graham ordered a large glass of local wine that was extremely strong in taste and with it he ordered a glass of aniseed aperitif. Again he was just happy to watch and observe the goings on in the square rather than urgently wanting to go somewhere and involve himself in something as he used to. These days he was happy to just watch the world pass him by as he found satisfaction in so many of the things that he had never noticed or cared about before Spain.

He could find enjoyment from food and company and satisfaction from a couple of alcoholic drinks rather than a barrel of beer or case of champagne. Graham Wright was a changed man and although he knew that something had changed within him, he would not realise for some time just how much of a change there had been within such a short period of time. As he sipped the French alcohol he began once again to return to thoughts of home and his imminent return there. He imagined how many of the people that he knew from home maybe would have forgotten him or assumed that he would never be returning to England. Some presumed maybe that he would return to the social scene with even more gusto than he had left with, another pretty, young flapper perfectly placed on his arm. He was quite sure also that there would be those who would not want him to return at all, he hoped that some of them at least would want to see him back home.

Graham smoked and drank the day away sitting at the little table on the main street whilst chatting to two people that he had disembarked the liner with before and really enjoyed the conversation. Graham bought the couple drinks and they reciprocated later on in the exchange. Bryan Sharpe and his wife, Freda, were from Cornwall and both were first timers on a cruise and, as Graham had been, in a state of culture shock having spent time in Spain and in France. Graham was pleased to discuss his experiences and it took him immediately to relive the happiest times of his life back in Spain with Aina.

The conversation ebbed away and Graham decided to take a stroll as the frustrations of the wind had passed on to somewhere else. Further away from the town centre and its busy square were elements that he had never seen before. Not far from the buildings that made up the houses and pavement cafes, were fields of green and brown that were far more rural and agricultural than he had expected so near to the town. There was a chateau that must have stood there for a hundred or more years, that had wooden barrels stored in pyramid formations all over the courtyard and small wagons full of grapes that had recently been harvested from the miles of vineyards that went practically from the rear of the chateau to high up on the hill as far as the horizon could be seen. The chateau was surrounded by a stone wall whilst its impressive staircase led up to doors on the second floor.

The whole place was full of money and tradition and was for Graham something that he had not expected to find when he had got off the liner. He was never someone who relished tradition and the age and tradition of the place was not as important as the location and the rolling countryside. There was at least ten Frenchmen sat around and standing supported by the grey stone walls around the premises, smoking cigarettes, reading newspapers and chatting to one another. There seemed to be precious little work going on but Graham forgave them for that and continued walking on down the hillside away from the vineyard.

Twisted, old vines clung to the supporting fences as the green leaves faced the sun soaking up all the precious rays that they lusciously took in to invest in the grapes that hung just above the ground. Graham had expected that the ground that they grew from would be green and abundant in wet fine soil. Instead small stones and rough gravel sat in heaps at the roots of each plant the complete opposite to the fresh green shoots of leaves at the top of each plant. Each plant sat in regimented military-like rows doing their duty in producing tiny green grapes that would be picked and fermented to produce wine sold all over the area and across the continent.

Graham continued down the hill for some time, until he could hear sounds that seemed like they were being made by people talking and clapping. After walking past the poplar trees that indicated the edge of the vineyard, he could see people playing lawn tennis, in doubles, on a well tended rectangle of green grass. Making his way closer, Graham sat on the grass at the side of the court and watched the goings on for a while in the afternoon light sunshine and slight breeze that blew across his face. After watching the game it seemed that he was being talked about although he obviously didn't know in what context.

Graham smiled in his inimitable wide, white smile, casually waving at the players and they returned the pleasant gesture to him. A tall lady of about thirty years of age walked over to him during the break in play and spoke to him in French whilst showing him with her left arm to the court. Graham instantly thought her to be polite and extremely stylish in her appearance. Her whole outfit was white with soft linen trousers that rose high up her body to her slim waist, tied with a white belt. The blouse that she wore was almost translucent and Graham was a little excited at the sight of her braless torso beneath its silk like material. Her black bobbed hair was topped off by a white, woven skull cap that clung tightly to her head and finished off a well turned out figure of a woman, fashionable and yet practical all the same. Graham replied to the woman in the best way he could.

The woman surprised him by then asking him to play tennis with her and the others in a mixed sentence of English and

French, which he found quite charming especially in the accent that she spoke with. The woman introduced herself as Michelle.

Graham had played tennis for years at an exclusive club and in a family tradition and had been considered, at one point, one of the best players at university with the majority of the games he played ending with him as the victor. As with any competition or challenge that Graham entered, he intended to win whoever he was playing and at whatever the cost. Graham agreed to the game as one of the two gentlemen opted to sit the game out in favour of their guest. Graham was delighted in the fact that he had been generously asked to take part in the game with three complete strangers in the grounds of such a grand and exclusive vineyard.

The sun was high in the sky and the breeze enough to blow the hair across the faces of the players but not too much to effect the game or annoy them. Graham got to his feet and walked to the tables by the side of the slightly yellowed grass court and placed his jacket over the back of a chair untying his tie and opening the collar of his white shirt which he unbuttoned by two holes. With that he was ready to play tennis in France and hopefully impress with his skills and of course the finesse and swagger that separated him from his compatriots.

Graham had been paired with the woman who had asked him to play in the game and he was glad at that for two reasons. Firstly, he thought that she looked like an accomplished player and secondly, he was looking forward to seeing her run and bend whilst chasing the ball in the revealing outfit that she wore. At the end of the day he was always a man and of course had his little feelings and desires that all men had inside them somewhere.

His service started the game as he energetically tossed the ball into the air and with full force launched it a few inches over the net with a hard swing of the catgut strung racket. The ball was immediately returned with attitude by the man that was opposite him and Graham struggled to run right into the corner of the court before flicking the ball back into the air and over the net. The small woman opposite Graham, with her black hair that was tied back behind her, was the exact physical reverse of Michelle and she certainly gave her all in returning the ball into the tall striding figure in front of her.

Michelle won the point after she placed the ball into the ground right onto the chalk of the base line. From then on whilst Graham made so many crucial points his own and clearly showed his experience, training and class. He was flustered and with each return of the ball had to work to achieve what he did. All three of his French counterparts in contrast were cool and reserved and seemingly made every point won or lost in total calmness and with such refinement.

The poplar trees that surrounded the private grass court rustled in the breeze and the coolness of the wind combined with the heat of the rural and coastal landscape, as birds sang and insects clicked in the distance. It was a perfect setting for tennis Graham thought to himself, and its impromptu nature made the occasion all the more special to him. The people he played with, he really enjoyed the company of, especially as they all courteously spoke in English in their conversations and Graham was able to comment as much as he could in French and feel part of the whole situation. Graham was happy to comment on Aina and his time spent in Spain, something that the two girls clearly felt was sentiment of the sweetest kind. The two gentlemen were very impressed clearly that he was a traveller and that he was unmistakably a man of money, taste and sophistication.

The game concluded with a blinding cross court return from Graham that won the match to which his new acquaintances applauded and congratulated him on a fine performance. Michelle ran across to Graham and threw her arms around him whilst quickly kissing both his cheeks in celebration. The five people sat at the table in the lush greenery of the French vineyard and drank wine that had been sown, grown, fermented and then bottled on that site. After fine food of several courses and more wine Graham chatted and talked over life in the little French town whilst Graham contrasted it with his much busier experiences of living in one of the most important and largest capital cities in the world, London.

He had been in France now since the morning and at four o'clock he left his French friends and made his way back into town to head for the Empress liner that sat in wait, now topped up with food and provisions for the remainder of the cruise. Graham knew that it was the final leg of the sea element to his little adventure and it was the penultimate one before he would re-enter London town via the train from Southampton.

The months that he had spent away had changed his life in so many ways and it was indeed the greatest thing that he had ever voluntarily decided to do. The biggest thing of course that he had found on his voyage of discovery had been the introduction of love and that had come in the form of Aina. The closer to home he was the further apart from her he became and it would sadden him consistently to think of that prospect.

An hour or so later, Graham and all the passengers scheduled on the liner were back aboard the white steel marvel of modern engineering and money, waiting to depart for

England. Just as it had done on the initial phase of the journey the sound of the ships horn sounded out across the French town as the flags flew high above the people waiting expectantly on the decks below. Graham wasn't one of those who stood on the wooden decking waiting for the giant liner to be pulled away into deeper water by the two little tug boats. Instead he waited below deck in a bar topping up his alcohol levels on top of the two fine bottles of wine and two glasses of aniseed liquor previously in the day.

Once the tugs had hauled the massive ropes connected to the liner until they were taut, the vessel started under its own steam and the chimneys began belching out smoke and the final leg of the trip was underway. Whilst headway was made in the ocean Graham Wright languished in the bar sitting at a table on his own in the corner of the room smoking a cigarette and knocking a large glass of whiskey and soda back. The ice cubes clinked as he replaced the glass onto the black wooden table in the dimly lit room, from drinking so little on his time away Graham concluded that he was going to stay in the bar for the rest of the day.

He knew that he didn't need to drink anymore to be satisfied with his life but the thoughts and tension of his arrival in England were clearly worrying him a little more than he thought it would do. The silent barman casually dried and polished a series of glasses behind the bar in between serving Graham with wine and spirits, something that was occurring with more and more frequency. Nobody had come into the bar for sometime but Graham was enjoying the silence that his hibernation from the rest of the ship was bringing him. In the corner of the dark room he sat alone with his thoughts and his memories and there was no mistaking it, he was missing his girl and the clouds that surrounded the ship seemed to be following him in particularly.

When Graham Wright surfaced from the depths of the bar where he had spent the last four hours, he was decidedly drunk. Making his way up the solid iron steps, his loose and stumbling person clung on tight to the rail, guiding him up to the now deserted decks. The liner continued onwards boldly in its path to England under brilliantly bright silver stars set amongst the black sky. Holding onto to the rails, Graham stood looking upwards just taking in the enormity and vastness of the sky above and the outstretching ocean before him. He knew that despite the pressures that he had felt, lived with and overcome over the last few years they were just tiny particles of a gigantic universe that he was now very much aware of.

It was then a matter of three more days at sea on the luxurious liner with all of its facilities and things to do but Graham wouldn't feel like doing any of them, he certainly didn't feel like flirting with girls at the pool or dancing at the club to the jazz band, he now just wanted the trip to be over, so he could return to normality; whatever that was. Graham instead decided to go the bed in his room and sleep for as long as he could manage. In his room Graham removed his clothes and got into the crisp fresh new sheets that had been laid by a maid that morning and melted into the comfort of the cotton like a letter in a giant envelope. Within a few moments his day time thoughts had been replaced by dreams as he entered a deep sleep. For a time he dreamt of Spain and in particular of Aina. He thought about her all night until the morning light woke him up in time for breakfast. As he arose from his sleep he yawned and wiped the sleep from his eyes but he had loved the fact that he woken up with the thought of Aina on his mind. He had been transported for what seemed like the whole night back to the time that he was at his happiest.

Graham made his way to breakfast after dressing and washing and sat down at a table on his own and ate copiously the sliced continental meats and cold cheeses that were served to him. With them were various pastries and fruits that followed onto his plate and without a thought Graham gulped and gobbled them up until he was ready to burst. He didn't feel like chatting and making small talk and so as soon as he was finished greedily eating he went back to his room. Apart from meal times Graham spent the remainder of that day and the first half of the next in his suite, in the library the bars or walking around the decks looking out across the sea as the English coast became closer. When it finally did appear faintly into view on the horizon Graham struggled to maintain his composure as he realised that all the demons that he had to face he would soon be meeting head on.

The famous sight of the hard and rugged cliffs of England, jutting up aggressively from the cold dark sea beneath it, was a vision of mixed emotion for Graham. He was pleased of course to be back at home in England but with the faces that he would have to reacquaint himself with he wasn't entirely sure if he wanted to be back at all. Birds swooped and glided above the land and down the cliff slides into and out of the water beneath it, whilst flocks of sheep wandered and meandered around on the grass that topped the sheer face of the rocks into the distance.

Out on deck, the mid November skies were grey and heavily waterlogged, surrounding the whole of England it seemed. The hot and sultry skies and light cooling breeze were left far away back on the continent, where summer seemed to last for much longer. There was, on his reflection, nothing that he wanted to see of England apart from maybe the lush countryside and immediately he realised that, now that he was on home soil almost. Hurriedly the tug boats were attached to the liner and it started to be dragged into the port at Southampton, where the industrious crew tied it to the steel capstans on the harbour side.

Chapter 9

The rushed pace of work now back in England was entirely different to that in Europe, where they seemed to work at an entirely different and much more lethargic rate. The boat was moored and the copious amounts of luggage started to be removed from the liner almost as it stopped. The speedy crew had a taxi loaded with Graham's luggage within half an hour and after exchanging the odd pleasantries with the driver they were on their way to the station.

The taxi cab arrived in the rain amongst a procession of cold, wet, black cars with passengers and luggage bound for various platforms on their way to home towns all over the country. Graham Wright had, of course, London waiting for him at the end of his train ride and after so long away he was unsure exactly how he would feel at the end of it. However he did feel that when he would eventually alight at the door of his massive estate on the green side of the city of London and know that money and security would protect him whatever the weather. His American loans, bonds and investments had amassed a small fortune for him and he lived in complete comfort and luxury from that.

At the station, the scene was as it had been at the port with a manic struggle from the perfectly pristine porters to get luggage onto trains in time for them to leave at the instant that they were timetabled for. When the train arrived, it was glistening with small beads of water from the rain outside that collected and ran down the shiny sides of the painted steel train dripping onto the rails beneath it. The platform was crowded with people all wanting to get to somewhere for some reason as fast as they could. With several trains in the station at the time, the smoke and steam surrounded the whole station roof whilst oil and coal dust collected on the tracks and on various points on the platforms.

Slowly and most grandly, the metal beast of a machine entered under dramatic glass folds of Southampton station roof and as the brakes brought the train to a stop, it let off a triumphant rush of steam that gushed across the platform. When the passengers that had been on the train had all alighted, Graham and the other passengers that had been waiting on the platform got onto the train and found their still warm seats or compartments along the train. Graham of course was in first class and located a compartment all to himself sitting down on the comfortable well sprung seats and relaxing before the train started off. All the optimism that had surrounded him on his outward journey had been replaced on the return trip with pessimism and concern for just what the future would hold for him. It was over an hour before the train drew up at Waterloo station, after stopping at seemingly no end of small stations along the way, and Graham was getting bored. As he alighted and was reunited with his luggage before it was transferred to a waiting taxi he briefly stepped outside into the cold mid November weather over London's old streets. All he had known for months weather-wise had been warm and comfortable if not predictable but now he was back to the colder, wetter but far more interesting weather of London.

The taxi moved off and after some half an hour's travel it made its way down Graham's street, across the light stone gravel drive and to his door. The driver got out of the taxi and opened

Graham's door allowing the quite reluctant figure of the owner of the great house to get out and walk slowly to the door. Once Graham was inside the giant and cold house, the bags were courteously brought in by the driver and when he had been paid and had walked out the door to his cab Graham Wright was alone with his thoughts and emptiness.

The darkness of his thoughts in returning to the house after almost a whole season away was impressively counteracted by the brilliance of the late evening light that streamed through the upstairs windows and flooded into the hall, that now filled with orange sunlight right up the wall and above his head. If he could have drowned in the late year's end sunlight at that moment then he probably would have, having stood around almost waiting for it to creep up upon him around him and above his head. The sunlight reminded him of each morning that he had lazily woken up in the hotel room in Spain and watched as the early day sun rose and politely lit the room inviting him to get to his feet and look out over the town. Each time he would push the curtains back and reveal a world that was bright and energising, warm and exciting.

Graham Wright had no ties, job, partner or siblings to concern himself over and the living in Spain had been easy. It wasn't an option for most people to just up sticks and get out of town to a place that so many had only even heard of but he had money, opportunity and inclination, so in the impatient ubiquitous way of the time, he just went ahead and did it. Now back alone in England without the wonderful experience of finding a girl that he clearly loved, he wasn't exactly sure what he should do with his time. He had no job because he didn't need one. He had no place to be or issues to resolve and with the issues at Bentley he wasn't sure even if the people he knew would accept him in their tight circles of social interaction.

After a comforting hour or so in the living room in front of the fire with a glass of red wine, Graham took himself upstairs to the cold and lonely place that was his bedroom and slept off the last few days of restless sea sleeping. In the morning Graham was awoken by birds in the garden that noisily twittered in the large oak tree, as they pestered and struggled with each other for berries and seeds that had fallen to the ground in the cold winds of the autumn weather. It was clear that birds outside would not be allowing him to sleep any further despite his restless turning and covering himself in bedding. By the time that he was dressed it was nearly lunchtime, so as there was little other than a few cans of food in the kitchens, Graham decided to go out into town to the new Woolworths tea rooms for something to eat.

The store was as grand as they built them with such inviting window displays that it seemed the whole of the city had turned out to see what was inside them. Above the sales floor was the restaurant that had only recently been installed. That too was busier than Graham would have desired it but he needed to fuel a big hunger and he had read about the place and wanted to experience it. Big in America the store serviced so much of what people wanted at fair prices and the fact that it was from across the Atlantic was a draw in itself for many including Graham.

The building was clad in white tiles and was in the familiar style of the 20s and stood proudly in amongst the traditional stone and brick buildings of the last century, looking bold and thoroughly modern. The food was fast and efficiently brought to his table, the ladies that brought it were smart and most courteous to him and other diners. Graham was most satisfied that he had visited and that his hunger had been tamed.

As he left the store, Graham was instantly made aware that the end of the year was rapidly drawing nearer as swirls of auburn, red, yellow and gold leaves lifted around his feet and across the street, lying in piles in doorways and at the side of the kerb stones. There was a chill in the air but the sun still shone although quite weak and pale making the walk to the car quicker than it had of been from it.

The car took Graham back via George Road until he reached home. On a whim he then decided to continue his journey to see Elizabeth at her home a few miles away. Elizabeth's home was a gorgeously quaint and isolated cottage by the river that had been situated there for generations in amongst some rare greenery in the sprawl of the rapidly expanding London. A slate roof topped a stone cottage that was completed with black wood beams across the whole length of every room. Small in size and yet huge in character and charm the home had been shared by Elizabeth and her mother since the tragic death of her father in the Great War ten years ago

Graham's giant, gorgeous, chrome finished car arrived at the cottage looking entirely out of place and was parked across the front of the cottage at a very random angle. Graham stepped out and walked to the door to the sound of water politely trickling down rocks in the river as it made its way down stream. Graham stopped for a second before reaching the door crossing over the river via a small iron bridge and standing in the centre of it looking out across the water downstream. It was peaceful for a moment and Graham gave himself to it for a moment or two before approaching to the door of the house and knocking on it.

Elizabeth answered immediately and was of course entirely surprised by the re-entrance into her life of a man she respected, cared for and regarded as a friend. He looked at the wonderful girl that stood in front of him with her long brown hair cascading down her shoulders and her low cut jumper that revealed a lot of her. She looked into his eyes and he looked into her's and within just a moment they were embracing and once more reunited as friends. Invited into the living room, Graham sat on the chair in the front room and stared at a woman that had saved him from himself so many times. He had never really been there for her and they both knew that although they both were happy to be in each other's company.

For an hour they talked about Graham's trip and all the wonderful new experiences that he had, although Graham then made reference to Aina and the love that they had found. Graham had expected his friend to whoop with joy on hearing the news that finally he had resolved an issue with his life that had been troubling him for so long and that for once for a rare moment he had achieved satisfaction. The drinking had been curtailed and the hopeless way that he lived his life had been turned around, all of which had made him more a complete man.

Elizabeth looked at him and smiled and said that she was delighted that he found what he wanted but her folded arms and sudden intake of breath told him a different story. He wasn't sure why she had said one thing but clearly felt entirely the other but he took what she had said and enquired as to her position on love. "Graham it's not something that I have much to talk about right now...I'm..." She looked to the floor and then quickly changed the subject. "I'm glad that you're happy Graham I really am." She seemed like she wanted to say more but persisted in holding back on revealing what it was. Graham still wasn't so sure about her conviction but proceeded with the conversation anyway.

Elizabeth admitted to deeply missing him whilst he was gone and that she had waited every day in the hope that he would come back, now that he had, a part of her that had been lost had returned. Graham loved that fact alone and would return to his house with a huge boost to his ego. He didn't of course need it as he knew that Aina was waiting, so far away, in Spain for his promised return but the knowledge that he was being thought of in a way above a friend. Elizabeth looked embarrassed; her long brown hair only partly covered her blushing cheeks as she looked to the floor and away from Graham. "I'm glad to be back Elizabeth, I'm glad to have you as a friend, you are so special to me." Graham was happy to make that comment as it was the last that was made before he left for his home and he wanted to make his position quite clear to her. He had once put their friendship at risk by misreading the situation and he certainly wasn't going to do it again in a hurry especially with the thoughts of Aina so fresh in his mind.

Later in the day, Graham visited James at his home and enjoyed a good hour chatting with him before agreeing to take a drive out to a pub in the countryside for a few drinks. The drive was exhilarating and most pleasurable as he had not driven for so long and he made sure that the journey time was kept to a minimum. The empty white sky really emphasised trees that were now just skeletal frames, naked from their leaves now that winter had started to cut into the year.

The huge engine of Graham's latest giant and luxurious car roared as his foot pushed harder towards the floor on the accelerator, birds previously settling down for the night became startled and rose up from the hedgerows and into the sky away from the roadside. There was definitely more than a chill in the air and the two men both wore their coats buttoned up, with scarves and flat caps, whilst they talked and reacquainted themselves with each other's lives on the journey.

The pub was a whitewashed thatched cottage that had already been a place of drinking, smoking, gambling and general social interaction for over a hundred years. The heavy oak wooden door creaked as it was opened and the two gentlemen walked inside and removed their hats and scarves as they did so almost in union placing them on a peg in the entrance. The age-old black, wooden floorboards squeaked a little and bounced slightly as they walked on them. At the corner of the room, along the main bare brick wall, was a fire that roared and crackled as it eagerly burnt up thick, wooden logs providing very welcome heat and warmth throughout the public house. The fire must have warmed generations of people as they quietly sat quenching their thirsts with beer or just slowly getting blind drunk on whiskey.

Graham and James sat by the side of the fire after pulling up seats and sharing a polite greeting with two old men sitting at a table adjacent to them. Together they chatted and talked about Graham's trip to Spain and recent happenings in London and it was a great time for the both of them. James was of course delighted that his friend since school had finally found someone that he wanted to be with and indeed was in love with. James revealed that his partner and he had become engaged and this sparked a real understanding that the two embraced for a moment over.

Eventually and inevitably the subject of their conversation rested on the race track and the incident that led to the death of one of his opponents and one of the main reasons that he had left the shores of England in the first place. As the dust had settled over the months after the death many who had originally blamed Graham had reduced their criticism and many that had not had an opinion had come out in support of him. It seemed for once all that Graham was trying to be was coming up roses. He was so relieved that he was, in the public mind no longer the criminal that he had originally been made out to be and that now it was like that a huge weight had been lifted off his shoulders.

The fire was re-energised by the addition of further logs onto the burning embers by the landlord, whistling as he did so and then rubbing his hands together to remove soot from them. His checked white shirt was open at the collar three buttons down exposing a string vest and a mass of white chest hair over an extensive beer belly. The fire warmed them on the cold day whilst they sipped their beers as the wind had risen to be most unfriendly outside. After three of four pints of strong dark ale each, conversation was fluid and a most welcome return to comradeship for two close friends. After another hour or so the drive back was even more energetic than it was on the way it was causing both of them to hold onto their seats as they entered corners and out of them. Graham dropped James off at his house, shook hands and then made his way back to his own home.

Along the route and near to his house, he saw what he thought to be Ottoline walking along the street near to Cooke's hardware store. Graham had a double take as he saw her for he was sure that she was pregnant. As he looked again he was convinced of it. He knew that this would be the last thing that she would ever want and would be a cause of much embarrassment. Graham thought that it was indeed most entertaining and laughed to himself as he passed her by, realising that the whole social scene of the bright young things would be shocked to know of her public mistake. He was sure that it would have been a mistake, surely it couldn't have been anything else.

As the year moved into December, the first flurries of snow began to fall as Graham watched the soft flakes slowly descend to rest on the gardens below them through the window. The initial flakes gently melted in a fleeting moment as they touched the surface of the ground after their lengthy descent from the white sky above. It was a good ten minutes before there was enough flakes to make a difference to the earth, to the trees and to all that they rested on as one joined another and then further ones. Gradually, over the hour, the snow had built up to a half inch or so of snow that settled and draped itself over everything that it touched, like a soft white cotton sheet.

At about 4.30pm after making himself some food in the kitchen, Graham decided to go for a walk to get out into the snow and to really enjoy the change to the environment, just to experience it. With his coat, hat, gloves and scarf he was ready to face the cold of the evening and eager to take a walk just for the sake of it. Once away from the entrance hall, a firm hand shut the front door and Graham's feet hit the snow with a most satisfying crunch as the fresh snow was made into the white carpet that was still being added to with every second by a million more flakes. There was no wind in the sky and so the flakes were free to float effortlessly to the ground as Graham made his way across the gravel drive to the gate and out onto the street. Behind the high wall of the garden, the street lamp glowed, casting a halo around it in the now mostly dark sky showing up the snowflakes as they gracefully descended around it.

The street was empty except for the solitary figure of Graham as he walked along in the snow with now cold and heavy shoes and yet he remained warm inside his thick coat. Further on, past the shops and newly erected war memorial, the snow was a little thicker and it was natural full moonlight rather than the artificial glow of the electric street lights that lit up the deep carpet of glittering snow beneath it. Still there was not a soul on the street but the lights in the windows of houses showed that they were perhaps staying at home instead. Occasionally they would look out of their windows to look at the snow on the street but they hurriedly re-drew the curtains before settling down with a book, the radio or to eat in the warmth.

Graham Wright felt very special to be there in that scene walking alone as he did up the high street. The footprints, as he turned around, were only his showing from which direction he had walked. He was alone and it was a special time for him even if it was not for long and he returned home feeling that the experience had been well worth it. The cold snow scene that surrounded London that night was so different to the heat and humidity that he had come to know from his time in Tarragona

He thought then of Aina and his isolation from her. He wondered just what his girl would have thought of the snow, in a setting that was totally alien to all that she had ever known, for he was sure that she would never have touched snow in her hands, or heard it crisp below her feet. He would have loved to have held her closely in the snow flurries, under the sparkle of silver moonlight.

The snow lasted a whole week before it melted and dispersed and although slightly warmer in temperature with the melting of the snow, with every day away from his girl, that had changed his life, he felt colder and colder.

James, his fiancée and Elizabeth agreed to spend Christmas with Graham at the house, along with Sally and William, who had recently become married. The six of them shared presents and a massive feast of food and drink that had been expensively assembled for the occasion. It was good for all of them to share special moments with friends, especially at Christmas when the air of happiness and considered kindness was at its annual high. There were party games and the latest music, snacks and silly behaviour for all and by the end of the four days that they were together, some great friendships had been made or reassembled.

When James, his fiancée, Sally and William had made their goodbyes and left to go back to their respective homes, Graham and Elizabeth were left all alone in the large expanse of house. As had always been the way with the couple, conversation was easy and for some time they talked and casually drank the afternoon away, Just after that, the feelings that Elizabeth had for him, that Graham may only just have realised, had combined with four days of drinking, friendship and frivolity. Elizabeth casually walked over to Graham's chair, bent at the waist, and without a sound, kissed his lips. For the briefest moment, Graham selfishly enjoyed the feeling of her delicate, soft, pink lips pressing against his and the taste of her kiss was exhilarating, but he knew that it was totally wrong.

Before he had travelled to Spain, he had briefly mistaken his feelings of friendship for her as the emotion of love, or more than likely, of lust. With this he had narrowly avoided destroying the friendship they had built up since childhood, now this was entirely different. Firstly from the way she was coming on to him and secondly he had a girl he was very much in love with. She may have been just half-way across Europe but she was there all the same and he had made her a promise.

He never thought that she would ever have kissed a man, not for a minute. With that thought he broke his lips from hers and moved his head to the side. Elizabeth stood upright and moved back to her chair on the opposite side of the room. She looked entirely destroyed, as if suddenly the life in her had forcefully been sucked out. Her usual complete air of calmness was instantly replaced with a somewhat dramatic and aggressive outburst towards Graham.

"I thought it was what you wanted!" she shouted, as tears welled in her eyes. She paused for the briefest of moments before adding to it with explosive suddenness and significant anger and tears began to fall down her cheeks. "You're impossible Graham. Four months without you, thinking of nothing but you. Five years of loving you... and for what? You're a sham Graham, a pathetic, shallow man."

It was an extraordinary turn of events and Graham could offer nothing to say to the dramatically, vociferous, female outburst that was being directed at him. Instead he looked at the floor by his feet, wishing it would open up and swallow him right there and then.

"I love you Graham. I've always loved you."

With that she walked straight out of the front door with her bag, slamming it shut as she did so. Graham watched her make a speedy course down the driveway and onto the streets before disappearing from his view behind the garden wall. Graham could hardly believe that what he had just experienced had actually happened but he did now know that something massive had changed with him and Elizabeth.

The New Year was another celebration for Graham, this time spent at James's house though, naturally without Elizabeth.

Glasses of champagne were drunk and coloured paper streamers thrown about as the old year of 1928 passed away and the first moments of 1929 began to unfold. The year that followed would herald massive social, economical and political changes that would affect considerable segments of the people of the world that continually became more and more local. There was nothing to indicate that however after the first few ticks of Graham's expensive handmade Swiss wristwatch but as the year reached October the world would change.

The alcohol that Graham had consumed that night made sure that he slept well and the thoughts of Elizabeth, that his head persisted in thinking about over the past few days since her revealing outburst, couldn't make headway. This changed as soon as he woke up feeling bad in himself that he hadn't invited her to be with him. He remained unconvinced however that she would have come anyway and in reality she probably wouldn't have even answered the call.

To ease his boredom Graham purchased a new car that he immediately took out to drive. Graham also purchased two new suits and ten bright cotton shirts ready for the summer, that were also purchased at a hugely exuberant cost. The latest radio and music players were also paid for, to ease the fact that he had nothing else to do with his time or with his money. At the bank Graham agreed to purchase more American stocks and bonds from financial establishments that were almost giving them away. It was easy money he was promised, as credit and investments were so inexpensive that a massive profit could almost be given with each one as a guarantee.

It was now April and Graham was still massively bored with his life as there never seemed to be anything to do, even with all the money that he had at his disposal. He could buy anything he wanted and go anywhere or do anything but it seemed that there was always a huge part of his life that he could not satisfy. He endlessly thought about Aina and the life that he had taken on in Spain, despite it now feeling a whole lifetime away and he wished he could be back there now. Over the next few days Graham Wright began to think about just what was stopping him going back there right then and he determined that there really wasn't a thing in his way.

As was his usual unmeasured thought process, he took the car and rushed to town to purchase tickets for the next available transport out of England to Spain, be it by boat or even by plane. It was likely that there wouldn't be many scheduled trips, if any routes to the continent for another couple of months or until the English weather was more predictable in temperament. There were obviously few that could have even afforded transport for such a journey and especially in the luxury and comfort that Graham Wright would require but Graham had the money and of course was never afraid to spend it to get what he wanted. Graham almost burst into the travel office, surprising the middle aged lady behind the desk so much that she dropped the book that she was reading. The clothes that the woman wore seemed to be from decades ago and entirely old in their fashion. There was complete silence with the exception of the persistent ticking of a large white and black clock that hung on the wall behind her. Around the other three walls of the small white plaster room were paintings of exotic or historic destinations that the company presumably arranged travel to. Graham was not interested in the ancient delights of Rome, Venice or the Eiffel tower in Paris, for him there was only one place that he needed to be and that was the coast of sun-kissed southern Spain.

Looking over the top of her glasses, the blonde haired lady informed Graham, in a rather dismissive tone, that there was no continental crossing until June and that there was no other way than by air and that too only had a couple of flights scheduled in the next month. Graham was hit for six with the news that his travel to Spain would have to be delayed for at least another few months. "Are you entirely sure?" he vigorously asked whilst gesturing his arms upwards and standing one pace further towards the desk at which she sat behind.

The officious response was immediate. "I can assure you that these are my timetables and this is my shop and there are no other crossings this month."

Other than a rather sarcastic thank you and goodbye, Graham said nothing else before leaving the premises to go back onto the High Street. Already Graham's mind was working on the solution and so he took his comfortable car to London aerodrome where he was going to attempt an entirely new approach to getting to Spain. Behind two antiquated, but still airworthy, Great War, Sopwith Camel bi-planes, there were several small single wing planes waiting to be flown somewhere and one much larger aircraft standing equally idle nearby. The larger aeroplane was a Lockheed Vega and was a very impressive machine. The morning sun shone brightly across the aerodrome and then reflected back in its highly polished aluminium exterior. Just to the side of the planes was the waiting area, where Graham anticipated finding a pilot that he could chat too.

The smartness of the pilots' beige coloured uniforms was finely tailored and their turnout was impeccable. The whole world of flight was still very much in its infancy and of course had only recently begun with the American Wright brother's 120 foot long flight in 1903. Rushed improvements came with the Great War and then it wasn't long before people began to realise the potential of making money with flight.

One seated pilot looked even more the part than the others did, in part due to the large blond moustache that was similar to an untamed garden bush; so much so that Graham wondered how he could even speak with the weight pressing down on his top lip. Before Graham had even opened his mouth, the man got to his feet and, with coffee cup in his hand, started a conversation with him. "I was in the war you know?" he rather pompously said and before Graham could interject he continued. "Yes a pilot you know? Teaching the Bosch a lesson; all very exciting hey?" Graham sensed an opportunity to speak but before he could was slapped on the back by the pilot who proceeded to repeat his last line for a second time. Eventually conversation left the subject of the Great War and got around to the topic that Graham wanted to talk about. Graham suggested that for a significant amount of his money and of course any costs incurred, that the pilot could fly him to Spain.

There was a definite hesitation as Captain Fredrick Rothchild carefully considered his verdict as to whether he would take him across the water to where he knew his heart longed to be. Passenger flights were still not a regular service offered, unless of course enough money was offered to the right people and Graham was sure that he had offered sufficient quantities of cash to persuade the trip to go ahead. There was the matter of the still slightly unpredictable weather for the time of year and there was the subject of obtaining fuel, supplies and a co-pilot but the prospect was now entirely possible it seemed, once the issue of money had been resolved. The two men shut themselves in an office at the back of the wooden building where they commenced talking about money. The figure that the Captain had been thinking of in his head was clearly a lot more than the amount that Graham had offered initially but following negation and promises Graham had convinced him to agree to the journey. The two gentlemen parted with a firm handshake and agreed on a date two weeks ahead, on Monday at 9am.

Graham rushed over to James's town centre grocery store and told him what he had just done. The store was busy but once the various customers had been seen to, James honestly expressed that he was unsurprised at the news and made sure that he wished his old friend the best in all that he was going to do and experience in his life. Graham immediately suggested a party to end all his parties as his leaving for Spain was probably going to be the last of Graham that people would see for some time. James agreed to it, laughing as he did so, knowing that although Graham had changed so much he would always guarantee a party with excitement and controversy in equal measure.

Graham parked outside Elizabeth's cottage and looked around for her through the windows of the home but he assumed that she was not home as he could see no evidence of her. The sound of trickling water from the lock and the rustle of the fresh green shoots and leaves in the slight breeze on the re-energised spring trees was comforting and serene. A boat further up the canal was negotiating the next lock, filled with coal as it busily carried out its heavyweight daily task of getting its cargo to houses, businesses and industry across London and beyond. Had it been the right time to just sit he would have, deep in the tranquillity of the beautiful and lush English countryside. Right now though he needed to speak with Elizabeth and tell her his news.

The last time that they had met, Elizabeth had revealed her affection for him and he still secretly revelled in the self-indulgent feelings that this had given him in his mind and more physically alone in his room when he had needed to think about such things. Behind the cottage, he found her in the vegetable garden, tending to a huge variety of tender plants that would with care, time, water and sunshine start to yield food and nutrients for the whole year of food.

She stood mopping her brow for a moment, in between digging with soil covered hands and a tired look across her face, resting on the handle of her spade. Her sleeves were rolled up to her elbows and a triangle of sweat was visible between her shoulder blades on the blue and white checked shirt that she loosely wore. The garden was clearly important to her and it was indicative of her that she cared so much about things that others of her generation maybe wouldn't have been so interested in. Elizabeth turned her head to see Graham as he called out to her from the white painted picket fence that surrounded the garden. "I'm sorry Graham." She immediately said before he had time to say anything other than her name.

"Elizabeth its fine, we are fine but I need to tell you something."

Elizabeth remained just where she was, resting on the spade and, without looking up, told Graham that she knew just what he was going to say. He told her anyway, despite the fact that he knew she didn't want to hear it and that it could potentially ruin the friendship that they had left. Graham figured that for the chance of recouping love and for the sake of his well being it was worth another few months away from England. Before he left to go back to his house he invited her to the party that he was planning and without even getting close to her physically he parted with a final comment to her, reassuring her that she was always on his mind. Graham felt frustrated in that he had once more upset someone that was his friend but he tried to focus on what he believed was right.

There was no time to worry about proceedings, in the next week so Graham concentrated on planning the late spring, early summer party that would be his send-off for at least another four months or so. He was going to invite all the people he knew and provide the best of times for all of them with music, food, dancing and alcohol. He telephoned who he could and visited friends that had things that he required. From stores in the city and in town, he ordered vast quantities of food and drink and arranged for them all to arrive on the next Saturday at the gardens of his house.

A gigantic white marquee would be constructed from the rear of the courtyard and out across the lawn that would house the tables and chairs for a hundred people and with them an abundance of food and alcohol that would fuel their ravenous greedy mouths whilst they were entertained. Entertainment would come from an orchestra of fine jazz players that were renowned for their art at all the best parties. Freshly fashioned mojito, mint julep and Bellini cocktails would be provided alongside the most costly champagnes and imported spirits would prove that expense to him was of no object. There was a comedian booked and with exuberant party gifts for all that attended, he would be doing all he possibly could to make the right boxes for them all and make the impressions he wanted to give.

Graham seldom used his brain to much extent as it had often bothered him to exude that much effort on any topic but when it came down to organising a party there was no other that could achieve such organisational perfection. By the morning of the day that followed, brown suited gentlemen were already banging steel poles into the fresh, perfect lawns in order to construct the marquee. Others were delivering food and drink in boxes and crates to the kitchens by the bulk load, as human chains were constructed from the vans to the door.

There would be something for everyone; Graham would make sure of that. From singers, dancers and performers to comedians and of course all the latest and wildest music he had it covered. Graham had ordered machines that manufactured doughnuts and candy floss when people asked for them and even had several one-armed bandits placed in the reception of the house for the use of his wealthy guests, with Graham taking his cut of the profits of course from their use.

Graham knew more than most that some people would do anything for money and so, armed with a few notes, he visited James's store and pushed them in the direction of an assistant that would obtain a hundred invitations and post them out to people that Graham either liked, didn't like or who just had money. Of course they were posted to the likes of Ottoline, Bonny, Florence and Sally, whether they would attend he wasn't entirely sure. On Friday the final deliveries and preparations for the party were almost complete and all seemed to be coming together for the final result to be a good one. He had requested that the band arrive in the morning of the day after ,to tune up and practice for the party that he had publicised as starting at 7pm and with the weather at its kindest, he knew that it would be a wonderful event for all.

Cars began arriving at 6.30pm and by one hour later were parked in the drive, in the street and right the way down the road into town on both sides for as far as he could see from the leaded upstairs bedroom windows of the house. The dresses that the ladies wore were all of the highest fashion and of the latest styles as they walked towards the house. Most seemed to wear the cloth hats that were rapidly becoming the way that women wanted to wear their hair and with the longest materials the ideal of a long slim curve-less figure was definitely the look to go for.

Seeing that the gardens were beginning to fill with his guests, Graham ordered the band to start up with as lively a tune as they could manage to get the party going. Within just a few moments there were guests already dancing or conversing with each other and creating the kind of exciting fluid evening that Graham had hoped for. With a fresh dry Martini in his hand he made his way down to greet some of the guests that mingled around the house and the gardens and out onto the lawns. Inside the marquee, drinks were being sloshed around and consumed as if there was going to be no tomorrow whilst nuts, crisps and confectionary were being devoured in a similar frenzied manner.

By 8pm there were already signs of much drunkenness amongst the guests and with the commencement of the comedian's routine, laughter and enjoyment were spreading though the party goers rapidly. James arrived and immediately made his way to where Graham stood at the front of the house and shook his hand sincerely in congratulations of the party that he had created. Florence and Ottoline had arrived in fantastic style with as much fanatical support as they had ever had at a party before, Graham was not surprised nor was he amused. He was determined that he was going to be the main event, it was his party and despite the dramatic entrance to the event from the ladies, he knew that by the end of it he would be what all the guests were talking about.

Ottoline was of course in a state that was most definitely pregnant, despite embarrassingly not having a husband or even regular boyfriend. However she tried to dress to hide it there was no mistaking that she was as some put it 'indisposed'. There was obviously a huge embarrassment to the whole thing but Ottoline was as obstinate and unrealistic in her whole attitude that she would carry on regardless. Florence would dodge and move with whatever was going on so long as she was never in jeopardy of losing face. He wasn't going to speak to them that night, he was sure of that, because he in reality couldn't be bothered to. It was important to him however to make sure that they attended so long as they saw that he was so much more without them.

There were bright stars that night above them that had emerged from the sky as the heavens became blacker with the descent of night time. Graham looked up at the sky and remembered his last party, standing out on the lawn with Bonny, thinking he had the world in his hands with a similar starry vista above him. That seemed so long ago now and he had become so much more of a man, of a lover and of someone with human feelings since then and that was because of Spain. He was a man of money and he owned a big house and allegedly he had friends and officially it was everything he needed to be happy. He needed more however and he would be returning to Spain to obtain it.

Graham from then on just drifted from guest to guest, charming and disarming ladies with his green eyes and polished, white toothed smile that resembled so much of what young ladies wanted sometimes. Gentlemen were inspired and eager to hear about his cruise and recent accumulation of European culture and lifestyle, whilst the ladies were keen just to listen to him and watched as he mingled and interacted with guests.

Through the house a young man was walking around on his hands whilst the reels on the fruit machines span and span to the fascination of the surrounding throng of people. Consumption of alcohol at apace continued all evening, with Graham and others drinking huge quantities of liquor to evolve the mood of the evening to that of manic.

Graham must have visited and spent time with all the guests that he wanted to be seen with that evening and whether it was to talk about racing, his trip to Spain or any other subject he was everything that night to so many and it was the confident, powerful side that pushed him for control that evening. Entirely absent was the self doubting or cautious side of him that had been an uneasy and yet very close neighbour intermittently through his life. It was his party, it was the biggest there had ever been and the party guests that danced and threw themselves into it certainly knew that he was the reason that they were there.

People ran wild that night under the influence of drink, music, youth, money and assumed freedom, inside a bubble that had by 1929 floated so high that would either make it to the stars or suddenly and explosively burst causing all the people inside to fall so far that they would never be able to make the climb again. But what did they care when all the dances, the money and the opportunity were flowing like water in an endless stream that led to somewhere fast. Where it would lead they were not sure but they followed it regardless. The party continued with kissing and all kinds of liberated sexual and random behaviour that blossomed all over the party, until the whole throng seemed to be brimming with frivolous and riotous excess. It was a party like no other. It wasn't a full summer evening for sure but it had all the feeling of one with the warmth of the late spring day continuing into the evening and the most temperate of nights being the perfect backdrop for the party to blossom in, amongst the swinging trees that surrounded the expansive grounds of the grand family house. The guests were enjoying themselves that was for sure and with an army of smart suited butlers serving all the food and drink that they could selfishly gulp down, they were well watered and fed, relaxed and free.

Graham looked out at the panorama from the walls of the courtyard across the scenes of guests dancing and he was convinced that he saw Elizabeth amongst them. He knew that he had to speak with her to resolve the situation that remained unfinished between them and that was just what he was going to do.

He was surprised when at last he had made his way through the gathering of people to reach her, to see a large cocktail in her hand, which she was regularly sipping from. Elizabeth didn't really drink and certainly not in large quantities and to see her doing the opposite was indeed a surprise. She wore a low cut, two part dress of thin material, that revealed so much of her that although as a friend he knew he must maintain eye contact, he found it slipping from her eyes to her neck and then to her chest. Rapidly he reverted back to her eyes as she spoke. A broad smile grew on her lips, that had been made up to look perfectly red and plump like a ripe apple. Without even a second thought she reached up stretching her neck as she did so before kissing him.

Some of the lipstick that had previously been on Elizabeth's lips was transferred to Graham's which she immediately wiped off with a plain, white cotton handkerchief. Smiling again she took hold of his hand and led him to where the dancing was taking place and together they joined in with the exciting black bottom dance that the whole party seemed to have been waiting for. Feet flew and skirts swirled as Graham and Elizabeth twirled around the courtyard with the other couples whilst the music played loud and fast into the evening.

Once the dance had finished and before the next started Graham and Elizabeth took a walk down to the lake right at the bottom of the garden and away from the party. With them Graham took a bottle of wine and together they sat overlooking the lake with the house in view with all its electrically illuminated iridescence. The lake was black as the night sky above it and its water was just as still as the breeze. Together they talked about the past, everything from their childhood growing up near each other, right up to the party, as the shared swigs from the bottle of wine that slowly diminished their worries and inhibitions. Elizabeth's hand made its way from the now empty wine vessel to Graham's shoulder and down his side as she pushed their two bodies closer until they rested entirely together.

The scheduled fireworks began from the roof of the house in a fantastic display of colour and sound rushing upwards into the night sky with explosive suddenness. The display was of course the best that money could afford and impressed every guest at the party, drunk or otherwise. The coloured explosions in the night sky were reflected across the water of the lake whilst Graham and Elizabeth looked out across the water.

Graham was so in love with Aina, he was entirely convinced of that but right there, at that moment, Elizabeth that he had for so long thought of as the perfect match for his life, was laid on the grass by his side with her hands all over him, clearly in the frame of mind that they should be together. Elizabeth was certain that if she could convince Graham that they were right together then maybe they would be and therefore his trip to Spain would never go ahead. Graham was of course now completely torn between the present and the future and between the secure and the fanciful. The alcohol, the exciting party amongst the temperate night sky, the fireworks and the sudden surrender of Elizabeth to him had taken him to the edge of reason, what he would do he just couldn't quite figure out.

He grasped her soft and expressive face, turning it to his before kissing it with passionate relinquishment and then holding her whole body and placing it next to his. It was perhaps entirely random of him for at that moment he acted in a way that he had never done before. He teased romantically just before he grabbed her loose fitting shirt and with a flourish, he whipped it right off her before throwing it to the ground, leaving her top half entirely naked. He had of course, despite their growing up together, never seen her in any way naked and just the first sight of her was entirely sexually exciting for him. Elizabeth was clearly surprised at his actions and yet was in no hurry to put her shirt back on despite not showing that she was happy to be in a state of undress with Graham Wright. She was convinced that she was in love with him and if he was being sexual towards her then that was all that was just so right for her. Graham obviously had ideas and removed his jacket, shirt and trousers. This left him with just a pair of undergarments that within a couple of seconds he had removed and thrust aside. Elizabeth was shocked and surprised at his actions but aroused all the same at the sight of Graham's completely naked body.

There was nothing else that she could do when faced with the thing that she desired, but to remove the rest of her clothes and stand on the side of the black, still lake with Graham naked next to her side by side. She of course had never seen him naked and yet despite their years together and with Graham putting it all on show she found it entirely impossible not to look and stare at his most personal of areas in the silver moonlight. Both of them desired the other but for that split second they just stood together at the edge of the lake with the fireworks still blasting stars into the sky and exploding excitement over the party beneath it. And then hand in hand they ran towards the still and dramatically cold water. Together they both leapt into the abyss plunging into the cold blackness naked, raw and wild at heart and mind.

The water was ice cold and Elizabeth screeched out as the temperature reached her naked body and aggressively shook it, Graham let out a loud call as he rose to the surface and pushed a hand through his hair and away from his eyes. Together they bobbed about for a moment before the whoops of exclamation gave way to laughter as the two realised the irrational act that they had just had just done. As soon as the cold became too much for them, they made their way to the edge of the lake before hauling themselves up and onto the grass like a pair of seals onto a rock. For a moment they lay on their backs on the grass laughing and then after a minute or two they put their clothes back on as the temperature desperately required that they did urgently.

He touched her naked stomach with his finger and drew circles around her waist and upwards between her breasts and then back down, to which she took huge enjoyment. She lay back looking at the stars above her head in silence hoping and wishing for so much more that she would have so easily submitted to. When Graham got to his feet, Elizabeth immediately realised that there would be no more that would pass between them in an intimate way and that they would return to being just good friends once again. It was not what she wanted and defiantly not what she had expected to happen but it looked like Graham had made up his mind as to what he was going to do. She was upset about the situation and Graham knew that. The temptation to continue with her had been immense but he had resisted in favour of returning to Aina, back in Spain. Once the party had been concluded some time into the morning he would be just a few days away from leaving the country and for where he had decided his heart wanted to be.

Returning to the party, his hair was dishevelled and thoroughly wet. Although there was no one who asked him why his appearance was a little less than the perfected article that it usually was, they all must have wondered at least why. Elizabeth decided to go home, her head was filled with a whole confusion of thoughts and ideas, from love right through to despair. Graham however continued on into the late night mingling and conversing with his guests. Some of them were by this point hopelessly drunk with a few even asleep in corners of rooms or laying across chairs and tables throughout the house. Graham didn't mind really, it was a party for them to all remember. Until he had spent another few months in Spain and then returned the party goers would have to use thoughts of this one as reason to wait until the next.

Unlike the last of his parties, there was nobody to share the moonlight with under the sparking starlit skies or to sit out and enjoy the peaceful night side by side with. He sincerely missed the opportunity but he knew that the dream that he held onto would be worth the missed chance. It would be immediate excitement traded for future satisfaction and he was prepared to make the trade. He knew that he would be returning to a reality that he had only recently realised was there at all.

When the final guests and hangers-on had left by foot or by taxi cab and the remaining cars had been driven away, there was just Graham alone in the fantastically sumptuous surroundings of his house that was now strewn with bottles, upturned glasses, tipped tables and general mess that had been thrown and left without care by faceless guests. The visitors were gone and the sound of a sonorous saxophone and triumphant trumpet had now faded into the slight wind that had built up around the grounds of the family home and in the trees and woodland that surrounded it.

The wealth of coloured cocktails and fizzing champagne that had been available at the start of the night had now run dry and the mass of expensive food that had been provided for the guests to greedily guzzle down their necks, had all been consumed or was lying wastefully disregarded. There had been dancing and there had been much frivolity. There had been spectacle and laughs but the party was over and it was time to call it a day. There would be people arriving tomorrow morning who would be paid to industriously clean up the debris from the revelry and abandon, in order to return the fabulous home and grounds to its former glory. Graham didn't care who had to clean up the mess, it didn't bother him, he had already made arrangements and paid for the place to be reset ready to be locked up for four months with his imminent return to Spain. It would be just two days before he would be making his way to London airport to fly to Spain and he would have to spend the next day packing cases for his journey. Right now it was late and Graham was half drunk and fully tired and so he retired to bed. It was a warm evening and he slept without bedding in order to keep cool during the night. He was thoroughly restless but the alcohol ensured that he got to sleep with dreams of fun and frivolity passing across his mind

. Chapter 10

The day that Graham was scheduled to leave, was a morning just like many others in a summer that was slowly gaining momentum in warmth and vibrancy with every day. He woke early to the restful sound of bird song, a blackbird searched for worms in the grass of the lawn whilst a wood pigeon called to its mate in amongst the blossoming branches of a tree just outside the windows of the bedroom. Graham pulled back the curtains and looked at the view across the lawns at the early morning summer scene and within a few moments with the wipe of his eyes, was ready to face the day. With a wash, a shave and a hearty cooked breakfast, he was starting to feel a little more human and ready to pack his travelling things that he needed to take with him on his second escape to Spain.

With his clothes and toiletries, he took a few gifts that he had purchased for the woman that he loved and was returning to within a day. He packed shirts and clothes that were lighter in texture, along with three suits and several hats, following his first visit his knowledge of what he needed to take and what he didn't. He was nervous and Graham was not a man that liked to be on time or in a specific place at a certain time, he was certainly not someone that wanted to rush to be anywhere in a hurry. There was no option however, for he knew that there was a plane waiting for just him that had cost more money than most people earned in half a year.

A taxi had been ordered to take him to the airfield and when it arrived the nerves that would be with him for almost the entire journey started to stir and rise up from within him. They whirled and whisked up inside his stomach and throughout his body as he greeted the taxi driver and showed him where the bags and cases, which he needed to take, were located. The last time that he had ordered a taxi to travel to the train station, the rain that had filled the sky had been torrential in its descent to earth from the clouds. The scene now, five months later, could not have been more different with a bright and brilliant sun climbing high into the sky, casting warmth and brilliance across the city. The taxi had loaded in it all the cases and bags that he required and Graham had climbed into his seat the taxi moved off on its way to London airfield. With every mile that the taxi cab got closer, the more the levels of his anxiety rose and fell as he edged further and further to the edge of the leather seat beneath him. It was a good half an hour journey, firstly through the swept, cobbled streets and black cast iron railings of the west side of the city before trudging through the smoggy industrial and traffic clogged east side. From then it was countryside until they came upon the group of six buildings of differing sizes and purposes and open space around it that made up the London airfield.

The aeroplane sat idly on the concrete, its metallic aluminium fuselage glinting in the sunlight as a couple of grease covered mechanics looked at the pair of tiny wheels on which the plane sat. The plane was mostly constructed from wood the way that it would have been ten years before and the thought of this was perhaps a little disconcerting for Graham but he knew that it would be the only way in which he would be flying. He was resigned to putting his faith in Captain Rothchild, his co-pilot and the wooden framed aeroplane and with the addition of luck that was all he was going to get.

The taxi was unloaded by the taxi driver and the bags were transferred into the underbelly of the plane with the assistance of one of the mechanics. Graham sat in the waiting area looking out across the airfield as he watched a small bi-plane build up its speed and ungainly take off into the sky and into the white puffs of cloud above. There were many that thought Graham a brave and courageous man for his driving at speed in the races that he had driven and in some ways he was.

There were some however that believed that bravery and stupidity was in effect the same thing. Graham was unsure at that point if this applied to the Captain and the pioneering pilots of the age. Even though Graham had the money, the possessions, the family history and all the acquaintances and friends that a man could ever want, he looked up to the man that now entered the room and made his way towards him. "Good afternoon Mr Wright, I trust that you are ready for our little...adventure eh?" A somewhat firm handshake from the pristine figure of Captain Rothchild accompanied his greeting and exaggerated raise of both blond eyebrows and slight sideways raise of the head.

"I'm ready Captain, how's the weather up there today?" he confidently enquired.

"Cloud and sun, not much wind, looks pretty perfect for it I'd say." He paused for a moment ensuring that there was nobody in the room who was listening before continuing with his conversation. "Look there is the matter of money my friend, I presume that you have the necessary?"

Looking Graham in the eye he persisted with his conversation. "I want to get the cash before we fly in case we crash hey!"

Graham resisted the opportunity to laugh or smile but instead he reached to the inside pocket of his tweed sporting jacket and produced a brown paper packet that he handed to Captain Rothchild. The money was immediately secreted away and with a further handshake the deal had been sealed and the flight was ready to commence. The Captain had no need to count the money as he was assured in his mind that Graham Wright was a man of integrity and business reliability.

Graham was convinced that the Captain would see him right in the flight to Spain and together they walked out onto the concrete and towards the plane. As they approached it, the two mechanics that had completed their seemingly very stringent tests and checks on the aircraft came towards Graham and the captain and with a simple double thumbs-up they signalled that the flight was ready to go ahead.

The interior of the plane was as raw and skeletal as the exterior, clad in metal but completed with a rough turquoise coloured carpet down the centre of the plane and four rows of three leather seats spread across the fuselage. Graham chose one of the seats and sat down as relaxed as he could be despite the nervous tension that was growing and multiplying itself within him with every second. There were four round windows on each side, one set for each row of seats. Through the one immediately to his right, he looked out across the grass that led away to open countryside beyond. Above, the sky was now blue and the clouds that had lingered throughout the morning had now been blown to other areas and conditions for flight seemed perfect.

Two thirds down each wing, hung below by what seemed the slimmest of supports, was an engine with a giant propeller that remained patiently motionless just waiting for the Captain to start the engines and to spin the propellers. Within just a few more moments, the propellers burst urgently into life with a white spark and a puff of black smoke and began to spin faster and faster until watching its rotations blurred Graham's vision.. The sound was an intense, dull droning and monotonous, that filled his ears whilst the vibrations from the engines rumbled throughout the whole plane and up though his entire body.

Graham's previous anxiousness, prior to that moment, was superseded by a little excitement as the plane's wheel blocks were removed by the brown jacketed mechanic and forward motion of the plane began at a slow pace towards the main runway. As the plane proceeded to its take off point it started to gain momentum and with it grew Graham's exhilaration with the anticipation of the plane taking off into the sky. The wings shivered up and down as they vibrated with the rest of the plane as speed increased and the sound of the engines became amplified as more thrust was applied to them from the man at the controls.

The view of the earth and countryside around the airfield from the window, became only a blur as the plane slowly and without warning lifted up from the ground beneath it the two front wheels initially then followed by the rear until the plane was unsupported by the earth and breaking free from the challenge of gravity. The whole plane felt suddenly like it had dropped as the engines took on extra strain before continuing to thrust the plane onwards and upwards at about forty-five degrees. When the plane had stabilised, the sound of the two wing engines became somewhat reduced, leaving only the droning background sound in his ears.

It was an exciting time and a free time and as the plane gained altitude towards the clouds and then entered into them. The ground and the increasingly minute features of houses, roads and towns beneath them began to become a green and brown haze of colour and movement. Soon after, the plane levelled and positioned itself in a direct route to cross the English Channel and to enter into the air space of France.

Graham unfolded a newspaper and read articles that kept him entertained for the following two hours until the plane began to descend. There was little to do up there in a metal and wood box with wings, other than to read the paper again and look out of the window. The clouds were fluffy and white and floated effortlessly together in the tranquil deep blue sky. There appeared little wind up there high above the earth and together the clouds formed what looked like a giant white quilt that naturally levitated in the sky.

The excitement and the nerves that had surrounded him for the entire journey in equal measure had instead been replaced by boredom and fatigue. It was approaching an hour and a half before the tiny, toy sized farmhouses and buildings started to grow in size as they grew closer with the descent of the plane towards ground. Graham watched from the small window to his side as the strip of land at one of the French aerodromes became closer and closer until it was clear that the plane would be landing.

The sound from the engines again grew in intensity as it worked harder to bring the plane steadily downwards. In the same way as it had done with takeoff, the fuselage began to shake and the seemingly fragile wings shuddered and shivered as it did so. The thrill of landing ended in the plane's steady touchdown on the ground and its eventual deceleration until it reached a stop. Graham was greatly relieved as he was entirely jaded by his whole flying experience, with the exception of the initial take off that he found most breathtaking and thoroughly gripping.

Graham took care of his necessary toilet and refreshment requirements before going for a stroll around the outside of the waiting area, smoking a cigarette as he did so. The wind was fresh and rejuvenating against his tired dry skin and his body felt a little stiff after the travel that had brought him to the middle of France in its green and rural heart. The plane would be refuelled, checked through and made ready for its continuing journey onto Spain but before then the intrepid travellers; Captain Rothchild, his co-pilot, Brian Roberts, and passenger, Graham Wright, would eat at a small cafe just a stone's throw away from the airfield.

Graham thought that the little cafe was typically French with its little round tables outside it on the cobbled street. It was shaded by the large canopy of a tree that looked ages old with its twisted branches and obscure gravity defying angles contriving and creeping over the walls of the brick building and street in front of it. They ate at one of the round, table clothed tables on the street ordering toasted croque monsieur sandwiches and freshly made local lemonade that came from a large jug half full of ice and pieces of fruit.

The food was a well appreciated gastronomic delight that, although simple in its construction and ingredients, was generously bountiful in its quantity and pleasingly satisfying in its taste. Graham said his thank you to the waiter and left a generous tip in sterling on the table before accompanying the Captain back to the airfield and the waiting plane that would, hopefully, be ready for its second journey from central rural France into the sunny savannah of coastal Spain.

With a few final checks the plane was ready for the three men to once again board and get ready for the second take off of the day. The captain and his comrade replaced their official looking hats, straightened their black ties and exchanged agreements to begin the flight. The plane was slowly positioned into the centre of the runway and as soon as the flash of ignition had sparked the engines to start up and the puff of grey smoke had been emitted, the pair of propellers began their spin which developed into a tornado-like whirl.

The plane started forward, rapidly gaining in pace towards a speed that would allow the silver metallic machine to lift of the ground again and eventually make its way to the next country and to the outskirts of its capital city, Barcelona. It would be a long flight and most probably once again quite tedious but the prize of almost omnipotent sunshine and the sweetest sublime return to the arms of the woman, that he was convinced that he loved, would make it all worth it. From landing in Barcelona, Graham would have to make his way own way to Tarragona, he was sure that a taxi, a car or a train would be going his way and that to get to where he wanted to go, there would be nothing that could stop him. Until then, the relentless drone of the engines and the sparse, riveted, aluminium insides of a totally empty aeroplane would be the setting for Graham Wright's journey. He had read almost every word in the copy of the 'Daily Telegraph' newspaper that now resided under his seat and so he picked up instead 'The Way The World is Going' by H.G. Wells. The book did engross him for a while and many of the issues and points raised he realised he had opinions of and thoughts relating to and that seemed to knock off about an hour from the journey and for that he was glad.

As the golden sandy coast of eastern Spain drew closer from out of the deep blue sea, Graham moved closer to the edge of his seat and stared through the window at the scenery below. The country seemed vast, endlessly golden and dry but sun kissed and as the buildings, roads and geographical features became apparent he realised all the charms and ancient spectacle that he knew he had missed so much since he last departed from its shores. The plane began to descend and as it did so there was a change in the engine sound and an increase in Graham's anticipation of landing and commencing the important final third of his journey.

He was sure that he could see the famous cathedral, with its pointed spires and impressive height, which dominated the skyline. Graham followed the streets with his eyes as the tiny features of the earth below slowly became clearer as the plane gradually lost altitude and drifted gracefully closer to earth. As the engine noise changed and the plane had dropped to a level that was close enough for it to approach the landing strip at Barcelona, Graham knew that the second third of his journey was reaching its conclusion.

When the plane finally landed and had reached its destination and the wheels had made their final turn, Graham Wright wasted no time in getting out and removing his luggage from the rear of the plane. It was with hearty thanks that he shook the hands of the two men that had bravely flown him from England through to the heart of Spain so that he could get to be with the girl he loved. She had no inclination that he would be seeing her soon and that, Graham felt, would ensure that it meant even more. Virtually as soon as Graham had walked out from the plane the feeling of heat and humidity struck him, just as it had done the first time he had arrived in the country six months ago. With it came the blinding brightness of the sun that reflected on the white plastered buildings and on the cobbled stones of the pavements.

Graham knew that money and confidence had and could get him very far in life and he was luxuriously festooned with both. With a flutter of his cash and the positive strut of his impressively large frame into the centre of the road, Graham managed to find a taxi cab that took him to a hotel near to the fantastically ornate iron structure of Franca station in the centre of Barcelona. He saw little of Barcelona from the window of his taxi but tired and ready for a cigarette a whiskey and a clean comfortable bed he wasn't so bothered.

The noise of traffic from the fifth floor of the newly constructed and grandly exuberant art deco building was enough to make Graham shut his window despite the heat and humidity that filled the room with an unwelcome feeling that he was still unhappy with, despite the fact that he had become used to it the last time that he was in Spain.

Unable to sleep after an hour of impatiently rolling and fidgeting, Graham redressed and made his way back down the restaurant and bar, ordered a whiskey and smoked a cigarette. There was life down in the bar, with the clinking of glasses and the chattering of the people that came and went out of the revolving glass doors and Graham liked it that way. Graham Wright also liked the fresh feeling of re-circulated air on his face from the massive blades of three fans that swirled relentlessly above on the suspended ceiling. Despite the comfort of the lounge area it wasn't long however before Graham decided to go outside and rest casually on a wall with a cigarette in one hand and a second tall glass of whiskey in the other.

The evening was fresh in its feel compared to the heat of the day and it was a pleasure to be able to spend time outside drinking and smoking in the evening, something that he couldn't do in London. It was only an hour or two before Graham was sufficiently full of fresh air, nicotine and alcohol and had allowed enough time for a change in the humidity so that he could achieve a night's sleep in his room. Graham returned to his room and within minutes of him resting his head on the pillow he was a sleep. With the thoughts of next morning's travel to Tarragona in his mind, his dreams were easy and worry free for the whole of that night.

The morning brought the expected brightness of sunshine through the dark, wooden, horizontal blinds and with it the smell of the white, pressed linen, bed clothes and the faint aroma of the paint from the recently furnished bedroom suit. The sunlight immediately reminded him of the hotel room in Tarragona where each morning he would wake and watch the slow ascent of sunlight from the corner of the foot of his bed upwards, until the brightness caught his eyes.

The hands on the clock above the bed were just reaching nine o'clock when Graham had washed, shaved and dressed and had made his way downstairs to eat breakfast. The room that had been set out for breakfast was a large open space, flanked with the flair of glass and the boldness of geometric shapes that had been styled in the most modernistic and gloriously exuberant way.

There were meats, cheeses and fruit in bowls, with ranges of cereals and pastries that were available for the hotel guests to choose for themselves, which was a new experience in itself for Graham that was more used to having plates of food brought to him than going to select it for himself. The food was simple but just what Graham Wright required for that morning and he rapidly consumed it before packing his bags and getting the hotel staff to bring his luggage down to the foyer and to call him a taxi cab.

When it arrived, the hotel staff again provided the service of baggage transferral, this time from the hotel foyer to the taxi, watched on by Graham who had already experienced the odd flutter of nervous tension with the thought of commencing the last stage of his journey. It was a full twenty minutes before the taxi was loaded and Graham had checked out of the hotel and paid the bill.

It was only ten minutes drive away from the iron pillars and stretched cast iron beams of the brand new and fascinating Franca station. The train that arrived at the platform was not as heavy or powerful as the trains that had taken him to destinations in England and made much less of an entrance or exit as it arrived. The train was smaller, sleeker and more streamlined than the English model and with fewer carriages. To complete the train, it had been painted in gloriously patriotic yellow and red and would provide the link between Barcelona and the home town of his girl Aina Maria Esquer.

As the shrill sound of the train letting off steam answered the call of the air from the whistle in the mouth of the station master announcing that the train was ready to depart to the first of its nine stops before it reached Terragona and then its terminus of Alicante. The coastal route of the train would provide some fantastic scenery for the passengers to savour and experience as they travelled along it. Some travelled to be with friends or relatives, others for business and some just for the hell of it, Graham travelled for love.

The journey would take an hour and in contrast to the laborious journey by plane, Graham relished the opportunity to see more of a country that he had fallen in love with. The sun was still rising in the sky and crept behind small puffs of white clouds and then out again as it did so, as if playing a game with

Graham as he watched. Each time it reappeared it would flash rays of sunlight at the train and through its windows causing Graham to blink and swiftly look away ready to play the game once again. The deep blue sea glinted with sunlight as the train continued on its journey, as the sandy beaches stretched out between the train and the sea with a grand curvature that enabled a fantastic view of the whole area as the carriages passed on.

As the train began to slow down and approach the station at Terragona, the nerves and butterflies that Graham had been feeling from within him began to rapidly increase in volume and sensation and somehow he knew that these experiences would only get more intense as he got closer to the town and to Aina. There was nobody to help Graham with his numerous bags, cases and luggage as the doors opened once the train had reached a complete stop and there were Spanish mutterings of discontent from the remaining passengers that Graham was taking too long to remove his possessions from the train. After Graham's struggle with his luggage the doors were shut and the train commenced once again on its coastal route down the country, under the heat of the Mediterranean summer sun that was continually growing in strength.

Graham waited for some twenty minutes for a taxi to arrive and it was a hot and flustered man that sat on the largest of his cases who came into view of the taxi driver as it eventually approached the road outside of the station. Sweat had formed on Graham's brow and he had removed his tie and jacket in order to try and keep cool. Once loaded, the taxi started off up the road towards the hotel that he had stayed at the last time and after helping him into the foyer, the taxi driver took his taxi away to some other destination leaving Graham to approach the desk and book himself into a room. It had been a while of course since

Graham had last used any of the Spanish that he had learnt with Aina but it felt like the correct thing for him to do and so he did just that. "Me gusta una habitacion por favour," Graham confidently said. He was however confused by the response in Spanish from the man behind the desk and that prompted him to instead speak in English but either way he now had a room in which to place his bags and wash. A team of young lads were mobilised to take his bags away up the stairs to his room. It wasn't the same room that he had been in last time but it was equally smart and well looked after and it had a view that looked out over the harbour to the sea. It was a pleasure for him to wash away the miles of travel from his brow, to change his clothes and restyle his hair before taking a few moments to rest on the bed. Graham would soon leave the hotel and make his way into town and to the square where just maybe he would see his girl and surprise her with flowers and kisses that he had been waiting so restlessly to give her once again.

Now rested and comfortably clean, it was time to walk along the coastal path and towards town. There were few people about that afternoon and Graham was surprised as there was no wind and the sun had risen to its pinnacle in the sky, bringing bright warmth and comfort across the whole town. The town was the same; nothing had seemingly changed in the centuries old square. The market was still actively busy with locals buying the food and goods, that they needed for the week, from the cheerfully noisy traders that continued in their well practiced manner until the time when they would pack up their stalls and head for home.

The orange and lemon trees were still bursting with bright round fruit in amongst shiny green leaves as he passed them by and he continued into the square and to the wooden benches where he had sat the last time that he had been there. It was comforting that the square remained unchanged and the overwhelming feeling that what he was doing was the right thing. As he sat there on the bench amongst the sounds and smells of the market place in the heat of the sun, he looked around for his girl but she was nowhere to be seen.

Soon enough he decided to walk down to the rocky caves and beaches to see if she were there. It was with an inner smug satisfaction and pleasurable warmth that he recalled the special and intimate time that Graham and Aina shared in the larger of the caves. The sea gently rolled up onto the golden sands of the beaches and softly dissolved into the grains of sand beneath them and then smoothly back to join the rest of the water. There were a few people swimming a little further out and quite a few more sunning themselves on the shore or entertaining children.

Graham climbed down the wooden staircase that zigzagged down from street level to the beach below. As he reached the bottom he sat on the bottom step and removed his shoes and socks and rolled up his trouser legs to his knees before placing his bare feet on the golden sands and walking towards the softly lapping sea as it rolled ashore. The soft sand was hot on his white toes and the bottom of his feet and he quickly swopped pressure between one foot and the other to equalise the heat. Soon after he began to jog to the clear water and enter into it with a splash. The contrast between the sand that had been heated throughout the day and the cool of the washing water was immense but it was over within a few seconds, then it was a feeling of just relaxation.

As the lone figure of Graham Wright made his slow meander in the sea, further up the beach he became aware that, despite the comfort of the sun and the holiday feeling of relaxation, he was still even without the slightest glimpse of the girl he had travelled so far and spent so much to achieve. He would complete the walk along the golden sands towards Aina's house where he was sure that he would find her waiting for him.

There was nobody at home when he approached the house and knocked on the door and the feeling was a sudden reality check that perhaps there was an abrupt and tormenting reason why he had paced the town, walked the beach and then called at her house and yet still there was no sight or sign of her. Urgently he knocked at the door again, this time harder, just on the off chance that she had not heard it the first time. The result was the same and so was the effect on Graham; that of mild dejection. Feeling that his time was wasted, he disconsolately made his way back in the direction of the hotel.

Stopping on the way at one of the sea fronted small cafe/bars, he decided to get away from the sun for a while and take a white beer in a bulky thick glass under a large umbrella that spanned the width of several of the outside tables with coloured fabric panels that were proudly blazoned with the brewer of the cold, malty, opaque beer that Graham Wright now drank in the sunshine. It could have been a wondrous dream to be out there in the sunshine of south eastern Spain looking out across the golden sands and the mild blue ocean. It was however no dream at all, as there was still little sign of Aina and that was why he was there in the first place.

Two further, long and intriguingly cold foreign light beers later, Graham paid his bill with the usual exuberance of a generous service tip and made his way back to the hotel. There was a change in the day as the fresh excitement of morning daylight turned into hesitant early afternoon and that then in turn transformed into tentative premature evening. With it there was a change in humidity, in heat and in brightness and slowly and surely the sun began to descend towards earth and as if submerged and possessed by the vast ocean it evidently disappeared from view.

As it descended into the ocean the colours that had been tightly contained inside it, began to run as if water had been applied to a painting. All the myriad colours poured into the vast sea and infinite skies and slowly drew themselves outward until their constituent parts were evident from corner to corner of the immeasurable horizon before him.

There was still the glorious haze of colours that spanned almost the entire spectrum, cast in watercolours, washed with a flourish of artistic unruliness, across the sky. Graham sat in awe of a spectacle that could not be created by man or his ideals and proved that the world was just such a large and contrasting place that it could provide no end of opportunity and possibilities for him and for all men.

With the descent of early nightfall, Graham decided to get back to the hotel and wash and change into something more comfortable and entirely more formal. Solemnly he changed in the small suite of rooms that the hotel had provided for him glancing out of the window he could see the dim glow of the lights that lit almost the entire way down the coastal path that lead to the taverns and restaurants at the end of the head of land that jutted out slightly into sea. He was convinced that he could just about make out a light that he had perceived to be the very same one that illuminated the cobbled yard in front of the little family run restaurant that had been where he had first met Aina.

He knew that this small, insignificant, rustic and slightly weathered place, was where his hopes and fears laid and that all he held dear would be there waiting for him expectantly, soberly and passionately. He wanted it; he knew it and he believed in it. He dressed and now got ready as suddenly as he could with tremendous haste and yet the upmost attention to detail like he hadn't paid towards himself for so long because he knew what would be waiting for him at the end of the rocky and isolated coastal road.

It was perceived in the fickle society set, that Graham Wright was never a man that emotion got in the way of. It was understood that he was not the kind of person that would be concerned by a woman and yet here he was feeling every moment, being moved by every second and doing all he could to be with the woman that he had changed his life for.

He left the building of the hotel and with a burst of pace he made his way up the dark and barely illuminated path to the outside of the restaurant and with an impulsive abruptness he stopped to compose himself because of the possibility of Aina being inside the small building overlooking the dark of the sea. It was a moment that he firstly wanted to be sure that he was ready to take on and secondly he needed to make certain that he could just savour for a moment the enormity of what he was about to experience.

Through the window, he could make out the familiar faces of the waiter and the manager who strutted around from table to table and to the kitchen and back with food and drinks. Sat at tables were customers already into the night enjoying their meals and each other's company he couldn't however see Aina but he entered the restaurant anyhow. Inside it was exactly as he had remembered it and within a moment of him entering and closing the door, he was embraced firstly by the waiter and then the manager, who were both delighted to see him again. "Senior Wright, you came back, I love to see you." He paused after another broad smile and then continued, "You have wine now?" Graham didn't need to answer and was instantaneously provided with a seat and a glass of wine. Soon after, food was placed in front of him and it felt like he had never been away. As before, he found the food to be perfectly produced and a delight that he had missed for such a long time, he was now content. Continually plied with drink and courses, Graham was beginning to think that he would burst and at the same time had once again been thwarted in his quest to reach Aina.

At half past ten two young girls walked into the restaurant and as soon as their coats had been removed and placed onto the pegs with the others, Graham's heart leapt around his chest wildly when he realised that one of them was of course Aina. As if possessed, he rose to his feet and pushed his chair backwards as he did so, standing for a second before he walked over to her. She turned to look at the man now within a yard of her and excitedly she called out his name and flung her arms around him. They kissed right there as they were, to rounds of applause and whoops of joy from the entire populous of the little seaside restaurant who knew exactly just what it meant to the pair of them.

They sat together at Graham's table and with an additional glass of wine for his girl, they began to chat and talk about all the things that they had experienced without the other and of course to underline just how much they had been waiting for the moments that they were now re-sharing. Graham talked about how he had travelled to get there and how much he had endured to be with her again.

When the couple had completed the consumption of their wine they left the restaurant hand in hand and walked to the path that ran along the top of the hillside, looking out across the night time sky that was sprinkled with a million sparkled jewels and a warm glowing moon that cast out its white radiance across the flat sea before it. There was no breeze and the heat of the day continued into the warm night time. Together they again embraced and with arms around each other they again kissed.

The kiss was what he had been missing for so long and had so desperately needed to initiate. It meant so much for all that it signified, all that it was and indeed all that it was not. Aina had patiently waited for him and from across the other side of the European continent Graham's heart had ached so much that it had brought him back to find the only one that could heal it. Money had allowed him to complete the journey but the origin of why he wanted to return and the fact that he had let nothing get in his way, were purely a result of following his heart.

Graham Wright had been a part of mad crowd of money wielding free thinkers on a crazy rollercoaster that had risen up to an impossible height, which looked as if it would never even reach its pinnacle. Within three months Graham Wright along with his playboy and flapper counterparts would then begin a relentless descent, without brakes, into the last throws of the decade. They would fall at unstoppable velocity before hitting the ground in a fantastically sudden implosion. There would be people that came out of it bloodied and battered and those that would almost be destroyed, Graham Wright would be one of them.

As black Tuesday hit the world and the financial markets of the United States collapsed, it would inflict an almost worldwide melt down of the values of money and what it could buy. Graham's investments would be blown away like leaves in a tornado, his house, his bank accounts and his cars would vanish from his possession and the financial viability of Graham Wright would total little more than the clothes that he stood in. Money was the very thing that had allowed him to play the game and to get into the giant bubble that had expanded so far outwards that the tension of is surface would become so thin that it would explode sending the contents of the decade crashing to the ground.

Graham had seen and experienced both the value and danger of money; what it could provide and just what it couldn't. When he had money he possessed so much and known so many people but at the same time they were possessions and faces that he didn't need. Graham Wright realised that the money he possessed could quickly become his downfall.

Now in Spain he had no more money than the few notes that he had in his wallet and yet he was wealthier than he had ever been. The summer that he had relentlessly searched for, he found in her smile. The love that had been so absent he realised in her heart, never had there been someone that he needed more or someone that he could do without less.